I0771540
JUST KILLING TIME
PAT CHAVIS

JUST
KILLING
TIME

PAT CHAVIS

ARPress
45 Dan Road Suite 5
Canton MA 02021

Hotline: 1(888) 821-0229
Fax: 1(508) 545-7580

Ordering Information:

Quantity sales. Special discounts are available on quantity purchases by corporations, associations, and others. For details, contact the publisher at the address above.

Printed in the United States of America.

ISBN-13:   Paperback   979-8-89389-782-1
                eBook   979-8-89389-783-8

Library of Congress Control Number: 2024922841

Contents

Acknowledgements

This book was a challenge to write, in that it describes some of the things I got involved with while on my job; the involvement sometimes was so deep that I found it difficult to leave things alone even for a few hours to go home. The characters are much like some of those co-workers and some things remind me of the people who taught me as I grew 'on the job.' Working with offenders can be stressing, as can employees who go wrong and disappoint you and others. I want to thank my 'teachers,' my family for their patience as I spent so much time at work, and my friends who supported me along the way. Balancing work and family was a continued challenge. I thank God for helping me to stay the course, in my work.

To Jerry T. Cole, who hired me and supported me as I advanced in the system, along with Bob Lewis, J. Boyd Bennett, James B. French, Lynn C. Phillips, and Ricky Anderson;

In memory of H. Leon Yow who praised our work, taught and challenged me with projects;

To Kenneth, Ashkea, and Adam, my husband and children, for your love, patience, and support;

To Billy & Minnie Lowry, Mom & Dad, for pushing us to go after dreams and work hard;

To Carol M. Williams, Stephanie Smith-Bell, Kathey M. Carthens, and Nora Hunt, for your endurance with this taskmaster and your continued friendship.

Comments:

This is a work of fiction. Names, characters, places and incidents are either the product of the author's imagination or are used fictitiously and any resemblance to locations, events, actual persons, living or dead, is coincidental.

Gabriel, Kaitlynn, Tristan,
Ashkea, Adam and Kimberly Chavis
With Love.

Chapter One

Having gone to breakfast, he had returned to his cell, shaved and neatly made his bed, and was standing on the threshold at his cell door watching the comings and goings of his roommates. Brent Galen, aka Buzz, stared at the Pod Officer as she patrolled the lower housing pod. He'd been transferred to the facility late in the evening the day before on the transfer bus for housing in the general population, and he was eager to learn how the staff assignments were made and what staff could be manipulated. Buzz had been labeled as a conniving individual who sought out those staff who could or would cater to him or do favors in exchange for a bit of information. At twenty-seven years old, he had not changed from that tall but skinny young boy who had been moved from foster home to foster home for playing devilish pranks and lying on other kids and foster parents to get his way, only to have things backfire on him when he ended up being placed in a juvenile institution for incorrigible kids. His parents had been killed in an automobile accident when he was seven, and having no siblings, he was taken in by his father's older sister, a spinster.

Buzz constantly got into fights with other kids at school, refused to do his school work and pay attention in class and argued with his aunt, who had grown weary and tired of dealing with him. She felt it would be useless to keep trying, and under pressures from friends, she finally gave him up for placement in foster care. At age seventeen, he ran away from the juvenile center with two other wayward youth and broke into a small-town donut shop late at night. He was caught and received sixty days in jail, and on release drifted from town to town doing odd jobs on the northeastern coast of North Carolina. Buzz, as he preferred to be called, was a rather nice looking man (or so he had been told) with dark brown hair, curly at the ears and on the nape of his neck, and greenish eyes. He had received his GED while on the prior prison term when he'd served three years for stealing checks out of a vehicle sitting at the coastal motel, where he had worked as a janitor. As he stood at the cell-door he thought about his life and how he had come to be back in prison for borrowing a truck and being accused of stealing it. As the judge had told him, Buzz had no credibility and was a scoundrel that could not be trusted, and if he didn't straighten up would spend the rest of his life behind bars or be killed by someone.

Looking down at his feet, he wondered if he'd ever get a nice pair of shoes or clothing that had been ironed—something his aunt had provided, for she took pride in seeing him dressed and polished in his appearance. Over the years, he did the best he could to have decent clothing that was clean and pressed, and he polished his shoes and work boots regularly, because he did care about his appearance. Over the few years past he had grown accustomed to wearing denim jeans with grayish-blue tee shirts with an unbuttoned plaid overshirt and had been comfortable. His Timberland brown brogans were so badly worn that jail staff threw them into the trash while he was awaiting his court hearing, and he'd been given a pair of high top sneakers. On prison admission, he was given three sets of new underclothes, with socks. The drab-olive green pants were so badly wrinkled, but then they suited him more than the baggy orange jumpsuits at the jail.

As the Pod Officer climbed the stairs and rounded the corner she saw him watching her. Looking at her wristwatch, she wondered what his story was but thought she'd learn that in time. Almost immediately the intercom came on with a screeching roar—"Count time!" Buzz felt the chills run down his back and he cringed. How he hated that roar. He had been in four community work centers in the past but this was the first time in an institutional setting, and he had a lot to learn.

The intercom roared a second time, "Count time, go to your cells, stand at the door!" Suddenly a white-shirted man suspected to be in his early 50's with dark hair graying at the temples with gold bars on his shoulders entered the pod as the steel doors opened, with two other officers accompanying him. Those inmates sitting in the dayroom, called a leisure hail, began going to their cells to stand. One of the officers yelled that the Lieutenant didn't have time to waste, and they needed to get a move on. Mentally, Buzz wondered why it took a Lieutenant and three officers to count a housing pod that had forty-eight inmates.

The Lieutenant called out, "Cell 0–1."

"Here, John Birchette, sir!" spoke the short bald inmate in a dirty tee shirt standing at the door of the first cell.

"Cell 0–2," called the Lieutenant.

"Sir, cell 0–2 inmate is at medical," spoke the Pod Officer, as she read from her clipboard. To conduct the head count took seventeen minutes. "Sir, pod count of 48 is clear," spoke the Pod Officer. The two extra officers left the pod as the Lieutenant stood talking and laughing with the Pod Officer.

Momentarily, the Lieutenant spoke to someone using a microphone penned to his left shirt lapel, clearing the inmates on the pod to be allowed to go back to the dayroom for leisure, to watch TV, or play table games. And he then left the pod. Most of the inmates went to the dayroom to sit around at the stainless steel tables to play card games, table games, or sit and watch the television in silent mode using the pocket walkman radios turned to the signal through which the television audio was transmitted.

The Pod Officer, a fairly young slender and attractive brown-haired female, stood in the dayroom writing in a notebook attached to a metal wall desk, as Buzz went to speak to her. "Pardon me, Ma'am, but when do we get yard privileges?"

"You can call me Officer Payne, not Ma'am," she spoke looking at him seemingly irritated, "and yard calls schedules are posted on the bulletin behind you," she responded.

"Oh, I hadn't seen it; I'm sorry," Buzz said. "I just got here," he said as he smiled at her, feeling stupid. At least embarrassed.

"Well, go read the board!" She walked away and engaged in conversation with another inmate who sported a handle-bar moustache, wore a gold rope chain around his neck, and a diamond earring in his left earlobe.

"Hey, don't pay her no mind, for she can be an inconsiderate smart-ass at times. She has her own agenda, and we aren't on it. Hey, I'm Titus Hawks, from cell 12. You're new here, aren't you?" spoke the fat guy leaning in one of the chairs next to the payphone on the wall.

Buzz looked at him, trying to make an assessment of the guy who sported eagle tattoos on both upper arms with an Indian motorcycle design under the eagle. He wore a skull earring in his left earlobe, and one certainly wouldn't miss seeing his rotten teeth once he opened his mouth to speak. His oily black hair was cut into a crew cut.

"I came here late yesterday from processing, but have never been in a large facility before, and haven't a clue about this place," Buzz spoke. "She is not a friendly sort. All I did was ask questions."

At that moment another inmate standing nearby spoke up to say, "She's not overly friendly, except with Jay. I'm Chuck Charles from cell 45. Good to meet you. And generally this place ain't too bad."

"Hello, I'm Brent Galen. Folks call me Buzz. I'm in cell 40."

Titus Hawks again spoke, saying he had been in other locations and the staff were much friendlier and took more time with the incoming inmates. He took note that Buzz had looked him over, with a lingering look at his tattoos. "You like my designs, huh?" he asked, holding out his arms for Buzz and Chuck to take a better look. "I did them myself several years ago when I rode out of Miami. Used to be with Hell's Angels down there. Lost two toes on my foot getting initiated; hell, it was worth it, 'cause those guys were great to be around. They helped me start a tattoo shop; I made a chunk of money. Every now and then, I can get in a few tattoos on some of the guys who have the bucks, and if my lady friend here can get the inks. Let me know if you want one." Titus Hawks walked toward the payphone, tapped another on the arm who was talking on the phone, and the guy handed the phone to Titus who began to talk to the individual on the phone while the other guy stood watch keeping other inmates from getting too close to overhear the conversation.

Buzz watched the expressions on Chuck's face, as it seemed that he was glad to be rid of Titus Hawks. They walked over to a wall of plate-glass, which provided a view of the wooded area of pines at the rear of the prison. Buzz learned that Chuck, 29, was from the Myrtle Beach area, in nearby South Carolina; was serving a twenty-year term for a series of breaking and entering crimes, with this being his second time incarcerated in the past ten years, and he had very few visitors. "Break-ins? Into houses, or what?" Buzz asked.

"Houses—rich people houses. You learn about them from death notices in the papers. Man, people tell lots of stuff in the papers, give you all you need to know. You read and wait a few weeks and go in. My last job had more alarms than I figured, and now I'm in here," said Chuck, shaking his head with disbelief that he got caught. He sat down and proceeded to recount his capers, educating Buzz. As the well-to-do older folks of Eagles Ridge died, he had learned from experience and study that the obituaries cited the residence address and occupants, mostly with family members living out of state who returned to their homes within two weeks of the funerals, leaving the spouse of the deceased in the house along except for a cook or housekeeper. Even the elderly were oftentimes left alone. Having worked in the landscaping and grounds maintenance business as a day laborer in the community, Chuck knew the Eagles Ridge citizens were the wealthy who had left the Northern states and moved to the North Carolina coast for a warmer climate, and less noise than in the city. Items he stole were mostly electronics, coin collections, silver, and things he could generally sell, but he always made his sales across the state lines into Virginia and Georgia, and generally used pawn shops for hand tools that he could always find lying around in garages.

"You said second incarceration?" Buzz asked.

"Yeah. First time I was 19, borrowed a car for a ride. The guy claimed I stole it. I got two years in prison—not like this place," Chuck said.

"For two years? Where'd you go?" Buzz asked.

"I did time at an older place in Wilmington, like a community work camp, and did eight months. Got paroled and worked at a golf course at the beach. Rich folks in and out, playing golf all the time, moving to the area, and lot of them always dying. I've done good getting stuff out of their houses, selling it off and living good for seven years." Chuck dropped his head, while slamming his fists on the steel table. "Oh, well, I'll be OK here. Maybe I can learn a trade in that school they have here. Food ain't bad either."

"How are the folks that run this place?" Buzz asked, to which Chuck responded, "Some OK, some are here to pass the time. Some will even bring you smokes and stuff, but make sure you know who you're dealing with. I've been in here a little over a year and generally keep to myself. That Titus is one you don't want to get friendly with. Word is he has some racket going in here with some staff and inmates. Thinks he's somebody, he does. Tries to push guys around who won't stand up for themselves. You'll see he's a mean one. He brags about being in the Hell's Angels in Miami, but he's in here for raping a college girl who had broke-down on Interstate 95 near Fayetteberg. Poor girl was going home to the North on college break. Hawks and two others stopped to check her out, but gang-raped her and robbed her and left her on the highway in bad shape. He brags about doing so bad and getting so little time for it. Only got 20 to 25 years for all that he did to that poor girl. Stay away from him, and you'll be better off."

"What about getting a job and a pair of pressed pants?" Buzz asked of Chuck. "What kinds of jobs can you get, and how much time off your sentence will you get?"

"Oh, they'll put you to work once they sit you down and talk with you. They want to find out what you can do, like job skills, work you've done on the streets, and stuff like that. You'll see a case worker in a few days who will ask all sorts of questions; those folks are the ones who try to work with you, especially if you have short time," Chuck responded. "Just pray you don't get stuck with Jesse Oxenberg or that Fran Russell; they're mean down to the bone and lie to you," Chuck said with a frown on his face. "You have to keep after them for anything you want to know, if you know what I mean."

"What do you mean; what's their problems?" asked Buzz, somewhat with a puzzled look on his face.

"They been here a long time, Man, and sit in their offices all day or just hang out all over the place. Word is they hang out a lot, or hide out, in that gym. I don't know 'cause I don't go there unless I'm told to. It looks like the prison heads would see it and listen to the guys who complain and write grievances on them. But they don't. I filed grievances on both of them, with nothing happening. Grievances sometimes get thrown in the trash, and when you get an answer to one you don't get a full response, or they discredit what you've said in the first place. So, most of the guys don't even bother. That Russell only likes to have black guys on her case load, and Oxenberg likes the guys who are into sports. Word is Russell is tight with that guy Jay in cell 26, as is Officer Payne. Watch yourself around him, and he's tight with Titus as well," said Chuck, while scanning the guys sitting nearest to them, and wondering if he'd said too much already, not really knowing a lot about Buzz. Chuck kept trying to figure Buzz out but seemed to like him right off. "Ain't never had a friend I could trust. Never needed a partner in my stuff. Mostly keep to myself, but I like you," said Chuck. "If you got a question, ask me."

"Yard time!" came loud and clear from the intercom system. "Yard time for Pods A, B, and C of General Population. Go to the Yard Door if you plan to go outside."

"Well, that's for me," said Chuck. "I need some fresh air; come on, Man. The outer walls of this place has pretty scenery, especially when the fall leaves change colors. Not much winter weather here and rarely see snow. But it smells wonderful outdoors, until rains drag that chicken house stink up here from down the road."

Chuck explained that a local chicken farmer had several huge metal buildings standing where he raised chickens for a chicken processing plant some distance away, and when it rained quite heavily for a day or two, the air carried a foul odor. "Oh, if you stay here long enough, you'll see what I'm talking about. But we just as well get used to it."

"Yeah, some fresh air will be good—check out the scenery too," said Buzz as he headed for the Yard Door.

The Yard held two half-size basketball courts, a shuffleboard area, a weightlifting shed with loose weights and a ragged bench press, and a dozen or so aluminum benches off to the side of the concrete pad. Two non- uniformed male personnel were talking to inmates at the basketball posts. Buzz and Chuck sat down on one of the benches to watch. "That guy you spoke of named Jay—isn't that him with the ball?" asked Buzz.

"Yeah, he's into basketball. Word from some is that he used to play for some team out west after his college years; he came home to North Carolina to visit a friend and some guy got killed when a bunch of them were drinking and Jay wrecked his car. I believe he called it vehicular manslaughter, killed his ball days," said Chuck. "Some say he was in college and on the school team, as a big-shot, and was into a lot of mess."

"If you guys on the benches want to play, come on down to the pad," yelled the tall black staff person with the green athletics pants and gold shirt. Buzz stood up and decided to have a try at it, and went down. He shook hands with several of the others, including the one called Jay. Jay Dillon was in his late twenties, tall, well built and sported a small, thin goatee on his chin, a handle-bar moustache, shaved his head and his sideburns dropped just below his earlobes. He wore a diamond earring in his left earlobe. He worked out everyday on the rec yard, and Buzz took note of his white and blue Nike high-tops, as well as the creases in his pants. The game went to suit Buzz, as he'd ended up on the same side as Jay and they had spoken to each a couple of times while on the court. As the game ended, they took a break together, sitting on the bleachers talking. Chuck was playing at the shuffleboards. Jay and Buzz talked sports, and Jay recounted his years playing college ball at Virginia Tech while on scholarship. Buzz seemed to like Jay right off, noting the boasting, and a bad gut feeling, but vowed to get to know him better, if he could, as Jay still had some time to do before parole eligibility and had offered to try to get Buzz a job on the rec yard as a janitor.

"Have you met Jesse Oxenberg yet?" asked Jay.

"Well, I'll talk with him about helping you," said Jay, who walked off in the direction of the staff person on the court in the green and gold outfit. Watching Jay as he walked off, Buzz thought may be he needed to carry himself with arrogance and still feel important to get along in here.

"Yard time is over; return to your housing pod. Yard time is over," called the person manning the intercom system.

While walking to the Yard door, Chuck caught up with Buzz. "See you speaking with Jay, be careful; check your back," said Chuck, who walked on ahead just as his name was called for reporting to the medical station. Chuck suffered from diabetes and had an asthmatic condition and was given a medical review two to three times a week. He had suffered a severe asthma attack several weeks prior and ended up being rushed to the nearest emergency room for a two-night stay in the hospital. Both conditions were being treated with medications and with staff checking him frequently.

Shortly after returning to his cell, Buzz sat down to read the orientation materials he had received while in the diagnostic center. The screeching sound of the intercom gained his attention: "Count time!" He knew he needed to stand at his cell door until the count cleared. As the count cleared, Officer Penelope Payne came to his cell and gave him a pass slip to report at 1:00 that afternoon for his Case Manager review. "Galen, take this and report to see Mr. Oxenberg in the gym next to the dining hall at 1:00 sharp!" she said, her tone of voice intimidating.

"Can I ask a question?" asked Buzz of Ofcr. Payne.

"Shoot," she responded, with "What is it?" eyeing him with disinterest.

"Will he be my case manager?" asked Buzz.

"I don't know…maybe…just go find out, and ask him that question," said Ofcr. Payne. "What is your story? Why you here?" she asked.

"Well, I borrowed a truck and the man lied on me and said I stole it, and here I am for three years. Up for parole at eight months," said Buzz with a sorrowful look about his face, "and I hope I can get out this time and relocate. I don't want to ever come back to prison. Well, thanks," he said as he took the pass-slip and went back to his bed to sit.

Ofcr. Payne watched him and wondered about Buzz. He didn't seem hard core as were many of the offenders in the facility and seemed to have a friendly side to him. She thought about his ease of asking questions and his seemingly soft-spoken voice, not like that loud aggressive tone from so many inmates. But she wondered why should she care about an inmate. Penelope Payne had worked at many jobs since high school, going from restaurant waitress, bank cashier, store clerk, factor worker and had come into contact with many men. The men in her life had borrowed money from her, her cars and so often returned them with empty gas tanks, and had oftentimes stolen money from her purse, leaving only to return to her small duplex apartment in a drunken state thinking they could spend the nights. She never let them into her apartment and turned them away when they returned the next time. Over time she had become insensitive and hard- nosed in building relationships with men. She had come to this job through a job fair where she sought a solid future in a job with good benefits and one in which she could look after herself on a long-term basis. Not a difficult job, she thought, but she easily tired of the crap of hearing the 'poor me' hard-luck stories of the men who were incarcerated and having to brush aside efforts of the male co-workers, many who were married and some who should have been on the inside of the fence doing time. She didn't hang out with many of the female staff because so many of them were just here to get away from home, to make a little extra money, or were just looking to have a good time with the men. There were some decent females working, but they had lives away from here, and needed to rush home to children, husbands waiting on them, or errands to run. Ofcr. Payne moved on to conduct her cell searches and other work.

Shortly thereafter, the intercom blurted "Lunch time! Pod A for General Population move to the pod door." Lunch time went by with no incidents, and Buzz appeared at the gym for his one o'clock appointment with Jesse Oxenberg.

"Sir, I am Brent Galen; most folks call me Buzz. I have this slip of paper to see you," he said.

"Yeah, Jay talked to me about you. You want to work on the rec yard or something like that, right?" said Oxenberg. "What skills do you have?"

"Well, I've been a motel janitor, done concrete work, washed cars and mostly odd jobs," said Buzz. "I can do general maintenance stuff. But I'd like the job of keeping the yard cleaned, storing the equipment, and stuff like that, and would appreciate your help," he said to Oxenberg. "Is there anything else if I can't work on the recreation crew? How much time off my sentence can I earn?"

Oxenberg motioned for him to go into an office nearby and sit and talk. They discussed Buzz's case file, with Oxenberg reviewing the case file via the computer system, and set up a case management plan to jointly discuss his case every ten days, and to review his case credits of jail time received and his work time to be earned based on good job performance. "Well, there are jobs in the sewing plant where inmates cut and sew to make tee shirts and underwear. You can do janitor work just about anywhere in the facility. We have no more openings for maintenance workers, which would be down your line of experience. They all pay a dollar a day, and you would earn ten days a month off your sentence. And if there's a real push on something special, you could earn extra time off your sentence. Get into trouble, go to the segregation and you could lose it. So, which do you want?"

"I like being outdoors in fresh air, so if it's all the same with you, what about the rec job?"

"Okay, you can have the job, but I expect you to report to work everyday promptly at nine o'clock to the rec yard. If it's bad weather, you come here to the gym. You will earn ten days a month off your time for your work. But the first sign of any trouble you need to come tell me. And what you think you might see you forget it, unless you talk to me. Understand?" said Oxenberg, further pushing the conversation with a question as to whether Buzz was into sports. Buzz answered that he never had much time for games or such, and would rather stay busy working.

"Yep, understood clearly, about the job and about any troubles," said Buzz.

Buzz went to the dayroom to watch a little TV, and thought he might write to his old friend David Simms. David was the manager of the motel where Buzz had worked for a few years, and he had supported Buzz by allowing him to stay in the staff rooms on the rear of the motel, use the motel laundry services, and wear the staff uniform. He had extended several loans when Buzz needed some extra cash, and even let him eat in the dining hall with no charge. David really thought Buzz would turn out to be okay in time, and believed him when he said he had borrowed the truck from the owner of the poolroom down the street. The guy had told some locals hanging out at the pool-hall after

Buzz's conviction that loaning his truck would jeopardize his vehicle insurance if it ever got out. David believed this is why he had Buzz charged with vehicle theft, but without proof nothing could be done to get Buzz's case back into court. Originally from Vermont, David Simms, a bachelor in his sixties, was an Army retiree who had settled at the coast to fish mostly, and he often spent time at the pool-hall drinking or just hanging out with friends. He'd met Buzz at the pool-hall one night, found that Buzz had been sleeping in the building after closing time, and offered him a job. That was five to six years before. With encouragement, he'd helped Buzz get into the local community college to take courses in vocational trades and had been proud of his accomplishments when Buzz earned a certificate in metal works mostly welding and blacksmithing, and a certificate in pipefitting and plumbing. This certainly helped Buzz in his janitorial and maintenance work at the motel, and had saved David a lot of money over time. Buzz knew David felt close to him and was a strong supporter, and wanted to keep in touch with him. Besides, David had said he'd be there when Buzz got out and that he'd have a job waiting for him.

"Hey, man, what are you up to?" asked Chuck, who came up to Buzz in the dayroom later in the day.

"Just writing a friend on the streets, who was probably my only friend out there. What have you been up to?" asked Buzz.

"Finally saw my case manager today, got a job where I can make some gain time off my sentence, and went to medical for some Tylenol. Have had a terrible headache," responded Chuck. "Lately I've been feeling poorly and having headaches a lot. Blood pressure has been up, and this time of year I am bothered with considerable sinus issues. I seem to stay tired, but the doctor just kinda passes it off. Sure hope this headache goes away."

"What job?" asked Buzz.

"Janitor in the clothes-house area," replied Chuck, "to start in the morning and I'll get to wear whites, and it's cool in there. Cool in the summer! And I can get clothes that fit and are ironed. That's special. And I won't have to be on my feet all day, and can sit and fold clothes. Too, it'll be warm in the winter around those dryers."

"Wow, man, that's great! I start tomorrow on the rec yard as janitor and in the gym if the weather is bad," said Buzz. "Oxenberg's my case manager, and he didn't seem bad—time will tell, I guess."

Chuck came back with, "Remember, watch your back with him."

They split off to go to their cells and await the evening meal. After the meal, Chuck went to bed early because he was a bit tired, and he thought his headache would ease off with sleep. He closed his cell door to reduce the noise coming from the dayroom chat.

Chapter Two

One Week later

"Hey, Buzz, wait up," called Jay, taking long strides, as Buzz was leaving the gym to return to his housing pod. "Been seeing you on the job—man, you work too much. You need to take a break every now and then. You need to throw some baskets with us. I can square it up with Oxenberg, if you need me to."

"Oh, I need the time credits off my term, so I can get on with my life. I'm up for parole in a few months, so I need to keep busy, but thanks anyway," said Buzz, who continued on his way out of the gym.

"Chow time for general population," screeched over the intercom shortly after Buzz had returned to his cell and showered. He sure hated that screechy intercom system and would be glad when it was behind him. He had received a return letter from his friend David, who was doing well, and sent well wishes to Buzz. Buzz felt that he really to prove to David Simms that he was turning his life around and would go straight when he got out. He'd thought that he would write to David after the evening meal.

"Count time, count time," came out over the intercom, followed by the words, "Huh, stand by your cell door."

That evening sitting in the dayroom watching TV, Chuck sat in the Rubbermaid plastic chair he pulled up next to Buzz. "How's the job going?" he asked.

"Great," responded Buzz, "but I see lots of things going on in that gym office, and it bothers me what I see. Man, some of the women here go in there with some of the guys, and their clothes are in a mess when they come out. That Oxenberg lets them in, lets them close the doors, and he sits out in the gym while they are alone for fifteen to twenty minutes in there. That one programmer with the red-flame hair, long legs, and flashy jewelry will stay in there with two to three guys about everyday. They say she's a hot one! Heard that Jay's one of her daily romps; he's got it made in here, if that's so. Ask me she's trouble. Been seeing that Titus Hawks in there hanging with Jay, too."

"Word is that Jay and her are an item here. Heard one time she's been married several times, and I've heard that she goes with that maintenance man, Tyler," said Chuck. "She better watch herself and not get caught, but I've heard word that she makes several hundred dollars on the side in here with the guys she's having sex with, and Oxenberg gets big bucks for fixing things, too. Bet Titus gets a cut on the action."

"That's bad wrong, man. If Tyler found out, bet he'd want to kill somebody," said Buzz. "But, maybe, she's not tied down to any one man, and certainly not if she's messing with guys in here. The law will get them sure enough, and I wouldn't want to be in that game. Get sent up for a long time, or so that's what they told us in the orientation sessions when I went through the processing center."

Inmates and all staff had been educated on the PREA laws, which are the rules and regulations covering the Prison Rape Elimination Act of 2003 enacted by the Federal government and passed on to all the state prison and county jail systems. Staff were prohibited from engaging in sexual activity of any kind with those offenders under their supervision, and reports of such conduct had to be thoroughly investigated, with vigorous prosecutions in the court systems. Each year the federal government received and studied statistical data on the numbers of reports, findings of investigations, prosecutions and convictions as well as the various ways and means for educating all employees and offenders in prisons and jails. Several states had imprisoned correctional staff upon convictions, with many having been sent out of state for periods of incarceration for protective reasons. In addition to this, the offending staff were required to register as sex offenders. Some offenders were aggressive at seducing the staff, yet the offenders were not prosecuted but were seen as the victims due to the interpretations of the law.

"And," said Chuck, lowering his voice even more and watching for eaves- droppers, "they forget that AIDS and STDs are still happening. That's a bad deal; it ain't for me."

Four weeks later

As Buzz finished his breakfast and headed for the gym, Officer Payne stopped him in the corridor. "Galen, you are being moved to another cell this afternoon. Same pod. Maintenance will be repairing that overhead light in your cell in the next day or so, so get your stuff together when you return to your cell," she advised him.

"Yes, Ma'am. Will I go back to that cell when the light is repaired?" he inquired.

"Don't know but we'll see, and quit calling me Ma'am. I've told you that before," responded Officer Payne.

"I am sorry. Keep forgetting. I was raised to always use respect when addressing a woman, and my aunt drilled that word 'Ma'am' into my head." he said.

"Miss or Officer would be better, so see that you remember that." Walking off, she threw him a stare, and turned to go on her way.

On the following day, the Maintenance Supervisor Marcus Torn himself worked on the light in cell 40, as well as cleaning of the overhead vent. Torn was a retiree of the U.S. Marine Corps, having served the last eight years of his service time at Camp LeJeune, N.C., and had grown to love the coast of North and South Carolina. On retirement, he'd sought employment in state service and had been offered a position in North Carolina's prison system at Glen Cove Correctional. At age 52, with ten years of service, he had observed a lot of things; he believed one could always watch and learn. A hands-on man, he did a lot of work despite having a team of eight in his section, but that, too, suited him.

After the supper meal, the Shift Captain McLeod had Buzz rehoused in cell 40 and later went to speak with him to ensure everything was fine. "Galen, that light will seem brighter, but it is repaired. Why you so fond of this cell?" asked Captain McLeod, "because Officer Payne said you wanted to come back to this cell." To which Buzz responded that he was just comfortable there and had a nice view outside his cell windows.

Buzz was steadily working, and Chuck had even managed to get him some pressed pants from the clothes house time to time. He had begun to feel more comfortable with his surroundings and had been interacting more with his inmate peers as well as attending more of the religious activities. Officer Payne personally checked on him from time and time and spent more time engaged in conversation with him. His friend, David Simms, had been to visit a couple of times. The good time credits for working had shown up on Buzz's record, and he had been surprised with Oxenberg had shown him the extra days off his sentence that had been sent in to the records office.

One afternoon in the gym, Jay approached him. "Hey, Buzz, how are things going? I see you wearing pressed pants and you got a pair of those new sneakers they brought in; you look sharp. You've even caught the eye of Faye Hondo in programs—she watches you. You know her?" asked Jay. "She's the red-head programmer."

"Nah, never spoke to her. Seen her, but that's it," said Buzz. "She sure spends time down here, don't she? Lot of guys be around her, and I guess she likes them, huh?" Buzz commented.

"If you want in on some action with her, let me know."

"Not interested," said Buzz, looking straight at Jay.

"Well, if you change your mind, get with me; otherwise, keep your mouth closed," said Jay, who gunned Buzz with his fingers as he walked off. Buzz had learned that gunning was the fingers being pointed at you as if a pistol was aimed at you.

That evening Buzz sat in his cell talking with Chuck who was sitting at the door's edge. He asked Chuck, "What do you know about Officer Payne?"

Chuck thought a minute before responding, pursing his lips and shaking his head. "Well, man, she is difficult to talk to. She's been here for a while and has had her favorites, like Jay; he's loaded, man, or that's the word. Has contacts in and out of the place. Talk is he's been a drug boss on the streets and at that bigshot college. He's supposed to be doing the time for that guy getting killed in a wreck but sold drugs for a bunch of town bigshots, and they owe him big-time, so he says. She thinks he's somebody. She's supposed to be straight but I can't figure her out and why she's always talking to Jay. Do you ever see her at the gym?" he asked.

"No, ain't seen her there and never hear her name there in the gym by anyone that hangs out there," said Buzz. "Jay asked me today if I wanted any of the action with Programmer Hondo. I said no."

"Buddy, watch your back good," said Chuck. "I'm off to bed. See ya."

Three months later

"Alright, folks, listen up! Word is there's a bunch of phones on Block B. You need to watch the inmates; talk to your snitches, and let's see what we come up with," spoke Lt. Peter Gibbs at the evening shift line-up. Gibbs had been working in prisons for twenty-seven years, of which he'd been a supervisor for correctional officers and Staff Sergeants for twenty-three years and had worked at four locations. He had been involved with female staff at most of the sites, which resulted in him being relocated, short of getting caught up in sexual harassment incidents. He'd been on the evening to night shift since he came here to Glen Cove Correctional, and he hated it. He walked the dorms and segregation housing constantly and spent a great deal of time talking to inmates and watching staff. Gibbs' strength was his knowledge of surveillance equipment and techniques for nosing out improprieties involving staff and the inmate population.

In his personal life his two wives had divorced him and left him broke. He worked in the daytime as a mechanic at a garage two blocks from his duplex apartment, in Glen Cove Village, since he had acquired mechanical skills over the years from having to personally service his own vehicle. He'd never been able to buy himself a new vehicle, since his alimony and mortgage payments kept him strapped for money. He had two house payments to make each month to the ex-wives, child support for one child, and $400 in alimony, all of which took about two-thirds of his income, so he had to work a second job to make ends meet. He figured that women were his bad luck and had promised himself that he would leave them alone and stick to his work. Gibbs seemed to be satisfied and strived to do a good job until his retirement. Besides, his kid was nearing eighteen and one of the ex-wives was contemplating another marriage, so he'd be gaining some of his payout in the near months hopefully.

"Alright, go to your posts!" he shouted, turning to exit the command room. "Keep an eye out. Do your locker searches and check those containers that could be used to conceal things."

"Hey, Lt. Gibbs, wait up," called Sgt. Jacobi. "Do you reckon the Super in the head shed could get us some more help?"

"What did you say? What do you mean 'super in the head shed?' Let's get some thing straight—that's Superintendent and don't let me hear you refer to him in any other way or manner, understand, Sergeant? And you can refer to him as Superintendent Colden."

"Yes, sir. No disrespect intended."

"Now to your question; I know we need more staff to man posts and do some searches, and he knows that too. I've spoken to him already but the budget holds up the hiring, and we'll have to do the best we can," commented Lt. Gibbs. "We are getting more cameras on the housing pods to help, and in the storage areas to help with surveillance for the special operations folks."

"Yeah, I've heard that," said Jacobi, "but keep after the boss up front. We need the people." Some folks thought of Jacobi as a cocky smart ass, as he was computer literate but exhibited little respect for others. He had been disciplined on two occasions for circumventing policy—taking shortcuts— although he achieved results, but he continued to make little change. It was past supper time, and since it was Tuesday, there would be several church folks coming to have religious services and the local AA sponsors. Lt. Peter Gibbs knew he'd have just enough staff to provide supervision and cover the housing pods. He certainly hoped there would not be an emergency to where he would need to send any inmate out to the local hospital emergency room, as he hated to run any location short-staffed.

The intercom screeched, "Church services in visitation will begin in five minutes—IDs required."

Buzz exited his cell, closed his cell door, and proceeded down the mezzanine stairs. Chuck caught up with him as they walked down the corridor toward the visitation room.

"Do these folks come here often? Where are they from?" he asked Chuck.

"Don't know, but local churches in the county I think," Chuck responded. "I've only come a dozen or so times. They have coffee and cookies, and some of the guys here do a group number on guitars and a keyboard."

"It's my first time; David wants me to go to church, thinks it will help me."

As the group took their seating, the older white-haired man with the black suitcoat, white shirt, and tie stood at the podium looking at the group and began speaking. "Welcome tonight, and it is our hope that you'll get a blessing from being with us tonight. I'm Reverend Thom Suggs from Beevins Baptist Church. It always warms my heart to see all of you come to join us as we worship and praise God for all He's done for us. Amen!"

As the older lady with the white beehive hairdo sat at the piano and began to play, the group stood at the preacher's signal of raising of his arms. Hand-me-down hymnals were opened and they all began to sing "Amazing Grace." The program came to an end some half-hour later with no concerns arising for the prison staff supervising the visitation room program. The inmates went to their cells immediately, seemingly in good spirits.

Reaching his cell door, Buzz spoke, "I enjoyed that," he said to Chuck. "Man, I haven't been in a church for years; I guess when I was in one of those foster homes. You've got a great singing voice."

Overcome with surprise at Buzz's comment, Chuck responded, "Thanks, Buzz. No one has ever paid me a compliment like that. Good night. I'm pooped right now; I'm going to bed." Going to his cell, he smiled for he had enjoyed the singing, seemingly thinking that it warmed his heart, and he began to think. He became quiet, entering his cell and sat on his bunk, staring out the small port-hole sized window into the darkness outside. Looking back in his life no one, except Mr. Jim, had ever paid him much attention and compliments were a rarity in his life.

Chuck's mother had been a factory worker who had shifted from one factory to another; she mostly tired from the people she worked with, and with three kids at age twenty-two to feed and clothe she was going to where she heard she might make more money. She had married at age seventeen to a local boy from the little village of Hamlet, N.C., who delivered auto parts to her dad's garage; after eloping, they had moved in with his folks. He'd left after the second child was born and his folks told her to move on, so she moved back near to Lumberton to live with an aunt and her husband, both of whom were alcoholics. Over time, his mother became pregnant for the aunt's husband, who was physically abusive to those around him including the children. Chuck could well remember being kicked around, hollered at, and even ignored by the mother as a young boy. He was farmed out to neighbors to do day chores as young as age four and then after school as he grew. He mostly enjoyed working with the animals on the neighboring farms, with a passion for young calves, and fishing on the farm ponds.

As soon as they could, his two sisters ran away from home, leaving Chuck alone, and when he turned fifteen, his mother died of pneumonia, so he decided to leave as well. He picked up odd jobs here and there, as he mostly traveled in rural areas and near to the coast; he had worked at camp grounds for a number of years with an elderly man who taught him the basics of plumbing, carpentry, and some bricklaying. Mr. Jim Cole was a man who had done labor for people all his life; he lived alone in a small cabin near a river, as his wife had died some years before. They had no children. 'Mr. Jim' as most folks called him had worked at mobile home parks and camp grounds near the state lake for a long time; he was patient and kind with Chuck, who grew to develop a strong fondness for him. In fact, Chuck remembered saying he loved Mr. Jim as he stood in the cemetery on the day of Mr. Jim's funeral. Some few days later, Chuck was working on a well in a mobile home park and had asked one of the men there to loan him his car so he could drive into town to pick up some parts and subsequently had Chuck charged with vehicle theft. The little money left for Chuck by Mr. Jim had paid for an attorney, not an aggressive lawyer by any means, but he did ask for leniency of the court. That was the first time in prison.

Chuck lay in his bunk that night thinking of Mr. Jim and how he had treated Chuck like a son. Mr. Jim was the closest one to ever show parental love, calmness in his voice when he talked to Chuck, and trust. Without him, Chuck sure felt a deep feeling of loneliness. He decided he needed to get himself into a trade school and get a better education, maybe even graduate high school, and build his own business.

Chapter Three

Early the following morning, the Facility Superintendent and his management team of two Captains; two Asst. Superintendents, Mitch Steele and Matt Ranham; and the Plant Maintenance Chief were making inspection rounds on the compound. The Superintendent oftentimes came into the prison during early morning hours before the breakfast meal to walk around, talk with night shift staff, talk with inmates at the breakfast tables, and watch his staff as they began the daily cleanup tasks and of getting the inmates out to their work details. He also found it interesting to watch the amount of scrap foods that the inmates threw into the food wastes buckets; he contemplated installing new rules where inmates would have to select the foods they wanted from the chow lines, thinking this would reduce the amount of foods wasted. He had a number of inmates that most referred to as his snitches, and he generally sat on the benches in the yard and talked with them; he also gleaned information during these talks about his staff that were a bit questionable, and about other inmates involved with staff more than allowed. Too, Supt. J.T. Colden was no fool, and he observed a number of things every time he stood in the housing pods, or stood in the observation towers or monitored the surveillance cameras in his office. Oftentimes, he would ride through his prison's parking lot and occasionally check on vehicles, especially when he noticed new and expensive vehicles. Just that same morning there were three new Mercedes sedans and one bright yellow sports car with a black convertible top and rather expensive rims, much like the Enkei racing series that he had seen with his teenage son. He would run the tags to determine ownership—how would any of his staff be able to have such luxurious automobiles he wondered? Colden didn't discuss his thoughts with staff until he felt they needed to know; he did much of his research himself unless he confided in his Personnel Specialist, in whom he had a great deal of confidence and trust.

Colden spoke with a number of the inmates in the chow hall, and felt pretty comfortable about the food services afterward. A few complained of not being able to get a job assignment for the extra time credits, and some asked questions about the policy on transfers to prisons nearer to their home areas. One rather loud inmate asked about getting thermal wear for the weather had changed, as winter was fast-approaching and the inmate told Colden he was always cold. Generally, Supt. Colden personally talked with the responsible staff when inmates complained of things having some legitimate basis, and he sent notes back to the inmates. After several hours of making his rounds, he went into conference with his team and shared notes on his findings on the inspections. He questioned the Captains on the rumors of the cellphones, and learned that staff searches had yielded nothing substantial. He asked about on-going investigations and the drug traffic, for he had already studied the drug testing reports, seen the number of inmates incurring disciplinary action for positive drug tests, and had arranged for division staff to monitor telephone traffic regarding drug activity. After discussion, he decided to set up a facility shake-down in the not too distant future; no date was determined, as he would tell his staff when they needed to know as well.

"Mr. Colden," spoke Capt. McLeod, "we are hearing of female staff hanging out too much in the gym and perhaps having sex with inmates, and we're monitoring that as well."

"Oh, yeah, what female staff?"

"Programmers, sir, but just hearsay from an inmate occasionally. Nothing concrete right now, but we're watching and listening."

"Stay on that, and keep me informed!"

Supt. Colden asked Maintenance Chief Torn to walk with him, as they left the meeting. "Let's check the fence, and talk." They exited the facility and began walking the northernmost zone, with Supt. Colden pointing out the weeds and growth in the area between the fences, referred to the cattle shoot or dog run. "Tell me, Torn, what is going on with your staff that they can't get this area treated with herbicides?"

"I've been out sick, you know, sir, but I'll deal with it today."

"Any word on those surveillance monitors in the lights you installed some time back in the inmates cells?"

"I didn't share that with anyone in my section, so I can monitor it myself, and with me just returning to work, that's a priority to do." Torn felt that he had installed the audio monitors in the right places, for the inmates were fairly new to the facility, and he had a gut feeling that he'd get lucky listening to their conversations with others in the housing pods.

"Well, get on this. And, get back to me at the end of the week," said Colden, "and, thanks."

Late fall

Buzz and Chuck had been to the religious services program earlier that evening and were sitting in the dayroom of their housing pod catching up on the talk.

"I hear Christmas activities here will be pretty neat, and that they're doing something new with foods coming in by church folks," spoke Chuck. "There's a church group organizing a Christmas program, with a play and singing. Special foods will be a good thing too."

"Yeah, but only cookies and cakes—not the good stuff like ham, greens, and cornbread."

"But that stuff has to be refrigerated, and we don't know how long it's been cooked and stuff like that. Cookies and little Debbie cakes, and moon pies are ok with me, man. Better than nothing, I always say! Come on, Buzz, let's be happy about it."

"Oh, I am! And you know, those church people are real nice folks, to think of doing something special for us in here."

"That Ms. Allabee, she wants me to try out for the skits, like Joseph in the program about Christ being born, and I said I'd think about it," remarked Chuck.

"Go for it, Chuck. Your hidden talents may show! It won't hurt, and I'd enjoy the play. When I was a kid at school, I always enjoyed watching other kids act out. Fun stuff."

Chuck responded, full of enthusiasm that Buzz supported him, "Thanks, my friend. By the way, have you heard from your friend, David lately?"

"Yeah, got a letter from him—he's OK. He says he plans to come up and visit me soon, and he has a surprise for me."

They sat watching a rerun episode of *MASH* followed by an older John Wayne western—*True Grit.* They liked each other, much like brothers each had never had, and each had developed a great deal of respect and trust for the other. Afterward, they went to bed.

It was past midnight and was relatively quiet on the housing pods for the general population. Counts had been conducted rather quickly and the Pod Officer for Block A had completed her shift narratives and was reviewing the inmate property sheets when Lt. Gibbs came through the electronic doors.

"It's quiet in here - any issues?" he questioned. Officer Mariel Gaben had worked the block for the past two years with no one questioning her as to how she managed the inmates or how she conducted cell searches, counts, or dealt with the inmates. "No issues; how are you doing, Lt.?"

"I'm doing well, Ms. Gaben; thanks for asking."

"Lt. Gibbs, tell me something, sir. I've taken the Sergeants' examination and passed. I've applied at two prisons and didn't get accepted or called for an interview. Any ideas why? What should I do?" she asked, and he noticed how she continually wrung her hands as if frustrated.

"Well, sometimes, prison managers are looking for people with a lot of service time. What or how long have you worked?"

"I've been employed for three years. The first year I was on the gatehouse entry team conducting metal detection on incoming staff, visitors, and checking IDs and purses and lunch containers. For the past two years I've been on rotation here in A Block on pods A, B, and C and I've had good performance appraisals," she said.

"Let me take a look at your application when you can get with me, and we'll see what you put on it," said Lt. Gibbs, "and you can call me Peter, when it's just us."

"I'll bring a copy tomorrow night, and I sure do thank you, sir."

"Well, have a good rest of the night. Call if you have a problem," said Lt. Gibbs as he exited the pod. "By the way, heavy rain outside."

As he stood outside the pod, he watched Officer Gaben as she patrolled the cellblock. She wore her uniform well, given she was quite shapely and petite, and her uniform had been crisp starched and pressed. Her make-up was limited to lipstick, a bit of eyeshadow, with a touch of perfume to her earlobes. Sporting small pearl earrings, she was rather nice-looking. He had never heard anything negative about Mariel Gaben. He'd also noticed the absence of a wedding band. He thought to himself that she'd probably make a good supervisor, and was really interested in doing a good job.

As the morning hours passed, the rain began to subside around noon. Counts occurred on schedule.

Staff shifts were managed without incident for the night's duration.

At first shift line-up, the Shift Commander McLeod spoke to his staff about the upcoming Christmas season programs and visitation as well as the special Christmas packages that the population could get in the mail from family and friends. The Division of Prisons had engaged in a program whereby inmate families and friends could pre-pay for certain food items and beverages that the commissary company would mail to the inmates in the two weeks before Christmas. The beverages were usually hot chocolate in powdered form and special coffees that hot water could be added to using the hot water taps in the housing dorms attached to the water fountains. The snack items were generally chips, cookies, gums, candies, cheeses, and sausages. The inmates would also be able to get fruits that were provided by the facility as well as pastries and punch and coffee provided by various local churches.

"Captain McLeod," spoke Officer Payne, "some of us have looked at the work schedules, and it seems that something is not right. Could we openly talk about this?"

"Raise hands for those of you who want to discuss this," he spoke.

Eight staff raised their hands, and Captain McLeod could see from their faces that they were frustrated, from their lips moving and heads shaking as well.

"What is the problem?" he asked.

Officer Payne spoke first, and said "I put in for Christmas week off, and I did that six months ago, sir, and now I am scheduled to work. I have worked that week for the past three years."

Another Officer on the back row of the line-up spoke up, "Sir, I'm Gideon Malloy, and I asked for a week off with my Christmas holidays, that's about ten days, because I've planned to go to Texas to spend Christmas with my kids. I put my request in four months ago, and have heard nothing on it."

"OK, what I will do is see each of you with questions after shift change. Each of you will contact your Shift Sergeant to be relieved to see me. Shift Sergeant Ben Hunt is your point of contact for this. He will schedule you, and I'll give him a sheet of times immediately after this line-up. Thank you for your patience, and we will see what we can do."

Immediately afterward, and for the next two hours, Captain McLeod spent talking with his officers. He arranged to have a meeting with Supt. Colden to work on getting his staff's time off, but he needed help to make it happen.

"Mr. Colden, I need your help with some staffing issues, sir. I know we are short, but several of my Officers are upset over being scheduled to work over the holidays. Several requested some holiday time off some months ago, but my shift is short nine officers. They have valid concerns, Sir."

Captain McLeod reviewed the work schedules with the Superintendent as well as the requests that had been submitted for the time off. Superintendent Kent Colden conferred with the Asst. Superintendent by telephone and with the Personnel Officer to determine what was going on with the hiring of the staff to fill the vacancies. He learned that several new officers were set to begin work the following day, and that transfers were being finalized to bring in five officers transferring from nearby prisons. "Let's get the transfers on in here," Colden told the Personnel Officer. "This will help you out, and if it falls short, get back to me," he said to Captain McLeod.

"Thank you, Sir," McLeod said on his exit. He decided to schedule each of the officers involved for a meeting the following day to advise them as to what would happen, and he felt relieved.

"Count time!" spoke one into the intercom system. Captain McLeod decided to go to the housing pods to observe his staff.

"Good morning, Lieutenant Adams," spoke Captain McLeod as he entered housing pod A of the general population.

"Good morning, sir."

Counts proceeded with no concerns, and Captain McLeod moved on to the gym to check on things. While standing in the hall, he glanced into a corner window, seeing a movement out of the corner of his left eye, as if a female had gone into the equipment storage with a person in inmate clothing. As he entered the gym, Jay saw him, said something to another inmate and quickly approached the Captain. The doors to the equipment room opened, with a female exiting with a clipboard in her hands, followed by another inmate.

"Hello, Captain, how are you doing?" she said on approach. "I'm catching up on the recreation equipment inventory for the end of the year, and I'm just about finished."

"Ms. Hondo, could we speak alone for a minute?" said Capt. McLeod.

Walking outside the gym, the Captain sternly reiterated the rules that she not go into any rooms alone with any inmate. She readily acknowledged them, but indicated that she needed to get her inventory done and could not get custody staff to assist.

"You can get a male program staff person to help you, Ms. Hondo, so you don't endanger yourself. Understand me clearly."

"Why, Captain, I'm not endangered; these guys take care of me," she spoke, to which Captain McLeod responded that they were convicted offenders and that there were certain boundaries. Again, he reminded her of the rules and suggested she go to her office. She walked off, as he stood watching her. He thought to himself: What is going on with her?

Captain McLeod re-entered the gym, walked around, talked with several inmates, and went into the recreation equipment storage room to look around. Jay watched him closely and wondered what if anything did the Captain suspect. Captain McLeod found the storage room to have shelving with basketballs, table games in boxes, and an assortment of other recreational items neatly stacked or in place. On the wall was another clipboard with an inventory that seemed to be monitored on a daily basis, as there were daily entries of equipment removed and returned. At least the gym or recreation clerk was doing something to account for equipment, or so Captain McLeod thought. It did seem unusual for the weight bench to be in the storage room when it could be out in the gym, and besides that it took up too much room to be in storage and could be a safety hazard for someone in there conducting an inventory. As he exited the storage room, he directed Jay to put the weight bench out in the gym immediately. He asked Jay the name of the inmate who came out of the storage room with Ms. Hondo. "Oh, that was Bill Judd, who checks out the new stuff to the guys, and he was helping her count the stuff," replied Jay.

"How many guys does it take to keep up with equipment? Aren't there four already assigned to recreation, or something like that?"

"We have to keep the floors clean, and the recreation yard, sir," Jay spoke, "in addition to all the stuff for the facility. There's all the new things Mr. Oxenberg expects as relates to those new standards for accreditation or something like that."

Captain McLeod walked off, with a questioning look. He thought this needed to be monitored a little more. He turned to take another look at the inmates in the gym, and locked his eyes on Brent Galen, a move that Jay observed. Looking at his watch, the Captain decided to move on to another part of the facility.

Sometime later that day before clock-out from assignments, Jay cornered Buzz, with a stern facial expression. "Hey, Buzz, anything going on? Why'd Captain McLeod lock eyes on you earlier?"

"Man, I didn't know he did. He looked at all of us. Means nothing to me. You make too much out of things."

"You'd better not be talking about what goes on in here, and you better hear me real good."

"Whatever," Buzz shrugged, throwing his hands into the air, somewhat dismissing Jay's threat. "Don't get paranoid, Jay!"

The population heard the screeching sounds first, then the message came through loud and clear, "Count time!"

That evening as the inmates were watching television, or doing whatever they needed to be doing, Buzz and Chuck were sitting in the threshold of Buzz's cell talking.

"Boy, that Jay is getting paranoid big time! Today, the Captain came into the gym; almost caught that Hondo woman with an inmate in the storage room. He ran her out. Jay thinks something is going, on and I'm talking about what goes on in there, just because the man laid eyes on me as he scanned the guys in there. It's almost scary how frantic Jay got."

"Watch your back, Buzz, because Jay will kill you if he thinks you're talking. He controls that game, and word is Hondo is driving a new Escalade that Jay paid for."

"Yeah, I saw her give him three new cellphones yesterday, and he handed her a wad of bills. He gave a phone to Titus Hawks right after. How is she getting that stuff in here, I wonder? She's gotten so cocky and arrogant, and she must never work 'cause she's always in that gym."

Chuck had an eerie feeling about Buzz's safety, and again told him to be real careful. "I've heard in the clothes-house that Titus Hawks is selling calls on a cellphone to guys; he's like a runner for Jay or that is the word. And he's doing a lot of tattoo business in that warehouse job he has in maintenance. He's supposed to be keeping up with their supplies and stuff back there, but he's done some fresh tattoos lately, and rumor has it he keeps his gear stashed in a maintenance locker. That maintenance man Torn will catch him sooner or locker, no doubt, cause he is sharp."

Chapter Four

Chuck, do you suppose you'll ever get another job? I mean with your health like it is, and you need the gain time, more so than that medical time credit stuff. You've been sicker a lot lately, haven't you?"

"I'm getting better—feeling better. I've asked for a job but can't do heavy lifting and being around chemicals; that bothers my respiratory system. Working around those cleaning detergents in the clothes-house, and all that cloth dust hasn't been good for me. Since I came out of there, I've got a bit better. I'd sure like to get more time credits. I spoke with Maintenance Man Torn; he's decent, it seems. And he strikes me as a sharp fellow, like I've said before. He said he'd see what he can do to help me out. He said they might give some extra time for guys to get out in an early spring release; something about easing the state's budget crisis. There's also a new thing about giving sick guys like me some time off their sentences who can't work but would like to." Chuck further commented, "Torn don't like that Hondo woman. He tried to talk with her about my time, and she wouldn't even talk to him. And he let it slip, but he's checking behind that Titus Hawks, and hopes to get him out of his shop. I could keep up with maintenance supplies easy."

"Hondo is playing a bad game, man. Some of those guys having sex with her are nasty heathens, and some of them are the worst homosexuals in here. She's got to be crazy or something. Captain McLeod made Jay get that weight bench out of the storage room, and she is hot over that.

Jay controls her good. And that Fran Russell comes around more than she should. Acting high and mighty. Believe she is jealous of Hondo or something. She don't stay in there but a few minutes at a time. How's your getting ready for the Christmas play?" Buzz asked Chuck.

"We've been practicing a lot, and it's coming along good. You coming to see the program?" asked Chuck. "I've been told I might get some extra time off my sentence for participating in this play; that would be terrific!"

"Yeah," responded Buzz, but one could tell he seemed preoccupied, and Chuck thought it was things associated with his observations of the goings on in the recreation gym. The both of them thought it was definitely wrong what was going on, but with them being in prison they felt threatened even discussing it. They both felt Jay was a danger to them and that he would either hurt them or kill them because Jay had a long history of assaults that were covered up for him, so he could play basketball in high school and college. There had been talk that Jay had been implicated in the murders of two college students but law enforcement could not prove it nor entice supposed witnesses to talk. On the streets Jay had friends who controlled drug traffic, prostitution circles, and had a gang of thieves who robbed convenience stores and small family-owned businesses. He may have been a big-shot ball player, but his circle of associations was certainly frightening, thought Buzz. Buzz and Chuck were continuously careful with whom they spoke, and decided it best to limit their interactions with others. More often they found themselves sitting in Buzz's cell talking, and that was okay with Buzz. He worried about Chuck's health and could see some decline in Chuck's energy level.

"Man, this play means a lot to me. I'm enjoying what we are doing, and I believe folks will like it. There are several guys who plan on a quartet singing, and they are really good," said Chuck.

"I look forward to this program, Chuck. Right now I'm bushed and am going to lie down. See you tomorrow. Usually you're the one that's tired, huh?"

"Night, my friend," said Chuck.

Lying in bed that night, Buzz thought of his life, his friends, and the things he had experienced in the past year. He really wanted to get out of the prison and become a better person in society than he had ever been. Times in prison were not what it used to be, and he no longer wanted to be in prison. He'd be up for parole in a couple of months, and was working for as much time credit as he could get. He finally turned over when he heard his cell door click-locked, and drifted off to sleep.

For the next week, the inmates rehearsed every evening for the upcoming Christmas play, and Chuck seemed exhausted more so than ever. But he was excited and looking forward to the play. So, he spent less time chatting with Buzz in the evenings and went to bed early. Buzz understood and acknowledged that, but he seemed to worry about Chuck's health.

Two days before Christmas

Around noon the intercom blared with an announcement about the Christmas play being produced that evening in the visitation hall. The inmate population needed to be on time as late-comers would not be allowed entrance once the play began. Chuck was excited; this opportunity meant a lot to him, and cell mates were constantly praising him about what they were hearing of his practice sessions—that he was good.

Chuck had committed himself to intensely studying the Bible, especially as it related to the story of Christ's birth, the trip to Bethlehem, and the impact of Christ's birth then and even in the present society. He thought a great deal of Joseph and how unselfishly he loved a woman who carried a child that wasn't his, but he also thought a lot about this special child called Jesus.

That evening about two hundred inmates attended the play, which lasted about an hour in addition to the quartet's singing of songs to celebrate the Christmas season. The performers received an outstanding ovation, and the fifty plus church visitors were excited and applauded them over and over.

The following day, special visits were allowed, and David Simms came to visit with Buzz. They shook hands and talked for an hour or so, and then blurted the intercom message that visitation was coming to an end in five minutes. David Simms vowed that he was seeing a positive change in Buzz and that he would be coming to visit more often. He also pledged to travel to talk with a parole board representative on Buzz's behalf.

"Buzz, it has been good to see you, and that change about you is good, my friend," said David.

"Thanks, David, it is always good to see you. I think of you often, and I would love for you to come back as often as you can," replied Buzz. "I wish you could meet my friend Chuck, and maybe you can one day."

"I'd like that, but take care of yourself in here," said David, as he turned to exit the visitation room.

That evening was Christmas Eve, and the prison staff had provided fruits and punch to the inmate population in the dayrooms as inmates watched the television, or played table games or just sat around chatting with each other. Buzz and Chuck sat in the cell talking, and Chuck could really see that David's visit meant a lot to Buzz. They talked a long time, and Buzz told Chuck how Fran Russell was spending time in the equipment room with Jay. Ms. Faye Hondo was still coming and going as usual. Both just shook their heads in disbelief, at the thought of people throwing away good jobs to satisfy sexual urges of inmates and the risk of contracting diseases and being caught and prosecuted. They discussed the idea of going to Superintendent Colden in confidence to let him know what was going on. But they also discussed other ideas: that he might not believe them and totally discredit them; that he would share the information with others and eventual word to Jay Dillon would leak; that Jay would hurt or even kill them; and that other staff might be involved and could frame one of them or both of things that could lead to more time in prison or loss of good time credits thus delaying any chances of parole eligibility. There was no way to determine what Superintendent Colden might do with the information. On the other hand they wondered what Captain McLeod might do if he were told; Captain McLeod seemed to be a professional who genuinely managed in a manner that was deemed 'right' and in line with policies. Buzz recalled how he sternly dealt with Ms. Hondo in the recent visit to the gym. In any event Buzz knew he certainly could not discuss any of this with his case manager Jesse Oxenberg, because of his association with Jay Dillon and Fran Russell.

Christmas Day was uneventful as to inmate disturbances; there were religious groups visiting and the day went well, with fruits and refreshments, especially cakes and pies, and coffee provided to the inmates. Given it was a holiday, there was a skeleton crew of staff working, with most of those being single persons with no children or families that dictated a need to be at home. Too, most of the staff favored the holiday wages to be earned in addition to extra time to take off in the near future.

As the evening hours progressed, Officer Mariel Gaben was making her rounds in the housing pod, and Sergeant Jacobi was standing in the dayroom chatting with some of the inmates, trying to get a feel as to how the day had gone. Most of the inmates feel the environment to be calm and generally positive; Officer Gaben did not sense any hostility and later commented to Sergeant Jacobi that things were okay. Sergeant Jacobi went on to make rounds in other parts of the facility.

"How's your week been, Ms. Gaben?" asked one of the inmates sitting in the dayroom watching tv. She responded that it had been "good" with a pleasantry smile as she was scanning the inmates, to include observations of those on the telephones.

"I heard that you are interviewing at other prisons, and hoping for a promotion, is this right?" asked the same inmate, a red-haired heavy set guy with a goatee, a wide gap in his front teeth and a large spider tattooed on the left side of his neck. He further added, "Sure would hate to see you go."

"Where did you hear that?" she asked, with a disapproving scowl.

"That's the talk at the chow hall, and even heard you're tight with Lieutenant Gibbs," said the red-haired inmate with a smirk on his face, as he walked toward her at the foot of the mezzanine stairs.

"Listen, young man, my business is my business, and I don't intend to stand here and discuss personal issues with you, and I'd appreciate it if you'd end that right here." Officer Gaben spoke in a high tone of voice and ascended the stairs to make rounds on the second floor.

"So be it, Ma'am, but I was just killing time and telling you what I heard," said the inmate. He then took a seat at a table with others who were playing cards.

Officer Gaben was angry regarding the rumors, as well as the fact that an inmate would ask her about her personal affairs. She wondered who was talking about her possibly transferring; she had only discussed this with Lt. Peter Gibbs but knew that staff in facility management would have gotten wind that she was actively going on interviews because of phone calls for reference checks. She thought that she would consult with Lieutenant Gibbs—maybe at shift change.

Chapter Five

Early January

Captain McLeod and Maintenance Supervisor Torn were sitting together in Torn's office listening to an audio tape of a conversation that Torn wanted to have Captain McLeod listen to. Torn had made it a point to vacate the maintenance area so that no other staff would attempt to listen in.

"Captain, just listen to this, and we'll discuss afterward."

The conversation was of two inmates discussing sexual activity going on in the gym area, of sex between inmates and female staff, of money exchanging hands, and of staff bringing in cellphones and cigarette tobacco to inmates. The names Hondo and Jay Dillon were mentioned more than once, as well as the voices having a sense of fear about them.

After the tape ended, Maintenance Supervisor Torn told Captain McLeod that the audio surveillance tape came from a device he had personally installed in the overhead light in a cell that housed one Brent Galen, aka Buzz, whom he felt was a decent sort of guy that worked in the rec area with Jay Dillon. He told the Captain that no one else knew about the surveillance device, and that he did not have Superintendent Colden's blessings to place it. He felt he needed to act alone out of fear that word would leak out, because so much had already leaked out from the facility administration, and he felt that Superintendent Colden was too trusting of others.

"You've done good, Torn, and have my blessings to keep this in place. We just need to implant or install some added surveillance, in the gatehouse. The guy, Brent Galen, is he a clean cut sort of tall one who works in the gym a lot?"

"He is clean cut, quiet, and sort of keeps to himself. And the other guy is a Chuck somebody—I can't recall last name, and he seems to be OK," said Torn. "But, Captain, I don't trust anyone in maintenance with stuff like this. Even Tyler's had a thing for this Hondo woman."

"I don't trust her at all. We need some kind of camera and audio surveillance in the gym and in that recreation equipment room, as well as the gatehouse. I want to know how she gets stuff in here, man, and quick," said Captain McLeod. "Give it some thought, and do your research. Let's talk in the morning over breakfast at the Waffle House in town, around seven A.M."

Capt. McLeod walked away thinking of things he had heard on that tape, and was quite worried. As staff Captain, he wanted to keep his job and wished that he could trust the supervisors, but he couldn't. And since Asst. Supt. for Custody & Operations—Matt Ranham—was out for extended sick leave, Superintendent Colden was relying on McLeod to ensure that operations were accord with policy. At least, he felt like Maintenance Supvr. Torn understood his position and would help. He went to the front gate house entry point to observe and determine how he could better monitor that area. On arriving at the gate house, he talked with the officers and positioned himself in the corner at the door that left the building going to the administrative building. In a mental picture of the area, he knew he needed a camera positioned above his head, with audio. He then walked out of the gatehouse, to stroll through the parking lot. Knowing that he needed to be cautious and not draw staff attention to his activities, Captain McLeod didn't stop at any particular vehicle but just strolled looking at all vehicles. One bright yellow sports car, a Corvette convertible with expensive rims, caught his attention, as well as a white Mercedes sportster with a license plate that read "ME." He mentally tried to record the license plate on the Corvette so he could determine ownership. He knew the Personnel Specialist had the skills to research this data and get what he needed, but wondered if he could trust her. He then went back to the gatehouse, and asked for maintenance to be called, and he asked for them to determine when they could sweep the parking or blow it clean, hoping this would satisfy those minds of persons who saw him walking through the parking lot. He also asked if trash barrels could be placed in the parking lot for staff to dispose of trash and in which they could empty their cigarette ashtrays, instead of dumping them on to the parking lot. He then exited the gatehouse and went back inside the main building, to speak with Vanis Goodson, the Personnel Specialist.

"Ms. Goodson, could we speak, please, ma'am?" he asked standing on the threshold of her office.

"Yes, Captain McLeod, come in and sit, please," she spoke as she closed the door and ushered him to the far end of her office. She had positioned her work space on the far wall away from her door, to avoid staff eavesdropping at her door. And she had placed a small radio on a shelf on the wall adjacent to the door, and kept it on daily. She enjoyed country music and also knew it would help to disallow anyone from hearing what might be said in her office.

"First, let me come to the point: Can I trust you?" he asked, and quickly said that she was taken aback by that comment.

"Captain, rest assured that I don't gossip and certainly, don't share anything that is confidential with others, except perhaps Superintendent Colden on a need-to basis. Also, my files are locked behind two keys, and no one has a key; those are in the emergency red key box in Superintendent Colden's closet that has to be accessed with his permission. Now what can I help you with?" she asked.

Captain McLeod then asked if she could search out vehicle records.

"Captain, you know we have technology which I can use for tracking records on vehicles. Do you have the license plates' data?"

Captain McLeod than gave her the license plate which read "ME" and the one which read MBA1119. In conversation, they decided that he would return the following afternoon for her findings; he thanked her and left.

Around 6:45 A.M. the next morning Captain McLeod gassed-up his vehicle at the local Sunoco station on Highway 242 and proceeded on to the Waffle House. He saw that Marcus Torn was already there, because one could spot his old two-tone brown and rusted Jeep Comanche truck in the parking lot. Going inside he spotted Torn in the rear booth, and took a seat across from him.

"You order already, Torn?"

"Just two cups of coffee. Thought you might want to order for yourself, sir," said Torn.

The waitress came on over with the two cups of coffee, and greeted Captain McLeod. "Hey, Buddy, haven't seen you in a while. Where have you been hiding?" she asked, smiling intently at him, ignoring Marcus Torn.

"Working, Maybelline, just working all the time. You've been doing okay, I suppose. And I want a big breakfast this morning, with grits, two eggs over easy, country ham, biscuits and grape jelly, please."

"And for you?" she asked looking at Torn. He responded that he'd have the same as his friend. Maybelline walked away to get their food.

"Well, what did you come up with?" asked Captain McLeod, and he hurriedly told Torn that they needed a surveillance camera in the gatehouse with audio.

Torn then told Captain McLeod that he had researched and a wall clock containing a surveillance camera with audio could be mounted in the gatehouse in addition to the same being placed in an illuminated exit sign over the door that allowed building exit. "It will cost about eight hundred dollars, and I'd have to install this equipment myself into the clock and sign in my office and then install them in the gatehouse, so no one will be the wiser. I don't think anyone would suspect anything but with that exit sign already there we'd have to damage it to justify a replacement," Torn said. "But we could say that the replacement meets accreditation standards and move on. Folks know we are changing things anyway because of our efforts to gain national accreditation. What do you think?" he asked Captain McLeod, who gave his okay to proceed. They discussed the purchasing aspect, and McLeod said that Torn could make the invoices and purchase orders to read for accreditation standards.

"What about the recreation equipment room?" asked Torn.

Captain McLeod then asked if an overhead ventilation square

would allow for a surveillance device with audio, to which Torn responded that he would prefer to replace the main overhead light with a special light that contained a surveillance with audio in the light framing mechanism, as well as add additional fluorescent lighting in the gym area. He further commented that he would install a back-up set in a ventilation panel that could be in the ceiling panels. He indicated that this was probably the most expensive part of the plan, and that he would prefer to shut down the gym for two days in order to do the work he needed to do. He would rather not have any inmates in there to guess what was going on or ask questions. Captain McLeod told Torn to get the materials ordered and get back to him so he could provide a notice to staff and inmates on the temporary closure of the gym. They proceeded with their breakfast, and departed for work.

Over the next few days, the weather changed to cold from mild more often than in the weeks before, with more rain causing inmates to have to spend more time in the gym instead of being allowed outside. This also meant more staff supervision in the gym, which concerned Jay Dillon, as well as fewer visits by Faye Hondo. The big-screen television was constantly watched by groups wanting to view sports games, using their pocket walkman audio sets linked in to the games. The pocket-sized walkman audio enabled inmates to listen to the games, even though the televisions were in a reduced audio mode, commonly referred to as silent TV. Others sat around the game tables, playing cards, dominoes, and checkers. The inmate janitors were constantly cleaning up trash, and wiping down the water fountains, but this suited Buzz who wanted to stay busy for it kept his mind on track and he earned extra merit time off his sentence when the gym was in full use on inclement weather days. He also slept better at night after a full day's work. Those spending more time in the gym included Jesse Oxenberg, his case worker, who enjoyed watching sports and talking to inmates about various teams, players, and scores. In fact, rumors abounded that Oxenberg was betting on the games with some of the inmates and kept notes in a book which he carried on him.

"Hey, Galen, how's the job coming?" he asked Buzz. "You're earning a lot of merit days for the extra work keeping this place clean. And your equipment inventory look good, or that's what Ms. Russell has said."

"It's a job, and I like to be busy, unlike most of these guys who are just in here killing time and hanging out," Buzz responded. "My parole eligibility is coming up this spring; do you think I might make it?" he asked.

"Don't know, with your priors and all, but there's nothing really assaultive. I guess we'll wait and see," Oxenberg commented, and walked on off in the direction of where Jay Dillon was sitting.

Oxenberg spoke to Jay about a number of things and remarked that a second big-screen television had been ordered to be installed on the wall opposite the existing TV and was to be delivered soon. Jay asked if that meant more scheduled TV viewing sessions, because mentally thinking that would interfere with what he had going on, and he didn't want more sessions. Oxenberg advised him that no added sessions but that some inmates were often complaining that they wanted to watch more movies or shows, whereas the majority in the gym wanted to see the games. Thus, one television would show games or sports channels, and the opposite television would be tuned into movies.

"Count time!" blurted the intercom system. "Dinner meals will be served a little earlier today, so go to your cells immediately."

That evening Buzz and Chuck sat in the cell chit chatting about recent events and how things were going. Chuck's asthma and diabetic conditions were much better, and he commented about being on medications which seemed to be helping him, although he didn't care for the daily insulin injections. The both of them were enjoying the religious programs more, and especially the Bible Study groups.

The following morning Buzz walked into the gym, seeing case manager Fran Russell sitting close at Jay's desk with her head leaned toward him whispering. Seeing Buzz walk in, Jay hollered and told him to come on over. "Ms. Russell says we have to do a yearly close-out inventory this morning of all our gym equipment, so we need to see your sheets on this, Buzz."

Speaking up, Fran Russell said the entire facility is having to recheck all equipment, and turn in the reports as soon as possible to the front office, and that she was told to eye-ball everything in the gym, and that an Officer was coming in to help her. "I would appreciate it if your listing would advise the location of the equipment to make it easier for us," she said to Buzz in a firm voice. At that point a tall male Correctional Officer walked in, introduced himself, and said he would be assisting with the recreational inventories.

"Well, let's get started then," she said as Buzz had given her a copy of his latest inventory, which he had done six days prior.

At the conclusion of the inventory, Fran Russell and the Officer left, and Jay thanked Buzz for his work. "You know, your inventory sheets were thorough and on the money. That helped tremendously. Thanks."

"Just doing my job," Buzz spoke, "and we'll continue to keep it straight."

An hour or so later, Captain McLeod entered the gym and advised Jay Dillon that the gym would be closed at twelve noon on Wednesday, and not re-open until Monday morning for additional lighting to be installed, an addition wall-mounted big screen television, and other noise reduction systems that would aid in national accreditation efforts. He further advised that all inmates would get their regular work time credits even though they would not be allowed in the gym.

"There will be a notice posted in the next hour, Dillon, so be sure you tell the workers to read it," Captain McLeod told Jay Dillon, "and this also pertains to you." He further advised that all program staff had already been advised accordingly.

McLeod watched Jay Dillon closely as he spoke with him. "Yes, sir, Captain, but I will need to be provided guidance on the television and how to operate it."

"Oh, the maintenance supervisor will instruct you on Monday," Captain McLeod advised Dillon, and exited.

Later that day, Maintenance Supervisor Torn met with Captain McLeod to ensure that everything was in order. In fact, Torn had contracted with a local electrician who would be assisting him install the lighting and television, because he did not want to use anyone on his staff for fear of detections to the surveillance equipment implanted in the lights and ceiling panel. Justification for this had been made since the electrician had worked on accreditation issues at the local jail in the physical plant areas, and extra funds had been made available for contracts of added personnel.

At the end of the week, all the work had been done in the gym by Friday evening, with the gym secured and Captain McLeod had given orders that the gym remained locked until his final inspection on Monday morning. "Good morning, Captain, how did the weekend go?" asked Superintendent Colden as they both exited their vehicles in the parking lot on Monday morning.

"I spoke with the Officer in Charge late last night, and things over the weekend went well. Rather quiet sir," responded Captain McLeod. "Sir, we need to talk this morning, and I'd prefer we have that discussion away from the facility, if at all possible."

"That serious, huh?"

"Yes sir. I need to bring you up-to-date on some things before you leave for that conference, or has that changed?"

"No, Captain, I still plan to leave tomorrow afternoon and return on Thursday morning," responded the Superintendent. "But, we can ride together to check those crews of inmates working at the county recycling center, around nine thirty A.M., and we'll go in my car."

They both entered the facility, greeting the gatehouse staff cordially, and both endured the usual entry inspection and walkthrough of the metal detections. Captain McLeod proceeded to the operations center, where he reviewed the weekend's shift narrative summary reports and reviewed the use of three and incident documents posted on the facility computer systems. He briefly met with the Lieutenant and the two Sergeants working in the custody office, and left for the ride with the Superintendent.

While exiting the gatehouse, Captain McLeod observed Maintenance Technician Ace Tyler carrying a box en route to the gatehouse. "What do you got there, Tyler?" he asked.

"Plumbing parts, sir, and mostly PVC pipe to repair those bathrooms in the lock-up center," responded Tyler. "They stay torn up, and we are continually having to do repairs."

Captain McLeod nodded as if to indicate he was aware of the continued repairs, and walked on to the waiting vehicle, with Superintendent Colden sitting at the wheel. On getting into the vehicle,

Captain McLeod looked back and saw that Tyler had already exited the gatehouse, which puzzled him because he didn't think that box of parts could have been inspected in such a short time span. Mentally noting this, he thought to himself that he would need to check on this. Was it logged in? Was the box of parts fully examined? Did Tyler get checked or go through the metal detection?

While traveling Captain McLeod gave the Superintendent a summary of things starting with his seeing Ms. Faye Hondo in the gym, coming out of the equipment room, the audio tape he had listened to with Maintenance Supervisor Torn, the installation of the surveillance equipment, as well as the concerns he had about certain vehicles in the parking lot and things he had heard about various staff. Superintendent Colden complimented him on his aggressive approach and advised him to proceed on, but to keep him posted. He also told Captain McLeod that he was right to be cautious as to which staff that could be trusted, but that he could trust Vanis Goodson in the personnel section.

On arrival at the recycling center, they walked around and observed what the inmates were doing, especially looking at the safety factors, the inmates' training on machinery operations, their work apparel, gloves and boots and headgear. They then moved on to look at the location where inmates took breaks, ate their lunch, where their foods and beverages were stored in the break room refrigerator, and the restroom facilities. Superintendent Colden frowned on seeing a public telephone mounted on the wall in the break room and asked if the inmates had access to this or was it usable with phone cards. The center manager quickly saw Colden's look and frowns, and spoke up anxiously hoping to answer in such a way as to relieve his anxieties about the phone. Moving on to walk through the recycling center, Colden wanted to talk with the inmates about the work they were doing and hear their views. As he did, they talked about the heavy lifting involved, the absence of midmorning breaks, lack of toboggans in cold weather outdoors, and various other complaints, and he advised that he would look into them once he and Captain McLeod returned to the facility Superintendent Colden and Captain McLeod felt pretty good about having gone to the recycling center and felt that staff there were certainly safety conscious, taking measures to ensure that worker and inmate safety was a priority.

Returning to the correctional facility, and having summoned Maintenance Supervisor Torn, Captain McLeod immediately proceeded to the gym where he visibly checked the equipment put into place to include the new wall- mounted big screen television. Jay Dillon and other inmates, in addition to several program staff, were waiting in the hall. In fact, he openly spoke about the added lights as the inmates were signaled to enter the gym. Raising his voice he spoke to the inmates, "All equipment in here, guys, needs to be taken care of because we will not be spending taxpayers' money on more big-screen TVs and continually buying basketballs, and that kind of stuff. I'm sure our legislature don't like frills in prisons."

As Captain McLeod scanned the inmates' faces, Jay Dillon watched him closely to see if he focused on any particular inmate for more than a moment. That not happening, Jay Dillon moved away toward his desk, as Fran Russell and Jesse Oxenberg stood looking around. Oxenberg spoke up about the lighting being so much brighter, and that it would help them get good reviews when the accreditation team came in, because the candle lighting output would be better in the evenings and that might help with using the gym more often for special programs. He also told Jay Dillon that the new television should be set for the sports games because it had a better picture, and the population would be in awe. Fran Russell spoke to Jay with sarcasm saying that accreditation was a load of bull and too expensive, and she turned to check the equipment storage room. As she opened the door, she spoke that she saw no difference there except to note that the shelving that previously been constructed of wooden two-by-fours had been replaced with heavy duty metal shelving racks, and it looked good.

"Count time!" came across the intercom, and it seemed much clearer than in the past when it was a screeching sound almost as if someone was dragging fingernails across a bulletin board. All the inmates proceeded to go to their cells.

Chapter Six

As Officer Penelope Payne conducted the counts in the general population with Sergeant Ben Hunt accompanying her, she spoke to many of the inmates on the block and inmates in B housing pod, though she was a bit more friendlier than in the past. Several still found her to be sharp-tongued and oftentimes heard her degrade inmates about their unkempt cells and personal hygiene. She habitually left lockers in disarray after her searches, oftentimes leaving hygiene item bottles opened, turned over, pictures removed from the locker walls and thrown on beds, all of which humiliated inmates.

The count was called in timely, and she continued making observational rounds, conducting locker and cell searches. The intercom sounded off that the inmates in the pod could proceed to lunch, and onto medication pick- ups. She watched as the inmates collected their ID cards and exited the pod, and she then proceeded to the dayroom to monitor those inmates who remained behind. She had glanced at the menu posted on the TV screen in the dayroom, taking note of the meal consisting of turkey sandwiches with fried potatoes, salad, and beverage, and thought that folks were fed up with turkey on the menus but that the food budgets benefited from the extra USDA meats provided to the state's prisons. A number of the inmates in the dayroom ate packaged chips or cheezees with soda purchased from the canteen.

"Officer Payne, you ought to see that new big-screen television on the wall in the gym," said a young man thought to be in his twenties who sported several tattoos on his neck, and wore his long dirty-blond hair pulled back in a ponytail with a shoestring. "Boy, this is the life, wall-mounted TV big as one at the theaters, hot foods, your own room, and we can kill time all day!" he spoke.

An older inmate with several front teeth missing, a receding hairline and thinning hair was sitting in a nearby chair at a table playing solitaire spoke, "Speak for yourself, you stupid lazy nerd! It ain't so great in here, with no smokes, no beer. And you need a bath!" he said as he pointed his fingers at the younger man. Officer Payne took note of the old man's brown and orange-yellow stained finger tips. She stepped forward and told him to calm down, but she could also dictate a foul odor about the younger man.

She turned to him and asked if he had showered lately, to which he responded, "What for?"

"Young man, your hygiene leaves a lot to be desired, and if you don't wash with soap today you will incur a disciplinary report," she said. She further gave him a direct order to take a shower, and told him that she would not tolerate his stink in the housing pod another day.

"Ms. Payne, want us to handle that for you?" said a big fortyish man with long unkempt hair, tee shirt rolled at upper arms, both arms full of tattoos sitting in a chair leaning on the wall next to the phone. "We'll clean him up, just give us the word," he commented.

Standing next to the man stood Titus Hawks, who spoke up in support of 'taking care of the problem' for her with the inmate. "Yes, sir, he sure could use a scrubbing!"

Officer Payne quickly told the inmates to stay out of it. She thought that they themselves didn't look much like ones to be telling anyone to wash or clean himself up.

The day went pretty quickly. Buzz and Chuck sat at the same table to eat their dinner, and sat around for an hour or so in Buzz's cell talking.

"Chuck, I might be needing to get me another job. Jay Dillon is more suspicious of everybody working in the gym and on the recreation yard, and he knows I don't like the idea of Ms. Hondo being in there all the time. And that Russell woman is always rubbing against him and being in that storage room with him. Ms. Hondo brought him more cellphones in there this morning, and I saw her give him a box of what might have been coffee. He now has a coffee pot hidden in a wall cabinet behind his desk. I saw him hand her a fat brown envelope! Dillon is always watching me, and he frowns all the time. I don't give Hondo or Russell the time of day. Oxenberg hides in there so he can watch TV, drink coffee, and just hang out!"

"I can't wonder but how they bring it in. Word is that man Tyler in maintenance brings stuff in for Hondo; he slips around with her I've heard," said Chuck.

"I'll just be glad to be out of here!" Buzz responded.

"Me too," said Chuck.

Shortly thereafter, the lights flashed, indicating that the inmates had twenty minutes to use bathrooms, or whatever, and get into their cells with the lights off.

The following morning when the intercom signaled count time, to be followed with break, two Officers were making rounds in the housing pod. Officer Payne looked in the celldoor window of the blond haired young man with the tattoos, as he had not moved on his bunkbed. She tapped on his door, and observed no movement. She tapped on the door again, and called for the control center to open his celldoor. As the door opened, she heard him moan, and she called for the second Officer to come help. As they lifted the blanket off the inmate, Officer Payne could see that his hair had been hurriedly cut, and he had scratch marks and bruises about his backside, legs, and arms. Using her walkie talkie she summoned medical staff and the officer in charge. Other staff came to assist, moving the inmate onto a litter, or a body carrier; he was conscious but unable to move able on his own. He was taken to the infirmary, where medical staff examined him, and began to arrange for transport to the local emergency room where he could be further examined and treated. As they later learned, the inmate had failed to take a shower the previous evening, and other inmates in the housing pod had dragged him into a shower after the evening meal, and had scrubbed him head to toe with a janitorial brush, with soap and Ajax, and someone had whacked his hair off with razors and shanks. He fought against them, and was beaten, and unfortunately he had been unable to identify his assailants. Captain McLeod had Sergeant Ben Hunt pulling video surveillance in the housing pod to determine what had occurred, who could be identified, and why the pod had been short staffed, as there had been no supervision of the restroom area.

The inmate called Murphy was transported to the local hospital by facility vehicle, and upon arrival was checked and provided x-rays to ensure there were no broken bones. His small finger on the left hand had gotten broken in the scuffle, and infection had set in where the skin was scrubbed raw in several places about the body. Still he told the staff in observation that he could not recall anyone's face among those who assaulted him, and he was determined not to tell anything, and when he was returned to the prison two days later, he advised the Superintendent that he knew nothing and couldn't recall faces or names.

For several weeks there were no serious incidents, and things were going rather smooth and quiet. Additional staff had been recruited and hired, and Assistant Superintendent Matt Ranham had returned to duty on a part-time basis. Facility operations were still delegated to Captain McLeod, until Ranham could return to work full-time. On a daily basis, Captain McLeod walked the facility making stops at the gym almost every day as well as walkthroughs in all the housing pods. But for a few weeks, Jay Dillon and Faye Hondo had stopped their activities, since both had a suspicious nature about Captain McLeod and his more frequent rounds. Even Fran Russell and Jesse Oxenberg were making less frequent visits to the gym. Buzz was spending more time on the outside recreation yard, since the weather was a bit more allowable for outside sports and leisure time. Even the days seemed to go quicker because there was so much more to do with maintaining a clean yard, handling more recreation equipment, as well as maintaining the gym area.

Two newly-hired officers had been assigned to the recreation and exercise yards, and they constantly walked the yard searching for contraband and talking with the inmates.

"How are you, young man?" one of the new officers said, speaking directly to Buzz, who was wiping mud off basketballs at the entry of the outdoor storage shed where sports equipment was held.

"Doing fine, sir," spoke Buzz.

"What is your name?" the officer asked, to which Buzz responded. "Well, I am Officer Davis. What do most of these men do out here?" he asked Buzz.

"Well, most of them just sit on the bleachers and kill time, talking and enjoying being outside in the fresh air, sir," Buzz commented.

"Well, carry on with your chores, as I guess you are one of the janitors," said Officer Davis, as he walked off.

Later that day, Jay Dillon asked Buzz about his conversation with Officer Davis. Buzz spoke that Officer Davis was just making an introduction of himself, nothing special or to worry about, and that Officer Davis stopped several inmates and spoke with them. But Buzz did indicate that both the new officers habitually searched the yard, and the yard equipment, especially the weight area and the cushion wraps around the basketball poles, and that was something he had rarely see other staff do. This too worried Jay Dillon.

At mail call, Buzz received a letter from the state parole board; tearing into the letter he learned that his friend David Simms had indeed traveled to talk with his assigned analyst about his parole eligibility. There were indicators in the letter that Buzz would be given a review in the next few weeks, and that David Simms had advised the parole authorities that Buzz would have a residence plan at his home. Buzz seemed to feel good about his upcoming review. After the evening meal, he shared his good news with Chuck as they sat in his cell talking. Chuck was elated at his friend's good news. Buzz also relayed the latest goings-on about Officer Davis, the reduced activity in the gym, and Jay Dillon's paranoia. The reduced activity in the gym was short-lived, because Captain McLeod's workload increased and he began to make fewer rounds in the facility causing Jay Dillon and Faye Hondo to pick up their games in the gym. Even the maintenance man, Ace Tyler, began to go into the gym more often than he ever had, and generally he had carried a box with him.

On occasion, Captain McLeod was on observation in the gatehouse, and noticed Ace Tyler enter with a box of PVC pipe plumbing parts; staff failed to inspect the PVC pipe, even though Ace Tyler had casually opened the box to show it was PVC pipe. With his suspicious nature,

Captain McLeod decided it best to let Ace Tyler take it on inside, and watch him.

Captain McLeod continued to spot-check the parking lot and have his reviews with Vanis Goodson. She had given him information on the two vehicles he had inquired about. The yellow Corvette convertible was registered to Jesse Oxenberg, and the white Mercedes sportster was registered to Faye Hondo. He had learned that Jesse Oxenberg's motor vehicle records carried two driving violations and he was looking into facility files to determine if they had been reported as they were supposed to, especially since one of them was a driving while impaired offense and the other was an offense of having a prescription bottle of controlled pain- killers in the vehicle with the prescription having been for another person. Captain McLeod also wondered how both these staff could afford the vehicles on their salaries. Jesse Oxenberg had been employed at the facility for two years and until recently had driven an older model Mazda pickup. Faye Hondo's driving record showed three speeding tickets on file in the past few months, all of which were from the adjoining state in a beach town, and all tickets displayed late night time elements on them as well. He figured he had his work cut out for him, and intended to learn all he could about the two staff, before going to Superintendent Colden.

As she was making rounds, Officer Mariel Gaben spoke to several inmates in the housing pod, mostly about the change in weather. She checked cells and performed locker searches, as usual, and her counts were well done.

Coming to Buzz's cell, she stopped, speaking to them, "You two guys are always sitting and talking. What's up?"

"Just killing time, Officer Gaben," spoke Chuck. "And it's quiet, and we just like each other's friendship. It's good to find a friend in here."

"I suppose so, but don't you ever watch television or read the newspapers?" she asked.

"Well, sometimes, ma'am, we can't do anything about what's in the news, so why worry about it? And there's not much on the tv," spoke Buzz, "unless it's an occasional western or a good action movie."

"I suppose," she remarked and walked off.

Buzz and Chuck watched her, as she moved about the tables of inmates sitting around in the dayroom, chatting with some of them. Buzz spoke, saying, "She seems okay, and tries to do a good job. She could be a better case manager than that Jesse Oxenberg."

"Yeah, she's okay. Heard is she is trying to go elsewhere for a Sergeant's job," said Chuck.

"Maybe she'll get it. That Oxenberg hangs out everyday now in the gym, and so does Faye Hondo and Fran Russell. They had slacked off a while, but they are back to bad business dealings," said Buzz. "Why, even that Ace Tyler out of maintenance hangs in there with them too much. He's on the dirty. He gave Jay Dillon a bag, and I heard it had cellphones, and dope in it. I saw him with a wad of rolled bills this morning, and he was stuffing the wad in Ms shirt. I believe they are all in cahoots," commented Buzz.

"Wow, Buzz you'd better be careful!"

"Yeah, that Jay Dillon watches everyone in there, and he's dangerous! But, man, I want no part of their dirty games."

"I'm tired, Buzz, and I'm going to bed. See ya," exiting the cell door and going to his cell.

Buzz sat and read his Bible for a while, before turning off his cell light and getting into bed.

"Count time!" on the intercom awoke the inmates. Afterward, they had breakfast, made medication calls, and those with assigned jobs went to their respective assignments. Sometime before lunch, Jesse Oxenberg went into the gym and spoke with several inmates, whom he had on his caseload. Buzz was on his list, and would see him after lunch, and had hopes that Oxenberg had news about his parole review.

"Mr. Oxenberg, we have an appointment, sir" said Buzz as he stood at the door to the programmer's office.

"Oh, yeah, come on in!" said Jesse Oxenberg. "How are things going with you? Still happy on the recreation janitor job? You always seem to be busy when I'm in there."

"Things are okay, sir, but I'm hoping you have some word about my upcoming parole review. I got a letter recently and am waiting for word."

"I got a copy of that same letter but have heard nothing else, other than I have to provide them with a progress report. I know you are working, going to religious programs, have no adjustment problems or disciplinary issues, and just generally doing okay," said Oxenberg.

"Yes, sir, and I go to those social coping skills and anger management workshops, when they are held," remarked Buzz. "My work time credits are still on mark, and I've worked some overtime to earn extra days off my sentence."

"That's to your benefit, and you are doing okay. Tell me something about that man who visits with you. He acts like he cares a lot for you. Does he have money? That might help speed up the parole review process, you know. Even the officers on your housing pod say you are not a problem child to theme," said Oxenberg.

"Money? How does that fit into this?"

"Well, a thousand or two dollars in the right hands could help get the parole board folks on the move," said Oxenberg. "Ask him if he could help you out and let me know. Anything else to talk about?"

"No, sir," spoke Buzz as he stood to leave.

"Well, as you've heard before, keep your mouth in check about things in the gym, and we'll see how things go for parole reviews," Oxenberg spoke sternly, with a strong look of warning to Buzz, as he dismissed him from his office.

Buzz returned to the gym, and on entering heard Jay Dillon's yell to talk with him.

"How are things going, Galen?" inquired Jay Dillon. "You had a meeting with Oxenberg; how did it go?" "Okay."

"Good; maybe parole reviews will happen in the next little while," commented Jay Dillon. "I know a lawyer who'd make some calls to the parole folks, if we could get him a thousand or two dollars in the hand. By the way, some new basketballs and table games came in that need to be added to inventory."

Buzz thought about this, and he didn't want to use David Simms or his money. David was a good friend, and Buzz thought that his parole would have to come in the regular way, and he had no intentions of even asking this. He went about his work on the inventory, ensuring that the new equipment was added, tagged and put into storage. That night he talked with Chuck, especially about the money issue, as he thought Chuck has more experience with these matters.

"No, Buzz, don't go there. Your parole will get a review because that's the law. Don't try to buy it. Lawyers just take your money and do nothing. That Oxenberg is playing a game with you. He's dirty and has played that game before with other guys. I've even heard his name come up about guys paying him lots of money to get prison transfers or changes in their custody levels. The word is that he's even been going out with inmates' wives in exchange for them to get transfers, custody changes, or extra gain time when they don't even have a job. He'll fall one of these days and ought to be doing time for some of the stuff he's done." Chuck was angry as he spoke, ending the conversation with saying that Jesse Oxenberg was "slicker than mud, and crooked."

"Chuck, you are a good friend too, and it helps me to talk with you," said Buzz.

"Man, let's go to sleep. I'm tuckered out. Going to my cell. Goodnight. See you tomorrow," spoke Chuck as he exited Buzz' cell.

Early the next morning the "count time" intercom signal was extremely loud. The day went well with no incidents. Marcus Torn, the maintenance supervisor, met early with Captain McLeod with a desperate sense to talk with him. They listened to the audio tape taken from the speaker system to the surveillance technology installed in the overhead lighting in Buzz's cell several times. Captain McLeod was visibly angry, and seemed to get worse each time Torn played the tape for him. "Damn that Oxenberg, he's been doing this the whole time he has been here! No wonder he's able to buy that expensive car!" spoke Captain McLeod.

"You know that too, huh?" said Marcus Torn, "and that's not the only car he has. And his phone line shows tons of calls to inmates' family members all the time."

"What do you mean?" said Captain McLeod.

"You do know you can check the phone computer in the electronics room and see where calls are going, how many and when?" asked Marcus Torn.

"No, I didn't. How does it work? Let's go show me," directed Captain McLeod, who stood up putting the surveillance tape in his coat pocket.

They went to the electronics room, where Marcus Torn demonstrated how the computer system worked, with tagging in certain room phones to be checked. He showed how one could check the phones used in the segregation control center, the control center phones in the general housing pods, as well as office phones. Captain McLeod had no idea of this technology, and was puzzled that he had not been made aware of it. Then he recollected that when it was being installed he was attending a four-week workshop on prison perimeter fence systems across the state, and it had slipped his mind. Further he inquired of Torn as to who had clearance to run the phone check system, and was pleased to learn that only Marcus Torn and Vanis Goodson in personnel had authorizations. Occasionally Mrs. Goodson would use the system to check phone calls when telephone bills were extremely high or a question arose about staff in control centers sitting on phones constantly.

Captain McLeod asked Torn to "run Oxenberg's office for me and let me see his," which Torn obliged.

Studying the print-out, Captain McLeod whistled aloud, "Geez look at these calls! Now, can we match these numbers?" he asked.

"Yes, sir," said Torn. "By individually plugging in the numbers using this code, it will show the inmate's PIN number that the phone number belongs to, like this."

"Boy, this is great! You have earned every dime the state pays you, Torn, and I appreciate your working with me on this. I appreciate your trust too," said Captain McLeod. "Would you run me a print-out for Oxenberg's office for the past sixty days and get it to me? please?" to which Marcus Torn nodded that he would do today.

By now, Captain McLeod knew he needed to sit down with Superintendent Colden and review the materials he had, as well as getting proper authorization to get law enforcement involvement in the investigations which needed to be done. However, unknowing to the Captain, Superintendent Colden was being drawn into the case on his own. Around late morning on that same day, he received a call from two people. It was a pleasant day and he had decided to take calls from family members and other interested parties to the inmates housed in his facility. The first caller had been a woman he thought might be in her late twenties to early thirties, and she was quite emotional crying and generally upset. She relayed to Colden that she had been married to an inmate for several years but married before he was sentenced, and they had two small children and she was struggling financially. She did work and a neighbor took care of the two little boys while she was at work everyday. In the past three weeks, she had had an unannounced visitor on two occasions who was an employee at the prison. His name: J. Oxenberg, and she had been led to believe that Mr. Oxenberg could help her husband move through the prison system and eventually get out in short time. Because she had no money, she had been forced into having sex with this Oxenberg fellow in her home while her sons were asleep. Oxenberg had beaten her on both occasions because she refused his demands, and he ultimately raped her. She wanted, and needed, to write to her husband and let him know what was going but she was fearful her husband would be hurt or even killed, because Oxenberg had told her that if she did this that he would see to it that her husband never came home. She was fearful of calling the police as well because of possible danger to her children. She needed help and was calling the Superintendent to ask or plead for his help. She indicated that she could provide Oxenberg's vehicle license plate to him, and that her neighbor had witnessed Oxenberg's vehicle being in her yard on both occasions. Her neighbor she said was willing to talk about this as well. Superintendent Colden told her that he would get back to her that day but he needed to do something that could help her.

Chapter Seven

Prior to going to work for the prison system, Superintendent Colden had served as a law enforcement officer in a couple of towns and had been in the military police while in the US Army when he served at Fort Bragg, North Carolina. Given his background and the things he had learned in years past, he knew he needed to enlist the help of the local police in the lady's community, and possibly the state's police bureau of investigators as well. He made some calls to contact some individuals with whom he needed to talk, but before he could get out of the office, the second disturbing call came from a man who identified himself as one David Simms, a friend to an inmate Brent Galen, aka Buzz.

In talking with Colden, Mr. Simms recounted having received a call the day before from one J. C. Oxenberg, who claimed to be an attorney representing the inmate Brent Galen and was working on a parole review. He indicated that if he could get two thousand dollars up front that he could persuade the parole folks to expedite Galen's review and possibly help get him on out of the system. However, he had spoken with Brent Galen, aka Buzz, just last night and was advised not to send any money to this man, and that Buzz thought this man to be Jesse Oxenberg a prison staff person. Buzz had told David Simms about his conversations with Jay Dillon and Jesse Oxenberg on money just recently. Buzz assured David that he was okay and needed to discourage David from sending any monies to anyone. Superintendent

Colden advised David Simms that he would definitely look into this, and that Mr. Simms should send no monies to anyone. Superintendent Colden was all too familiar with scams committed everyday involving inmates, and was not surprised with the current situation. He did ask if Mr. Simms would talk with the law enforcement and himself in person if he could arrange it, and Mr. Simms agreed to do so. He also assured Mr. Simms that Brent Galen's welfare would be a top concern for him. He wrote down Mr. Simms's phone number and residence address for further information, and put it in his pocket. Leaving his office, he advised his secretary of his plan to be out of the office on business and she could contact him by cell phone if needed. He proceeded to an appointment with a local police Captain, who was to meet him in the local District Attorney's office with an SBI agent.

Walking into the local courthouse, he checked the marquee to determine where the District Attorney's office and proceeded on, fully acknowledging on entry that he was apologetic for being late but he had gotten tied up on the telephone. He provided a full introduction of himself, and thanked those present for agreeing to meet with him. He immediately began providing the reasons for the meeting, with focus on the two phone calls as well as suspicious activity going on at the facility and indicated that he felt he would be getting additional information shortly based on the installation of the surveillance equipment. He asked that local police meet with the inmate's wife and neighbor, and that more frequent patrols in their neighborhood be made; in the interim he would be working to relocate the victim's husband from his facility elsewhere for safety reasons. His thoughts were that if the staff person saw police in the area with more frequency on patrols that the staff person would stay away, until the police were ready to question him in the assaults and rapes. During the meeting, his cell phone rang, and it seemed that Captain McLeod needed to meet with him urgently and briefed him on the telephone. Superintendent Colden told Captain McLeod to bring what he had to the courthouse, and meet him in the main lobby. Once the phone call ended, he briefed the others on the information he had received, and they all agreed to hear it all and then decide on an approach to take. Captain McLeod arrived and shared his information, to include the surveillance tape, the information on the two vehicles and telephone computer tapes on the phone calls. All present agreed that Superintendent Colden needed added help from their respective offices. Discussion focused on their need to sit down and interview Brent Galen, aka Buzz, about what he was observing while working in the gym, and the approach to be taken because he would need to return to the prison afterward and they needed to ensure his safety. Eye-witness accounts were deemed important, and they needed to start with that, without letting on that they were investigating. It was decided that they would issue a court writ to have Buzz brought to the courthouse for an interview on a revisit to the theft of the truck for which he had been convicted, based on new information received in the case. But to set the stage it was decided that the District Attorney would send a letter to Buzz to let him that the case was being re-opened because of new information, and that he would be re- interviewed in the near future. Buzz received his letter in two days and was anxious but excited at the prospect that the case was being reviewed and that perhaps he might be found innocent and released. He shared his news with several people to include Chuck; Jesse Oxenberg, his case manager; Jay Dillon, in the gym; and others. They all wished him good luck and hoped he get a fair shake; Buzz was certainly on cloud nine. The writ arrived, and Buzz was transported by Captain McLeod because the facility could not spare an officer for the trip because they already had six officers out on trips and court orders before the writ came in. On arrival at the courthouse, they proceeded to the Office of the District Attorney, who was waiting with the SBI agent and the police department Lieutenant who had been assigned to the prison case.

"Sit down, please, Mr. Galen," spoke the District Attorney who introduced himself, and the others. "First, I want to apologize to you for misleading you. You have been led to believe that the incident of a stolen truck for which you were convicted and sent to prison is being reinvestigated, and that is why you are in this office. That was told to you as a cover for your being here today, and I must ask that you not disclose to anyone what we are discussing. However, I will work on the truck case, separate and aside from our conversation today. I understand you work in the prison recreation area on the rec yard and in the gym, is that right?"

"Correct, but can I ask a question?" spoke Buzz.

"Go ahead," spoke Superintendent Colden.

"You lied to me to start with," said Buzz looking at the District Attorney, "in that letter, to make me want to come talk with y'all? But why?"

"You used the word lie, but we wanted to keep you safe in the prison, and not have people wondering why you were coming to this office, so it was easier to say it was about the stolen truck case," said the District Attorney. "But I do promise to look into that case and I want to talk with you about it, but first talk to us about what's going on in the prison."

"Okay," responded Buzz. "There are staff bringing things to a guy named Jay Dillon, and two females who are employed there who are having sex—I think—with inmates and maybe staff. Jay Dillon has threatened me if I opened my mouth about what I've seen going on in there. He's suspicious, but he's tight with this woman named Fran Russell and has stuff going on with another named Faye Hondo. Faye Hondo is always in the gym, in and out of the equipment storage room with inmates, usually for ten minutes or so. Those guys slip money to Jay Dillon before they go in. When they come out, they comment, like 'she's hot,' 'she's on fire today,' 'git more of that soon,' and so on. Their pants are sometimes undone, and her clothes are wrinkled, or twisted, and her lipstick is smeared and her hair is disheveled. Then Jay Dillon gives her money. Sometimes I've seen her bring him cell phones or hand him bags with cigarettes, and some of the guys say she brings him dope. Titus Hawks who is housed on my pod is involved with Jay Dillon, as I've seen him give Hawks a cell phone. Word is Hawks sells phone calls and does tattoo work."

"How long has this been going on?" asked Superintendent Colden.

"I've been in there about five months now, and it's been going on during the time I've been there. I don't know about anything before my time going in there to work."

The SBI agent spoke up and asked whether he could name some of the inmates that had been in the equipment room with Faye Hondo, and Buzz said he could find out what their names were but there had been so many of them. He asked how they came to be in possession of cash monies, and Buzz told how they suitcased money in paper form in their butts, and some kept dollars rolled tight and lodged into ink pen barrels. The prison staff didn't check ink pen barrels, and seemingly didn't know how to check things like ink pens, chapstick containers, and watches. He told how inmates wore dead watches, where the watches had been gutted so that the watch could be used to conceal things like dope and tightly-folded money, especially large bills. The SBI agent could recall a conversation where legislators didn't think inmates should have jewelry, because of their bartering and trading, given that prisons had wall clocks. He then asked Buzz if he had any idea as to the amounts of money that exchanged hands over a week or two, and Buzz answered that he "had no idea, but saw a lot passed."

"Describe this equipment storage room, please," spoke the District Attorney.

"Well, it's about a ten by ten, with shelving on the rear wall that holds table games, extra sports equipment, and a weight bench in the corridor area. It's a neat room, with a light overhead. No windows." Spoke Buzz.

Captain McLeod spoke up, "Where did the weight bench come from?"

"Oh, it's the one you told them to take out a while back, sir. But, Jay Dillon had it put back a week or two back," spoke Buzz. "And there's one of those self-defense cushions in there on the bottom shelf, with some janitorial cleaners on the shelf with rags."

The District Attorney proceeded to move the conversation along, asking about other staff who spent a lot of time in the gym.

"Well," spoke Buzz, "that maintenance man, Tyler, is in and out of there a lot, carrying a box of stuff. Jay Dillon goes through the boxes and hands it back to Mr. Tyler. I've seen Mr. Tyler go in that storage with Ms. Hondo several times, and he puts his hands on her rump area right there in the gym."

"What about the Russell you mentioned earlier?"

"She's tight with Jay Dillon, always rubbing his neck, kissing on him, and putting her hands on his back. She gives him stuff, too."

Captain McLeod then asked Buzz who else knows this stuff, to which Buzz remarked that he only talks with his friend Chuck about it, because he didn't trust other people and if anything leaked to Jay Dillon that he'd probably be hurt and it would be serious. He then spoke about the inmate who had been beaten, with his hair cut using shanks and scrubbed with janitorial brushes, a case with Captain McLeod readily remembered. Buzz said, "Jay Dillon gave the orders to take care of that inmate, Murphy, I believe is his name. Some of us believe Titus Hawks followed Jay's order."

Buzz then asked a question as to how he had been fingered to be talked with. Captain McLeod spoke up saying that because Buzz worked in the gym and was trying to keep a clean record that they thought he might know something and might talk. Nothing was said to give a clue about the surveillance equipment in the overhead light in his cell.

"Let's move on, please," spoke the District Attorney. "Would you give us a written statement on all of this, Mr. Galen?"

"Yes, sir. But can we talk about why I am serving time for stealing a truck that I didn't steal?" said Buzz.

"In a minute, but let's finish. Can you do this in a week and give me names of the inmates who have gone into that room with Ms. Hondo?" asked the District Attorney.

"Yes, sir, but I would need to write it here. I wouldn't want to write it in the prison and have someone finding it who would search me."

The District Attorney indicated that he understood and would set it up to look like Buzz was being returned to the District Attorney's office on the truck case. He then asked Buzz to talk about the stolen truck case, and Buzz told his side of the story, and suggested that his friend David Simms be questioned because he had found out some things on that as well. The District Attorney gave his word that he would follow-up on that.

Speaking up, as an end to the interview session, the District Attorney addressed Buzz, "You don't need to mention this meeting other than to say that we are reinvestigating the stolen truck case for which you are incarcerated, and that we have heard your story and reviewed the court transcript. And, that we are going to re-interview witnesses and will have some decision or some action in the next few weeks. Do you understand? If someone asks how your case got our attention you can just say that the truck has again been stolen and wrecked, but the complainant's story doesn't add up. But the best action is to not discuss the case at all so you don't slip up and say something, to raise someone's curiosity, not even to your friend."

Buzz responded in the affirmative, that he "understood very well, and I thank you for your time, sir."

Superintendent Colden and Captain McLeod asked Buzz if he thought he'd be okay to which Buzz spoke in the affirmative. Captain McLeod placed Buzz in the normal transport restraints and proceeded to take him back to the facility. Superintendent Colden continued to have conversation with the others, and learned they were in the process of determining of how the two vehicles in question were purchased because there were no outstanding bank loans on either vehicle. The District Attorney was in the process of obtaining a judge's order requiring the dealerships which sold the vehicles to provide documents on the vehicle sales, and was in communication with the Internal Revenue Services and the state revenue office on obtaining copies of tax documents for Faye Hondo and Jesse Oxenberg. Too, the State Bureau of Investigations was conducting interviews with the alleged rape victim and her neighbors, as well as tracing the tickets that were on record for Faye Hondo from the adjoining state. Superintendent Colden agreed to continue matching the phone calls from the facility to inmate numbers, and turn his information over to the SBI, and they would in turn talk with the persons at those inmate home numbers to determine other inmate wives that might talk about questionable calls or visits by prison staff or other activities to include propositions made to the females. Those in the room would be touching base with each on a daily basis, and later make a decision as to when they needed to meet in person. They hope to coincide the meeting with the inmate's deposition, but knew there was a need to expedite their actions so as to not jeopardize the inmate's safety and well- being.

Chapter Eight

The District Attorney made good on his promise to reinvestigate the truck theft, and the next day sent an investigator to locate and talk with David Simms. He told them all he had learned from his trips into the poolroom, about the vehicle insurance deal and what the locals hanging out at the poolroom had told him. The investigator then proceeded to the billiards hall to talk with the guys who generally hung out there drinking and shooting pool. Several guys were ex-convicts who wanted no more trouble, and confirmed David Simms's story that the truck owner had, indeed, loaned the truck to Brent Galen, aka Buzz, who had been sleeping in the building just to key an eye on the place after closing hours. The investigator advised the District Attorney of his findings and worked to subpoena the truck owner to the District Attorney's office for an interrogatory and deposition statement, within forty-eight hours. However, the truck owner had heard rumors that the guys in the billiards hall had talked to an investigator, and had taken off on the run. The investigator had his work cut out for him because it was important that he locate the owner and have him appear in court.

"Count time!" over the intercom later that evening found Buzz lying on his bunk after the supper meal, recollecting the happenings and conversations that day. He knew he had to avoid discussing his situation. After the count procedures, Chuck came by his cell and stopped in for a minute to chat and asked if he thought his case might get an honest review. Buzz said he "thought so, but we have to wait and see what they find out. I feel okay about it."

"I hope things turn out good for you, my friend. Are you going to church services tonight?" Chuck asked, letting Buzz know that the prison gospel band was playing and singing. Chuck had joined the group, playing an acoustical guitar. And he occasionally played the keyboard instrument, as well as sang.

"Oh, yes, I'm going. You know I would not miss hearing your group."

In a few minutes the intercom system blurted out that those going to church services needed to make their way to the visitation room, as the services would begin in five to ten minutes and those not already in there at commencement would not go in. Buzz and Chuck proceeded to the visitation room.

Lt. Peter Gibbs and Officer Mariel Gaben were in the hallway at the entrance to the visitation area scanning the inmates' identifications, and watching the visitors from the local church. At exactly seven o'clock that evening the visitation room doors were closed, and Lt. Peter Gibbs signaled for services to begin, and he left, leaving an unidentified Sergeant in charge. The minister briefly spoke to encourage some of the inmates to get involved in the preparations for the upcoming Easter program whereas there would be a skit on the Resurrection of Christ, with a special hour devoted to a gospel singing that the Superintendent had approved along with some well known professional athletes coming in to talk about their faith and personal relationships with God. The minister then engaged in prayer and proceeded to allow the gospel band to sing a song before he moved into his message. After his message, the gospel band played a few songs with the last song being a congregational hymn, followed with prayer and closing remarks.

Exiting the services, Buzz expressed his praise for the gospel singing group to Chuck, saying that they "were so great tonight."

"Thanks, Buzz," responded Chuck. "The instruments are new, and we are gonna start practicing more often, so we should get better."

The inmates proceeded back to their cells, with some going to the dayroom to watch television or make phone calls on the payphones. En route to his housing pod, Buzz glimpsed the television and saw that the station was devoting the week's shows to John Wayne movies, so he decided to sit and watch *McClintock.* He went to his cell, retrieved his pocket walkman, and went to the dayroom, and picked a table on the outer edge and sat down, motioning for Chuck to come over and sit with him. Chuck had gone by the canteen and purchased a couple of bags of chips and two soft drinks, and offered one to Buzz with a bag of cheez-bits. Chuck carried his pocket walkman in his shirt pocket because he listened to gospel music more and more every day, along with country music. The time passed rather quickly, with inmate movement continuous in the dayroom as well as inmates in and out of the showers. The movie ended, with commercials indicating that other John Wayne movies would be playing for the next several days. Both Buzz and Chuck had decided they wanted to watch some of them and said goodnight to each other and others as they proceeded to their individual cells, just a few minutes ahead of the intercom's squeal for "Count time!"

The following day, Chuck suffered a severe asthma attack while leaving the chow hall after breakfast, and was taken on a litter to the medical station and later transported to the local emergency room. The incident was upsetting for a number of the inmates from his housing pod, and Buzz, because they felt that medical staff did not attend to him as quickly as perhaps they should have. And rumor had quickly spread that Chuck had also suffered a heart attack while he was in the medical station awaiting the arrival of the local emergency medical services transport vehicle. One inmate who was in the medical station at the time described how he saw Chuck yell, grab his chest area at his heart, and pass out.

Someone asked if Chuck was unconscious and did anyone provide him with CPR, and the inmate said he saw a nurse rush over and start working on him and that "she did try to do CPR, but I don't know from there because I got pushed out of the way."

Buzz asked several of the inmates in the housing pod to get word to him if they heard anything, that he needed to get to his job in the gym because of equipment inventory needing some work.

Arriving at the gym, Jay Dillon hollered at Buzz, letting him know he was late and that Ms. Russell had been in there two times looking for him so she could review the inventory. Buzz advised Jay Dillon that his friend, Chuck, was sick and he was worried, and wondered if Jay

Dillon had heard anything. It soon became apparent that Jay Dillon had not heard of the possible heart attack although he did know about the incident in the dining hall. At that moment, Fran Russell entered the gym, walked over to Buzz and sternly asked where his equipment inventory was; Buzz had retrieved it from his locker in the gym and gave it to her. She scanned the document, and told Buzz to go recount the new, unused volleyballs and the checkerboard sets on the storage shelf. Buzz opened the storage room door, and propped it open with a chair, as he was finding himself to be more claustrophobic and he attributed it to being confined in a cell. He checked on the two items and provided those numbers to Fran Russell, who found his numbers or count to be correct.

"Well, they sure don't coincide with what accounting is showing for the new balls purchased in the past six months," she remarked, looking at Jay Dillon. "Accounting is showing they have purchased and paid for sixteen new volleyballs, and you are showing a dozen new balls in stock."

Buzz thought for a minute, then spoke, "There were some that were loaned to another facility, weren't there Jay?"

"Yeah, that was a few weeks back on Mr. Oxenberg's orders, and those balls were given to him in a cardboard box, and he was to get the paperwork done to show them as loaned out. Didn't he talk with you on that, Ms. Russell? Said he was going to."

Fran Russell looked at Jay Dillon and back over at Buzz, with a stern look on her face. Buzz spoke, "Look on my back sheet and see if I didn't make a note of that."

Flipping over to the back sheet of the documents, Fran Russell saw that notes had been made on a certain date, with a time element on it, Jesse Oxenberg had removed four new volleyballs from the gym's equipment inventory room for loan to another prison, and was going to consult with Ms. Russell to advise her. "Well, you certainly did note it to cover yourself, but no one told me anything! Thank you and next time," she said, looking at Jay Dillon, "you need to let me know!"

"The same applies to the difference of count for the checkerboard sets, Ms. Russell," spoke Buzz. "Look at my notes on that as well."

Fran Russell looked at the notes and saw that Buzz had documented the removal of the board sets by Jesse Oxenberg. She signed the documents and walked out, and others could see she was in an angry state.

"Wow, I've never seen her in such a state before. Wonder what set her off this morning," commented Jay Dillon.

"Yeah, I wanted to ask if she'd heard anything about Chuck."

Jay Dillon tried to calm Buzz and told him to do something to get his mind off Chuck, such as cleaning the storage shelves, cleaning at the outside weight pile or something.

Some time later when the "count time" signal blurted, Buzz proceeded to his housing pod, only to hear that rumors were spreading word that Chuck was critical and in intensive care at the local hospital. This word spread through the dining hall as the inmates ate lunch, and Buzz asked several staff what they knew only to be told they knew "nothing." Officer Payne told him she'd try to find out something and get back to him, but could only tell him that Chuck was at the hospital, condition unknown.

That evening Buzz went to the religious services held and was pleased when the minister mentioned Chuck's name in his prayer. After the program, Buzz sat alone at the corner table watching the John Wayne movie in silence, and went to his cell immediately after. He found it difficult to sleep that night, tossing and turning in his bunk, with Chuck on his mind seemingly all night. In thought, he felt a deep sense of loss because he thought of Chuck as a brother, and he was worried. Finally he drifted off to sleep during the night and awakened just prior to count time.

At breakfast, Officer Penelope Payne told him that she had heard that Chuck did suffer a heart attack and was in the critical care unit at the hospital and might need surgery. Buzz thanked her for telling him, and asked her if she could keep him posted on Chuck and she smiled and agreed to do so.

The day's weather was mild, with some sunshine, and Buzz was working as janitor on the yard. He was cleaning out the storage building and installing new shelving for better storage of the outside recreation equipment, breaking only for his lunch meal. When he had completed the project, he went to his housing pod and showered just in time for the intercom blurt, "Count time!" After the supper meal he returned to his housing pod, to his cell, and decided to write to his friend David Simms, but didn't get too much past letting David know what had happened to Chuck. Closing his letter, he put it in the mail collection box, and sat down to watch television, hoping to get his mind off Chuck. Afterward he went to bed tired and really wanted to get a good night's sleep.

"Count time!" blurted the intercom, awakening Buzz. Getting up he hurriedly washed his face, shaved, and got ready to go to breakfast. While waiting on the doors to the housing pod to open, two Officers came in to search cells and lockers, and did check five to six cells without incident. The inmates were allowed to proceed to breakfast. On exit from the dining hall, Officer Payne told Buzz that Chuck was going to have some kind of heart surgery from what she had heard in the medical station. He thanked her, and proceeded on to the gym and to the recreation yard to work on rewrapping the basketball goal posts. He knew he needed to keep busy, but continually thought about Chuck, the goings on with the District Attorney's office, and his parole review. He worked all day on the recreation yard, and stopped at the gym in the afternoon to record his work on the day's work log because it was an accreditation item that needed to be documented. He had been told that accreditation reviewers looked to see if and when equipment storage areas were cleaned, how often the goal posts wraps were tightened or relieved of slack, how often the basketball pads were painted, and the condition of the weight benches as well as frequency of repairs.

The work log was hanging on the inside of the storage room door; he rather quickly went in, opened the door and found Jay Dillon engaged in a sex act with Faye Hondo. Jay Dillon became outraged, hollering, "Get out!" Buzz quickly closed the door and glanced around to see the inmate watch-out staring at him. The watch-out had been so engaged watching the small television on Jay Dillon's desk that he failed to see Buzz enter the gym and didn't see him go to the storage room door. Jay Dillon came out of the storage room, angry, followed by Faye Hondo who left the gym in a hurry.

"Man, I could kill you!" barked Jay Dillon focused hard and intent on Buzz. Turning to look at another inmate, he pointed his finger, shakily, saying, "And, you," he yelled at the inmate watch-out, "get out of here, but you better keep that mouth closed!"

In a state of shock, with his hand clasped over his mouth, Buzz stammered, saying, "Man, I haven't seen anything!" Buzz sat down in a nearby chair, and said that he just wanted to note his work on the log and go take a shower. After a while, Buzz retrieved his logbook, made his notes and left the gym, going to his cell to take a shower and await supper. Jay Dillon made a mental note that Buzz was still visibly upset on his departure, and thought he needed to stay away from him for the next day or so.

That evening after supper, Buzz went to his housing pod and cell and kept to himself reading and he went to bed well before the call for the lights out. Awaking early the following day, he got up and washed his face, shaved, and brushed his teeth and dressed, and awaited the call for breakfast. Just as the call for breakfast was made, he saw two officers with somber looks on their face go into Chuck's cell across the dayroom with white plastic bags, followed by Sergeant Ben Hunt. He could see that they were bagging all the items of property, placing all bedding items out on the floor, and going through all Chuck's mail and books in his wall locker. They removed all things from the wall above the bunk, and from the storage bay under the bunk. As if frozen, Buzz just watched, wondering what's going on, yet too scared to ask a question. He saw another inmate walk toward the Sergeant and ask, "What's up Sergeant Hunt?"

"Just go on about your business and let us do our job," responded the Sergeant with his head down. Finishing up, the two officers left the housing pod with the bags, and Sergeant Hunt arranged for the dorm janitor to thoroughly clean the now empty cell. He then departed the housing pod, leaving only Officer Penelope Payne who had come in for observation duty. She then proceeded to tell inmates to go ahead to the dining hall for their morning meals. Turning around she saw Buzz focused on Chuck's cell door, with a strange look on his face. Walking over to his cell, she spoke, "Galen, aren't you eating this morning? Breakfast will do you good."

Buzz asked, "Can you tell me anything, Ms. Payne?"

"All I have heard is that his surgery didn't go well; he's very critical and not expected to come through, but if he makes it through the next few days he'll be sent to a prison hospital for recovery and possibly rehabilitation services."

"Thank you, Officer Payne. I'm not hungry, and if it's okay I'd like to just stay in here for some quiet time."

Sometime around noon, case worker Jesse Oxenberg summoned Buzz to his office, for the intercom rattled off several names of inmates to go to their case manager's office.

"Mr. Oxenberg, you wanted to see me, sir?"

"Come on in, Galen. How are things going with you?"

"Not so good, sir. You must know my friend Chuck is in a bad way?"

"Seems I heard something about him, but he might come through it. Let's talk about you. Anymore word on the parole review? Did you ever think anymore about a lawyer, and did you ever talk with your friend Simms about the money?"

Buzz responded that he was not going to ask his friend for money, because he didn't feel right about, and that he had not heard anything more from the parole board. He just figured it would take some time.

Oxenberg could see that Buzz was preoccupied over his friend Chuck but proceeded to ask how the rec job was going.

"It's still okay, and I appreciate the extra time credits, Mr. Oxenberg. The weather is getting better, and I've been working on the rec yard a bit more and straightening up in the equipment storage building on the yard in anticipation of the accreditation reviews. When the paint comes in, I'll get the basketball pads repainted. Right now the weight bench on yard number two needs to be reupholstered but we don't have the foam to stuff it," said Buzz.

"I'll get that ordered today, if I can, and I'll talk with maintenance on the paint. I've checked the equipment shed and you did a good job installing the shelves, but the shed needs a good coat of stain and varnish."

Buzz responded that he would get the stain applied as soon as he could if the weather held to allow a day or two drying time, and then he would apply the coat of varnish weather permitting with a couple days drying time. Then he asked if Mr. Oxenberg had received any word on the progress report that he had submitted on Buzz, and Mr. Oxenberg indicated "no" and given the current agency's priority for work on classification reviews that he "didn't expect to hear anything anytime soon." Oxenberg further told Buzz that he intended to credit him with extra merit days for the staining and varnishing of the building they had discussed, and hoped that would help in his case. Buzz let him know he would appreciate that, and stood up to leave the office, when Oxenberg said that he hoped his friend got better.

"I hope so, too, and thanks," said Buzz, leaving the office.

For the next few days, there was no word about Chuck, other than his possessions having been placed in storage. Buzz did receive a letter from his friend David Simms, who acknowledged that he was still waiting on word from the parole board, but was doing well. He also indicated he has doing some renovations to his house, and had enlarged one room and added a bathroom, which would be Buzz's quarters when he got out. To keep busy, Buzz continued his work as recreation janitor and attended religious services.

Captain McLeod had gotten back on somewhat of a schedule of making rounds in the facility, although not routinely making them every day or on any particular time schedule. He had been checking on maintenance purchases, and reviewing the work orders especially for bathroom repairs and pipe replacements. It seemed that Ace Tyler from the maintenance department had been bringing in a substantial amount of PVC pipe, and Captain McLeod had watched the surveillance tapes from the gatehouse and failed to see anyone physically checking that pipe. While making rounds in the facility, Captain McLeod had even seen boxes that resembled those containing the PVC pipe sitting in a corner in Faye Hondo's office; he wondered why those boxes had not been maintained in the maintenance section or recycled. He met with Marcus Torn, maintenance supervisor, one afternoon to review his findings, and it seems that there were only a few work orders for bathroom pipe replacements to be made, yet there had been substantial purchases of three inch PVC pipe. They then learned that an order for more pipe was to be picked up over the next couple of days. Captain McLeod then decided to follow the pipe on its entry into the facility, and so advised Marcus Torn.

The next morning, Marcus Torn, made Captain McLeod aware that Ace Tyler would be coming in late because he had made plans to go pick up the PVC pipe on his way into work. Captain McLeod watched the gatehouse via the surveillance camera monitor in his office. Ace Tyler was not searched, nor did he walk through the metal detector and the box was not checked. Walking through the corridor, passing the hallway leading to the maintenance section, Ace Tyler proceeded on toward the gym and inmate housing pods area. Captain McLeod intercepted him just as Ace Tyler approached the operations hall, and asked him to come to his office, for a minute.

"But, I need to go check the bathroom in the gym. I understand it is stopped up right now," Tyler spoke.

"Well, it will keep for right now. Is there a work order on it?" asked Captain McLeod. "Let it keep. Just come with me, please." Captain McLeod escorted Ace Tyler to his office, stopping by the Operations Center to pick up the Lieutenant on duty to accompany him. Once they entered the Captain's office, he advised Ace Tyler to sit down and pointed to a chair. Walking to the chair, Ace Tyler positioned the box under the chair and sat down. Captain McLeod summoned Marcus Torn to his office. On arrival to the Captain's office, Torn was asked what he knew of any problems with the bathroom in the gym, and he knew of none and hadn't been advised of such.

Captain McLeod then directed Ace Tyler to give the box he had placed under the chair to Marcus Torn. "For what?" asked Tyler, "it's PVC pipe parts." All could detect Tyler's nervousness, and the Lieutenant then positioned himself in such a manner at the door as to block an exit. Marcus Torn reached for the box, but Ace Tyler was in such a state that he dropped the box causing the lid to fly open and PVC pipe to fall out as well as packs of cigarettes, cigars, and small plastic bags with green leafy substances.

"I can explain this! It isn't what it seems, Captain," mumbled Tyler, and he sat down.

"Just sit there, Mr. Tyler, and be quiet! You will have your time to tell us about this," Captain McLeod spoke in a loud tone, pointing his finger at Tyler.

Captain McLeod and Marcus Torn picked all the contents of the box off the floor and placed it on a side table, emptying all the box contents. Upon close inspection, they determined that the contents had been taped to the insides of the PVC pipe to where one could not readily see it. Captain McLeod then directed Ace Tyler to empty all his pockets onto a second table, and upon doing so, he was found with four packs of cigarettes and two cell phones.

"Sit back down!" spoke Captain McLeod, who then picked up his telephone and summoned a Sergeant from the Operations Center to bring a camera to his office immediately. The Sergeant was told to photograph all the items on the tables and to make several photos of the PVC pipe and the box. While this was going on, Captain McLeod went to an adjoining office and contacted Superintendent Colden and advised him what had happened. Superintendent Colden called his police contact and asked for police presence at the prison. On arrival the police Lieutenant was escorted by Superintendent Colden to the office of Captain McLeod, where Ace Tyler was then questioned by the Superintendent and the police Lieutenant.

"How long have you been doing this, bringing in cigarettes and stuff, Mr. Tyler?" asked Superintendent Colden, who looked at Tyler without batting an eye, full of intensity, and very direct. In fact, rumor had it that staff were scared to death of Superintendent Colden if he caught you in the wrong.

"For about five months now."

"Why in the pipe?" asked Captain McLeod. "And how many cellphones have you smuggled inside? I am going to assume the bags are filled with marijuana? Tell me: how much money have you made on these deals over that period of time?"

"I've only brought in about four phones counting those two. I saw the pipe used on my last job in the juvenile center where I worked prior to coming to the prison," spoke Tyler. Feeling the pressure, he further added "And the bags have marijuana. I suppose I've made around forty-five thousand dollars, but understand I needed the money for medical bills for my son, who is deathly sick and needs some really expensive surgery."

"Forty-five thousand dollars? How did you get that money from the inmates?"

"Mostly cash, and sometimes it got left in a can down the road in the edge of the woods or mailed to me at the post office."

Captain McLeod then asked, "What post office?"

"In the village— Glen Cove. Inmates' family members would send me money orders or cashiers' checks. Cash usually came in the can, and I picked it up when I went home."

"How much are the cell phones selling for to the inmates," asked the Superintendent, "and are they selling calls on them?"

"They cost me twenty-nine, ninety-five and I get one hundred and twenty nine dollars a piece for them. I've heard they sell calls for twenty bucks for five minutes."

"How much cigarette tobacco have you smuggled in, and how do you sell it?" asked Captain McLeod.

"A pound costs me six dollars, and I get a hundred dollars for it," said Tyler, "and I've heard a cigarette goes for five dollars. Just hearsay from some of the inmates. I'll work with you if you'll help out on this, please," pleaded Tyler. "I've got four children; my son is so sick, and my wife can't work because he needs her at home with him everyday."

The police Lieutenant then asked about the can and how that came to be. Ace Tyler said it was his idea, and that it was a white can about a gallon size sitting in the dirt behind a large pine tree off beside the road, next to a vertical white pipe near the stop sign at the left entranceway to the prison. He further told that inmates' friends also paid for him to bring stuff into the prison, usually dope which they left in the can with the money, with notes. He claimed he didn't ask questions but handled it for the money. He emphasized the need for the money more and more, until he broke down, becoming emotional. Captain McLeod produced a handkerchief, gave him a bottle of water from the office refrigerator, and waited a few minutes for him to regain composure.

The police Lieutenant questioned him as to the recipient of the phones, cigarettes, and marijuana, to which he declined to talk until he could talk with a lawyer. Ace Tyler's work identification badge was taken, he was handcuffed and escorted out of the prison, and placed into a police vehicle waiting outside the prison. The box and all the items were placed into a plastic bag, and turned over to the police Lieutenant. Captain McLeod directed the Lieutenant and Sergeant to complete written statements as to their observations and actions, after which those statements were witnessed and photocopied with the originals given to the police Lieutenant, along with copies of the photographs. The Lieutenant and Sergeant were then instructed to return to their normal duties but not discuss the incident further other than documentation into the shift narrative for the day's events.

"Good work, Captain," said Superintendent Colden.

"I'm glad you refrained from mentioning that surveillance we have in the gatehouse, sir," said Marcus Torn. "It'll serve us well, I'm sure."

"I don't want to expose that at all, but I appreciate your help, Mr. Torn. We are a good pair," said Captain McLeod, shaking Torn's hand. "I guess word is spreading like wildfire in this place! The poor guy! If only he'd sought out agencies that could have helped him, and we could have helped with some fundraising for the boy's case. We might not have been able to raise a lot, but he would have his job. Now he's heading to prison, facing the Internal Revenue agencies for costs associated with that untaxed money, and his family is headed for the welfare rolls. What a disgrace and a shame for his family. Oh well!"

The police Lieutenant assured them he would alert the State Bureau of Investigation as well as the state and federal revenue agencies, and thanked them for the assistance and cooperation. And he indicated he would keep them posted on developments as to the charges made, bond, and news media inquiries. He further stated that on his way back to the station he intended to spot the can, photograph it, and retrieve it for additional evidence.

Superintendent Colden left to return to his office to alert his chain of command and public information offices as well as to compose an in-house memorandum terminating Ace Tyler's entrance into the facility, and terminating his security clearance in the computer system. He then advised the personnel specialist to do the necessary paperwork terminating his employment based on his admittance to actions deemed criminal, and subsequent felony arrest.

At the dining hall, during the lunch meal, the inmates were talking about the arrest of the maintenance man Tyler, and the rumor mill mentioned he had a gun in his pocket that he was caught with, that he had brought in some drugs and cell phones, and other versions as to what had happened. Superintendent Colden and the police Lieutenant had talked by telephone on the charges lodged against Tyler, as well as potential bond, and had agreed to have him watched and followed to determine who would visit him in jail, and if bond were made, to have him trailed to see whom he would meet with. Colden was especially interested in prison staff who might seek Tyler out. The police had also advised the revenue services agencies on the arrest and developments to include the admission of guilt to accepting inmate monies for drugs, cigarette tobacco and cell phones smuggled into the prison.

The following morning the local newspaper carried a headlines story:

LOCAL PRISON EMPLOYEE ARRESTED ON FELONIES

Yesterday, an employee at Glen Cove Correctional Institution, Ace D. Tyler. was arrested and faces felony charges for possessing and smuggling cellphones, cigarette tobacco, and marijuana into the correctional facility, and remains in the county jail on bond set at $150,000.00. An employee at the prison in maintenance services for more than two years, he was caught smuggling the items inside plumbing parts. Tyler faces first appearance hearing in court within 48 hours, and if convicted, could be subject to charges by federal and state internal revenue services. Other personnel actions are forthcoming, according to the Superintendent, for failures to comply with prison regulations on entry and admissions. Glen Cove Correctional houses 942 medium adult male offenders from ages 21 upward.

In the dining hall, inmates were talking about the front page story in morning paper; word was abuzz about the housing pods, as it had been elsewhere in the prison and among staff in the shift briefing room. Superintendent Colden had briefed his shift managers, section heads, and then met with staff in the room, to include staff from other sections and the security/custody section to advise them as to the arrest of Ace Tyler. He then proceeded to emphasize the strict adherence to policy, further adding that all supervisory personnel would enforce those policies to the letter and for staff to see him if they didn't understand policies. He then added that if there were any staff who had any information relevant to the arrest, that they could contact him and would be free from any repercussions for their information. Thanking all staff for their cooperation and attention, the Superintendent left the room, turning the briefing over to Captain McLeod. Captain McLeod again re-emphasized that "policy will be followed. Do I make myself clear?"

He turned the furtherance of the briefing session over to the Shift Lieutenant, adding his expectation that future shift briefings will include a comment on adherence to prison policies on the entrance and exit policy. Staff were subsequently dispersed to assigned posts in the prison, and shortly thereafter the intercom blurt "Count time" was made. The population counts went as hoped with no incidents.

Buzz had gone to the gym to pick up some equipment to be taken to the recreation yard, and to pick up additional pole wrap fabric and foam inserts for the basketball courts. Jay Dillon showed him and others the daily morning paper; Buzz sensed he was being studied for any facial expressions or body movements that one might think or perceive as indicators that he had talked about seeing Ace Tyler in the gym at times. Titus Hawks was there, watching him as well.

"I heard it yesterday in the dining hall, and even heard he'd brought in a gun. That would scare me. How did it go down— do you know how they caught him—who caught him?" asked Buzz in a non-expressive tone.

"Man, you sound like you don't care what happens here," remarked another of the rec janitors.

Looking at Jay Dillon, and at the other inmate, Buzz commented that he was there to do his time and get out, and that is what he was working to do—get out of prison. "Jay, have you seen that yellow strapping tape we got to wrap the basketball poles with?" Buzz asked, as he turned to load his equipment in a basket.

Jay Dillon stuck the newspaper under his arm, walked to his locker and retrieved the roll of yellow strap. Handing it to Buzz, he said "I hope you make it out. Let me know when the poles are finished, so I can let Oxenberg know the inmates can use the basketball courts, and you need to do it quick because I hear they are upset that the basketball courts are shut down to wait on this repair work."

"Will do," said Buzz as he pushed the basket through the doors, keeping his head forward and walking casually, stopping only to retrieve his bottles of water from a chair, and to pick up a roll of the foam that had fallen off the basket. Another inmate in a few minutes left the gym to follow Buzz and to help him wrap the poles. They wrapped the poles with the foam which was six inches thick, and taped it in place, only to come back and place the blue pole wrap fabric around the poles. They then wrapped the poles, placed the yellow strapping tape around the pole at the top, around the middle, and at the bottom. They had been told to do this because it was a factor to the accreditation standards for the recreational yard, and the tape had to be at least two inches wide for visibility.

"Well that's a chore to cause you to sweat!" spoke Buzz, who sat down on a low bleacher to drink from a bottle of water.

Watching Buzz, the other inmate spoke, "Yeah, but not like Ace Tyler is sweating I bet! Titus Hawks is sweating too, cause some folks are tying him and Tyler in cahoots because Tyler let him do his tattoo business in the maintenance warehouse."

"Oh, well," remarked Buzz. "Why don't you go tell Jay Dillon we are done with the poles. I'm putting this equipment in the storage building, and I need to check those shuffleboard courts for erosion before Oxenberg hollers about it again." And turned to push the equipment baskets toward the storage building, and walked on off.

"See ya later."

"Yeah, I'll get let him know. See ya later."

The intercom blurted that lunch time would be in fifteen minutes and that all inmates on the recreation yard needed to report inside. Buzz had checked the shuffleboard courts, and written his sheets to let Jesse Oxenberg know that he needed fill dirt for not only three shuffleboard courts but the four horseshoe pit areas as well, and he recommended a concrete ramp at the equipment with a canopy top as well. Going into the gym, he gave the sheets to Jay Dillon to give to Jesse Oxenberg; Jay Dillon asked about the concrete ramp and the canopy top, and was told that Oxenberg said it needed a better appearance. With the new stain and varnish on it, this would only and certainly enhance the building's appearance and help with the accreditation review. Jay Dillon agreed, and laid it on his desk, and turned to see Fran Russell turn red-faced as she passed Buzz at the door, as he left going to the dining hall.

"What's up?" asked Jay Dillon of her.

"Anything out of him?" she asked.

"Nothing, and he acts like he doesn't care. I believe him. He just wants to get this time behind him and head on about his business, and he's still worried about that guy, Chuck," commented Jay.

"Oh, well, heard that guy died, didn't make it after that surgery. I believe that was yesterday too. Folks were so excited over Tyler's arrest. I came through medical earlier; heard the doctor and nurse supervisor talking about some problems with his medications while he was here that they are checking on. But don't say I told you!" she said to Jay Dillon. Pinching Jay Dillon's cheek, she said she'd see him later and left.

After lunch, Buzz had gone to the canteen to get some soda and a candy bar when an inmate from the housing pod stopped him.

"Hey, Buzz, I was in medical to get my pills a while ago and heard your friend, Chuck, died. I'm sorry, man. He was a good guy."

"What? What did you say? When? How? What happened? I hadn't heard a word! Tell me!" said an upset Buzz as he grabbed at the inmate's arm to hold him in place.

"I just heard that he had the surgery but something backfired, and there was something about another heart attack. Guess he just couldn't take it. Happened yesterday sometime. He was still in the hospital. Buddy, I am so sorry. I know you and he were pretty tight. If I hear more I'll tell you," as he walked off.

Entering the gym, Buzz sat down in a corner chair, put his snacks on the floor and dropped his head, placing his hands over his head. Jay Dillon saw him come in, and figured he needed some time alone, so he thought he'd encourage the others to let him alone. Later on Buzz walked over and told Jay Dillon what he had heard, and told Jay that he needed time alone for the afternoon and wouldn't be working. He headed for his housing pod, and decided to go see Jesse Oxenberg.

Knocking on the door, an upset Buzz failed to wait for a response, opened the door to find Jesse Oxenberg and Faye Hondo in a compromising position on the loveseat in the alcove of the office. He hurriedly slammed the door, and sat down in a chair beside the door to await Oxenberg's exit, which happened momentarily.

"You blasted fool! Who do you think you are coming into my office without my saying so? I'll have you put in segregation and written up, you confounded idiot! You'd better keep your mouth closed on this and you'd better hear me real good! What is it you wanted anyway," yelled Oxenberg, who took note of the facial expressions on Buzz.

"I heard Chuck was dead and wanted to ask if you knew anything. I'm sorry…I'm sorry…but I just thought you might know something. Please don't put me in segregation; I didn't see anything at all. I am sorry," pleaded Buzz who began to break in tears, sobbing so that Jesse Oxenberg gave him his handkerchief.

"Galen, I heard something earlier but I haven't asked anyone to confirm it, but I will, and I'll get back to you today, okay?" said Jesse Oxenberg.

"Do you promise?" asked Buzz. "He was my best friend in here."

"I will go in just a few minutes, and will get back to you. Wait till you calm down before you walk out."

In a few minutes, Buzz handed Oxenberg the handkerchief, and stood up to walk out. "Promise?" he looked at Oxenberg.

"Yes," said Oxenberg.

Chapter Nine

Buzz went to his housing pod, and sat on his bunk in his cell, staring out the small four by twelve inch window onto the recreation yard. Pulling out his Bible, sent to him by David Simms, he scanned pieces of old paper in it. One was an old Indian prayer, with the words that read something like O Great Spirit whose breath gives life I am small and weak, and I need your strength, and Buzz thought why did that Great Spirit take the life of his best friend. The next piece of paper held the words of remember those in prison taken from the Bible at Hebrews 13:3; he had been given that in a brochure by a visiting religious services minister. Then, Buzz studied scripture in the Bible regarding the death of Jesus Christ, later focusing on a bit of paper that noted a verse in Proverbs 18 at verse 24 which Chuck favored which read 'A man of many companions may come to ruin, but there is friend who sticks closer than a brother.' Chuck had often times cited that bit of scripture and smiled at Buzz, sometimes making reference to him as his brother and good friend. They had often talked about death, and he remembered another bit of scripture that Chuck cited from the book of Ecclesiastes 7 at verse 2, which he had written in the margin of Proverbs 18, which read 'It is better to go to a house of mourning than to go to a house of feasting, for death is the destiny of every man.' Buzz then dropped to his knees beside his bunk and began to pray.

As Buzz finished and sat on his bunk, the intercom blurted, "Count time" and as Buzz glanced at his door window he saw Officer Penelope Payne watching him, and he noted her facial expression. She asked if he was okay, and he then responded that he was fine, and thanked her for asking.

That evening Jesse Oxenberg called for Buzz to come to his office, and advised Buzz that Chuck had died from a subsequent heart attack. He also asked Buzz what he knew about Chuck's family because there wasn't much in his file and management couldn't seem to locate any relatives.

"Chuck's life wasn't good. He was badly abused as a boy; his mom died from pneumonia during his teenage years. She'd been living with an aunt, whose husband abused her, raped her and beat the kids. Chuck was farmed out as a kid. His two sisters ran away; he didn't know their whereabouts and never heard from them. His dad? I never heard him say anything about him except that he'd abandoned them when he was a little fellow. Chuck was taken in by an old man he called Mr. Jim; he's dead too and buried somewhere near to a state lake that has a campground and mobile home park nearby. It sure would be nice if Chuck could be buried near him, though. Do you think I could have Chuck's Bible, that is, if no one claims it? Chuck liked my friend David, and David liked him. Can I call David tonight? I'd like for him to know."

Jesse Oxenberg said that he'd follow-up with the Shift Commander on the phone call, and see what he could find about the Bible and anything else Buzz might would want. Then he opened conversation about the intrusion into his office that day, and threatened Buzz that he'd better not think about opening his mouth about what he walked in on. Buzz agreed.

The phone call was arranged and the call was made to David Simms, who was saddened to learn of Chuck's death. Simms then promised Buzz that he would contact the Superintendent to determine disposition of the body, and if he could intervene he would attempt to locate Mr. Jim's cemetery location and see if he help to have Chuck buried nearby. Buzz thanked him repeatedly, and that night thanked God for bringing friends to him and thanked God for the gentleness he had found in David Simms. He thought that he, indeed, had found two brothers, with Chuck gone on and David Simms still present, but he prayed that he would again meet his friend Chuck. Buzz slept well that night, awakening before the count buzzer. He took his time washing off and shaving and dressing in his neatly pressed pants and shirt.

Just before the count, Officer Payne came by his door, and said, "Good morning." He reciprocated with "Good morning,' and continued to stand at the door to await the "Count time!" blurt.

That day Buzz carried on his janitorial duties in the gym and on the recreation yard. In the afternoon, while writing up a sheet for the items he needed for the rec yard, Jay Dillon approached and asked him did he walk in on Jesse Oxenberg and Faye Hondo. Buzz asked Jay Dillon what was he talking about, that nothing like that had happened, to quit trying to set him up and just leave him alone. He kept writing the list of items needed, handed it to Jay Dillon, and walked out of the gym, went to his cell to await chow time for the supper meal. After supper Buzz attended religious services, returned to his cell, and went to bed early.

Awakening the following morning, he went to breakfast and then proceeded on to the gym where he got two bottles of water for the workers and onto the recreation yard where he used fill dirt to backfill areas around the shuffleboards and horseshoe pits. The eight bags of cement had arrived and he had decided to go ahead and build the ramps that would enable him to more easily push the equipment baskets in and out of the storage shed. He had gotten the used lumber to build the temporary frames to hold the concrete, and had taken a break to sit down in a chair by the shed to drink a bottle of water, when another inmate came from the bleachers and offered to help him. Buzz was appreciative of the offer for help, accepted it, and told the young man to sit and talk for a minute so he could finish his water. They were laughing and talking when he saw two inmates running from a housing dorm onto the yard hollering at someone on the bleachers. An inmate, whom Buzz recognized as a maintenance helper, came off the bleachers, spoke with the two who had given him a copy of a newspaper which he scanned; he threw the newspaper onto the bleachers and hurried back to the dormitory with the two. Several inmates gathered around the bleachers, while one inmate read the newspaper aloud.

Afterward, an inmate hollered at Buzz's helper and threw the newspaper toward him, saying, "Read this, Martin. Read it. It's bad news. Real bad." Martin picked the newspaper up off the ground, brushed off the dirt, and scanned the front page, while shaking his head and mumbling something that Buzz couldn't comprehend. Martin seemed to have read the article several times, constantly mumbling and saying 'no, can't be,' and 'why.' Having stopped looking at the newspaper, he looked off while shaking his head as if to disbelief what he had read. Standing, Martin hit his leg with the newspaper, and threw the paper down on the ground. Walking off in the direction of the dorm, he was heard to mutter the words, "This ain't good, ain't good at all," and "what next."

Buzz picked up the paper, sat back in his chair and read the item several times to fully absorb the statement made.

ARRESTED PRISON EMPLOYEE
COMMITS SUICIDE IN JAIL

Ace Tyler, former maintenance employee at Glen Cove Correctional Institution, arrested and in jail for various felony charges stemming from his admitted smuggling of drugs, cell phones, and tobacco was found hanged in his cell late last night. A night jailer was on duty making rounds when he saw Tyler hanging, summoned for help, and rushed into the cell to cut Tyler's body down from the overhead plumbing pipe from which the body had been suspended. Two shoestrings from his work boots were found around his neck; he was examined by a jail nurse who pronounced him dead. The law enforcement agency, jointly with the SBI, are investigating the incident but sources close to the family indicate that Tyler left a composition book with notes to his family, and detailed notes on the prison activities for which he had been arrested.

Buzz returned the newspaper to the bleachers, and continued to work on constructing the frames for the ramp. Once the ramp frame was finished, he heard the lunch buzzer and proceeded to return to the gym to wash and eat, which went without interruptions. He returned to the yard, built the ramps and poured the concrete, but it went slowly because he had to do the work alone and haul buckets of water from the water spigot next to the dorm but had to wait on the yard Officer to turn on the spigot each time and set the spigot cage in place. The spigot cage prevented inmates from tampering with the spigot, and was locked after each use with a steel padlock. The Yard Officers carried the keys as well as the keys which held the water hoses in place on the dormitory wall behind cages as well. At the end, he proceeded to cover the ramp with plastic to shield water just in case it rained as were the forecasts on the morning weather report. He decided it was so close to closing of the yard that he would go wash up in the gym, check on his inventory notes, and go take a shower. Immediately after checking his notes, Jay Dillon approached him, asking him if he had heard of Ace Tyler's suicide.

"Read it in that newspaper thrown out on the yard; it's out there on the bleachers. Did he have a family, or do you know? I'll say a prayer for them if there were, but I'm going to wash up and wait on supper. The concrete is poured and setting. I covered it with plastic just in case of rain." Buzz walked off from Jay Dillon without turning his lowered head. Going to his housing pod, the inmate talk was all about Ace Tyler committing suicide and speculation on what he said in those notes.

The intercom blurted, "Yard closed" and about fifteen minutes later blurted "Count time!" Following the count, the supper meal went without incident, and mail call occurred just after Buzz returned to his cell. He had a letter from the Superintendent's office, which he tore open and read.

Dear Mr. Brent Galen:

Due to circumstances that have made it impossible for prison management to locate family or next of kin for deceased inmate Chuck Charles, Captain McLeod spoke with you and advised me of your feedback. He also did mention your contacting a David Simms by special telephone privilege; Mr. Simms has contacted my office to inquire about assisting with body disposition and a funeral service. Though this is highly unusual and not covered in prison policies or state regulation, I am inclined to accept Mr. Simms's assistance and will confer with the Facility Chaplain on this. Be advised that Captain McLeod has also recommended that the Chaplain conduct a facility memorial service for those housed with inmate Charles; I plan to authorize that service. Thank you for sharing your information as regards Inmate Charles's family status with Captain McLeod.

Superintendent Colden

A second letter that he had thrown on his bed caught his eye; he saw the state parole office address in the upper left corner in bold letters. Tearing it open, he read that his parole was still under review but that the parole office had been advised that the crime for which he had been sentenced was being re-investigated with some outcome in the near future contingent upon law enforcement being able to locate and apprehend the complainant in that case. Buzz thought to himself that this may lead to good news, eventually. He went to bed wondering what he might expect, and tossed and turned all night, finally getting up, rereading his mail, and decided to write to David Simms.

Morning counts went without incident, as did the breakfast which was hot pancakes with maple syrup and butter, eggs, maple honey sausages, or ham slices, with orange juice, milk, and a banana.

Officer Payne was on patrol in the dining hall, spotted him, and when she came to his side of the dining hall, cordially asked how he was handling his friend's death and had he spoken with the Facility Chaplain. He advised her that he was okay, and thanked her for asking about his welfare. He then responded to her that the Facility Superintendent was going to allow a memorial service, which the Chaplain was going to handle. "Or so he said in his letter I got last night," said Buzz.

She commented that the memorial service was a kind thing to do, and walked on off to finish her patrols.

Buzz left the chow hall and went to the gym, where he spoke to his co- workers and Jay Dillon. He learned the rain was not to begin until the afternoon, so he decided to go out on the yard and check the concrete he had poured and formed yesterday. He removed the plastic but decided to replace it and let it stay in place another day for good measure. He then went back inside to the gym, to talk with Jay Dillon hoping that he get another review of the accreditation standards and ask if Jesse Oxenberg would walk the recreation yard and determine if there were any other items that help enhance their physical health and leisure opportunities program. He sat down and reviewed all the things that had been done on the recreation yard, and Jay Dillon thought everything had been completed that Jesse Oxenberg had directed them to do. The canopy materials had not been approved, and it was on hold pending the review by the facility maintenance manager because of a need to have a wind factor and site review on the project, as it was felt that the proposed project needed to be constructed so it would withstand strong winds up to 100 miles per hour. Jesse Oxenberg had told Jay Dillon he was working on that with Mr. Torn and hoped to get an answer within the next few days or so. Buzz had told Jay Dillon that he had worked on constructing canopies at the motel where he had worked in years past, and was versed and knowledgeable in wind measurements, tie and support rods, and support poles. After ending their conversation about the canopy, Jay Dillon asked how Buzz was doing with dealing with Chuck's death, commenting that he had noticed Buzz' grieving and that he was aware that it had hit him hard.

"I'm handling it. I'm glad that Superintendent Colden is allowing the memorial service. It'll help bring some closure. But I'm good, and I thank you for your regards. Well, the rain must have started; those guys are soaked, pointing to numbers of inmates re-entering the building from the rec yard. If you don't have anything else for me to do, I think I'll go get a nap," said Buzz, getting up and walking away.

Upon entrance into his housing pod, he noticed two Officers who were searching cells and lockers, and within a few minutes Captain McLeod entered and motioned for Buzz to come speak with him. It seems that Chuck's personal property was mostly junk but it was felt best not to throw away the Bible in his property. Since a number of staff had referred to Buzz and Chuck as church partners, because they always attended religious services together, Captain McLeod wondered if Buzz would like to keep the Bible. Buzz was pleased and advised Captain McLeod that he considered it a wonderful gift and he would treasure it always. Captain McLeod told him that he would get it done. One of the two officers came over and advised Buzz they needed to search his cell and locker, which was done timely with no incident or contraband found. Buzz entered his cell where he sat down for a while, and then lay down for a nap, because he suddenly felt somewhat drained and tired.

He missed the lunch meal, for he had slept, not hearing the signal. He then decided to write a letter to David Simms, and was sitting on his bunk composing the letter when he heard his name come across the intercom that he was to go to the Chaplain's office immediately.

As he walked into the dayroom, several inmates said, "We're sorry for the loss of your friend," or made other empathetic comments to acknowledge his grief and loss. He nodded his head and proceeded on to see the Chaplain, who was watching for him.

As Buzz approached, the Chaplain extended his right hand toward Buzz and said, "Young man, thank you for coming to see me. Come in and sit down, let's talk."

"Thank you, sir. I appreciate what you are doing in this. Chuck was one of the best friends a person could have had."

"Tell me, how is it that the two of you got acquainted? Was it here or did you know him prior to coming to Glen Cove?" asked the Chaplain.

"He introduced himself to me when I got here, and I kinda liked him right off, sir. He could laugh and talk, and talked about himself right much and how it was growing up. I guess I might have felt sorry for him. I think he felt like a throw-away kid, in that he didn't think what family he had cared for him. Especially after his mom died. He got quiet a lot. You know he felt the one man in his life, Mr. Jim, mattered to him, and he to him. Chuck was as close a friend to me as no other, except maybe Mr. Simms. I believe you've talked with him— David Simms?"

The chaplain responded that he had shared conversations with David Simms, and he let Buzz know that David Simms thought the world of him and had developed great respect for him, and was especially delighted in the positive change he had seen come on Buzz as well as happy that Buzz had given his life to trying to live in a Christ-like way. They talked at great lengths, but the Chaplain could see that Buzz was troubled, and prodded him to try to get to the root of that trouble and fear. "Son, what's troubling you so?"

"Chaplain, can I ask you a question? There's much devilment about in this place, and I've seen stuff that's bad wrong and I'm so afraid someone will be killed. Can't talk about it because I want to live to get out. How does a person keep on doing wrong and hurting people, even in here?"

"Well, my dear man, evil exists among men, and they themselves have to learn to change, and if not, judgment day will come. Others turn away from it and go a different path, and do change for the better. Prison is, and can be, a rather difficult place because of the environment and caliber of persons forced to be housed together. You've done well, and I wish you to continue in that regard, and I hope to see you get out. I urge you to continue to study God's word, and not let others tear you down. I'm always available any time you feel like talking, and I understand there are things you wouldn't want to talk about, but I'm here if you need me," said the Chaplain. "Let's pray and then talk about the memorial, if you will." They went together in prayer, and moved into discussion about the memorial service that the Chaplain had planned for the following day in the visitation hall with the service open to any inmate who wanted to attend. Buzz asked if the facility inmate gospel group could be allowed to play and sing, and the Chaplain responded that he had already planned to allow that, and asked Buzz if he would want to say a few words.

"Thank you, maybe a few words, and I'd like to thank folks for their comments and good thoughts about Chuck," responded Buzz.

"Good. I'll call you during the service, and if you the need to refrain all you need to do is nod your head. You're not pressured into doing anything. Is there any particular Bible verse or scripture you would be interested in us reading—perhaps some favorite of Chuck's?" asked the Chaplain.

"Sir, his favorite song was "Amazing Grace" and reading the Lord's Prayer. He had a copy of that song taped to his locker; he tore it out of one of the hymnals. He hated that he did that afterward. I know people have done worse but that wasn't too bad a thing. He tore it out so he could learn it, and he sure did learn it, and learned to play it on the guitar. Well, sir, I sure do thank you." Buzz stood up to leave when the Chaplain gave to him a small black Bible that had seen wear but was serviceable.

"This was Mr. Charles's Bible, and I was instructed by our Superintendent Colden to present it to you. It has that paper copy of the "Amazing Grace" which you spoke of in the front flap. May God bless you, young man. I will see you tomorrow at the service, and thank you for seeing me," said the Chaplain as he opened the door for Buzz to exit.

"Thanks, sir," said Buzz, as he wrapped the Bible into the fold of his left arm, and shook the Chaplain's right hand. Going back to his cell, Buzz had a good feeling that things would be alright. He thought they just had to be okay. Then the signal sounded: "Count time!" Buzz thought, that's okay too. Count procedures went as usual with no incident, followed a short term later with the evening meal of salad, fried chicken, mashed potatoes with gravy, green beans, corn, crescent rolls, and pound cake. For the first time in several weeks, Buzz ate heartily and drank two glasses of tea. Returning to his cell, he decided to watch the evening news in the dayroom. Some time later, the news reporter made mention of an on-going investigation surrounding Glen Cove Correctional Institution and deceased prison maintenance employee, Ace Tyler, with comments about a wall-locker in his workshop behind his home which was found to contain large sums of money, a detailed diary of activities, drugs, tobacco and an assortment of papers on taking items into the prison. The noise and inmate chatter silenced, with several comments made afterward: 'I wouldn't want to be in those shoes;' 'Someone's in big trouble;' 'They are gonna hit this playhouse;' and various other remarks. The news segment ended, and sports highlights began. The inmates' noise went back to a normal level, despite silent television in place. Several inmates tore their earphones off and pocketed them, going to table games, playing cards, or just conversation. Buzz showered, and sat up til the last count before going to his cell to sleep. Anxious, he found it difficult to sleep and lay in bed staring out his cell window most of the night. Awaking the next morning he was alert and standing at his cell window for morning count, and proceeded to breakfast. En route to the dining hall, he saw a notice on the memorial service posted on the hall bulletin board near the library:

NOTICE TO INMATE POPULATION

A memorial service will be held in the facility visitation room at 7:00p.m. to celebrate the life of Chuck Charles. All interested inmates are welcomed. Bring your Bibles for scripture reading. The prison gospel band will perform and sing.

....Facility Chaplain

Finishing his meal, he proceeded to the gym, hoping that Jesse Oxenberg would again discuss work that might remain as regards the accreditation standards. Upon entering the gym, with other assigned workers, he saw Faye Hondo, Fran Russell, and Jesse Oxenberg at the rear engaged in conversation with Jay Dillon. On seeing the inmates coming in, the staff dispersed but seemed to carry worried looks as they passed, going to the door leading out of the gym.

One of the other workers asked, "What's up, Jay? They look worried."

Jay angrily told the inmate to 'shut up and go clean that bathroom.'

Jay was sitting on a newspaper on the corner of the desk; he pulled it from under his leg and handed it to a tail slender well-built black inmate who wore a diamond in one of his front teeth and had reportedly been a star college athlete, until caught selling drugs on campus and betting on the college basketball games. Buzz had seen this particular inmate in close conversation on many occasions with Jesse Oxenberg and Ace Tyler as well as passing pieces of paper. The rumor-mil indicated the three of them conspired with Jay Dillon to handle bets in the prison.

Buzz spoke up and asked Jay Dillon if he had spoken with Jesse Oxenberg about looking at the yard, to which Jay Dillon said a flat 'no.' Jay Dillon then pointedly asked Buzz if he 'saw it?'

"See what? The bulletin notice?"

"No, you jerk! The news about the prison?"

"Yeah, I saw that bit on TV last night. So what?"

Grim-faced and short-tempered, Jay pointed his finger at Buzz, saying "Well, you just remember what I've been telling you or there'll be another memorial service around here, in case they come around asking you questions!"

Buzz spoke and said he was going to the yard to pick up the trash, and walk out. He checked the concrete ramp and was pleased with his work. Tearing off the plastic, he folded it for future use and stored it in the equipment shed. Replacing the padlock, he took a small trash bag and walked over the recreation yard picking up trash, and bits of debris. He sat down on the bleachers to rest for a while, and held general conversation with other inmates who had gone onto the recreation yard to play basketball or engage in other sports. He was talking with another about the memorial service but overheard two others talking about the newspaper story and some general gossip that a big prison search and shakedown was about to happen. For the rest of the morning, he went about his time sweeping out the equipment shed, putting air in basketballs, and cleaning water coolers used on the yard. He was ready for lunch, and had started to go inside when the buzzer sounded 'lunch time.' He was also wondering what the District Attorney was doing on his case, thinking it was time to hear something. After the lunch meal, he went to the gym to return to his assignments, and was met by Jay Dillon, Jesse Oxenberg, and Captain McLeod who had been talking with some of the other gym workers, advising them that the gym would be closed for the remainder of the day and that they could take the afternoon off and return in the morning. All the inmates were sent out, with Jesse Oxenberg walking out behind Jay Dillon, followed by Captain McLeod who locked the gym door.

On arrival at his housing pod, the patrol Officer on duty announced 'mail call' and began to call out names of those receiving mail After several minutes, with inmates asking if their name had been skipped, or if they received a letter, Buzz heard his name called and went to get his mail, finding a letter from the local District Attorney's office. Hesitant, he momentarily wondered what the letter might say, thinking his case had been found with no merit, or that they needed more time. He tapped the long white envelope against his fingers, giving it much thought, and thought that maybe they had found something that could help get his case back into a courtroom. He thought it best to go to his cell to open and read the letter, hoping it was some good news. He needed some good news. Going into his cell, he removed his shoes, sat on his bunk, and slowly opened the envelope.

March 22, 2011

Dear Mr. Brent Galen:

Be advised that this office has re-investigated the matter of a stolen truck for which you were convicted and sentenced to a term of incarceration in the Department of Correction. We are now in possession of additional evidence, and are prepared to discuss that with you. A meeting with you has been set for this discussion and you will be notified as to that date by your Facility Management. Thank you.

xxxCharles Fredrick, District Attorney

cc: Supt. Murray Colden

He read the letter several times, wondering what additional evidence had been found. He felt some sense of relief. Folding the letter, he placed it under his pillow, and decided to read his Bible, doing so, until the "count time!" intercom signal came loud and clear. Closing his Bible, placing it on his pillow, he washed his face and stood at the cell door for count. When the 'count clear' signal was made some half hour later, he exited the cell wondering why it had taken so long, and decided to take his walkman with him to the dayroom to pass the time, watching the television. Positioning himself at a side table, he became interested in one of the game shows being aired, Let's Make a Deal, and he thought it had been a long time since he had seen that program. Buzz watched television until the evening meal, after which he took a shower, dressed and sat on his bunk to await the memorial service. Hearing the intercom message on the memorial service, he left his cell and proceeded to the visitation room with his Bible in hand. He was pleased to see that the room was almost full of inmates; the gospel band was at the front among a number of visitors he had recognized as being persons who came to the prison to provide the religious programs. He saw the Chaplain, who then motioned for him to come to the front and have a seat. On opening the service, the Chaplain spoke about friendships, respect for mankind, and God's love for all people irrespective of circumstances in one's life, social status, and race.

He spoke about God's love for Chuck as a person. The gospel group played a number of songs, with one of the group's members speaking of Chuck's new love for the guitar. The moment came for Buzz to speak, and he spoke briefly about his new found friend, and thanked those in attendance for respecting Chuck enough to give their time to attending the service. He also thanked the prison management for allowing the service, also echoed by several other inmates. The service went well; Buzz was satisfied and felt some sense of closure with Chuck's untimely death. Re-entering his cell, he bowed his head in prayer, and slept well that night.

Chapter Ten

"Count time!" brought him from his sleep early the next morning. He jumped to his cell door to await the count procedures to clear, and washed his face, shaved and brushed his teeth, and dressed to await the breakfast meal. Breakfast that morning was hot waffles, with syrup, eggs and two strips of turkey bacon, toast, and an orange, with coffee and apple juice. Buzz ate all that was on his tray, and on taking his tray to the departure rail, was met by Sergeant Ben Hunt.

"Inmate Galen, please come with me," spoke Sergeant Hunt, then escorted Buzz to the Operations Center, where Captain McLeod told him of the writ for him to be taken to the District Attorney's office that morning to discuss his crime case. The Captain directed the Sergeant to handcuff Buzz and transport him to that office by 8:30 that morning, and to advise District Attorney Charles Frederick when he arrived. Sergeant Hunt followed the directives received, did a search of Buzz, and had him sit in a nearby chair while he obtained the prison folder, medical record, and keys to an available vehicle. Notifying the operations clerk to enter the writ and transport, Sergeant Hunt escorted Buzz to the vehicle, and departed the prison grounds.

"What's going on, Galen, with this writ? More charges? You in trouble or something?" Sergeant Hunt asked, once they were in the vehicle and traveling.

"I sure hope not. There's supposed to be new evidence that I didn't steal any truck that I'm doing time for. Guess we'll find out soon enough, huh?" replied Buzz.

"Good luck on that!" said Sergeant Hunt. "How much time you got anyway?"

"Got three years—up for parole soon. But I've done jail time and a prior term; that might hurt me. If I can get out, I plan to stay straight and never come back. I believe I've got myself together. Hope to get myself a job, find a church to go to, maybe one day have me a family, but I got to do better down the road," said Buzz.

"Yeah, you got to get yourself straightened out first, and I believe you are working on that, from what I hear about you. Even the prison staff often mention how you seem changed for the better. Hope you get things worked out," spoke Sergeant Hunt. "Well, we are here. Let's go inside and see what they say."

Sergeant Hunt handed the writ to the officer presiding at the entry desk, and advised that Brent Galen had a meeting with District Attorney Charles Fredriek. The officer told them to sit down, and she proceeded with writ in hand toward the District Attorney's office. In a few minutes, she returned and advised that Mr. Galen could go on in and that Sergeant Hunt could have himself a cup of coffee in the adjoining room if he wanted to.

As they stood, Sergeant Hunt said, "What? I'm not to escort Galen in there?"

"No, sir. Mr. Fredriek said for you to go have yourself a coffee," she said. "Oh, and you need to remove those handcuffs from him before he goes in."

Sergeant Hunt removed the handcuffs and opened the door for Buzz to go inside, also sticking his head in to advise that he'd be in the adjoining room if needed.

"Sit down, Mr. Galen. How are you doing? I'm expecting others to join us momentarily, so just have a sit. Do you want coffee or a soda?" asked the District Attorney.

Buzz accepted a Styrofoam cup filled with coffee and took a seat across from the man, nervously shaking the cup, almost spilling it on himself.

Taking note of this, the District Attorney asked, "Is it too hot? You can use that end table to sit it on if you'd like."

"Thank you, sir. I'm just a bit nervous."

Momentarily, another door opened and in walked Superintendent Colden, the police Lieutenant Buzz recognized from the previous meeting, Captain McLeod, and another individual who identified himself as one Jared Taylor of the state bureau of investigation. After exchanges of pleasantries and filling cups of coffee, everyone sat down, with eyes on Buzz. The District Attorney opened the floor with reference to Buzz's case, and discussed a review of the evidence and introduced a written statement that the truck owner had made which in short indicated that he did lie and perjure himself in the initial criminal investigation and during the court hearing. Also, he disclosed other witness statements taken from individuals who had heard the truck's owner admit that he lied on Brent Galen so as to not jeopardize his vehicle insurance.

Almost emotional, but elated to hear the truth, Buzz couldn't hold himself from asking the question, "What does this mean, sir? Am I free?"

"Hold on, Mr. Galen; let me finish, please. Yes, you will be freed. I have already met with the Resident Senior District Judge, and he has signed a court order authorizing your immediate release. I will in just a few minutes provide a certified copy of that Order to Superintendent Colden; my secretary is now faxing a certified copy to the agency headquarters as well. You are free to go, Mr. Galen. But I do believe we also have some unfinished business, and we will get to that in a few minutes after we take a break. Right now, I want to ensure that the prison official waiting outside is provided a copy of this, so he can get on back to the prison. I will return momentarily, gentlemen," said District Attorney Fredrick, who exited the room with a document in his hands.

Teary-eyed, Buzz dropped his head and wept, being patted on the back by Captain McLeod, who had given him a handkerchief as well. The District Attorney returned to the room and asked everyone to get back to business at hand. Buzz was then asked if he would write his statement on the activities he had observed, being detailed with names as much as possible even if it meant nicknames or aliases. He was asked for dates if he could recall, and anything he had witnessed since their previous meeting, or things he had heard that were questionable. Superintendent Colden spoke up to say that they wanted to do everything humanly possible to protect him from harm, and emphasized that he not mention the statement to anyone, not even with his friend David Simms. He also commented that plans were to note a fictitious release address in the prison computer system for Buzz, and that Buzz should not make contact with anyone at the prison at all, to which he readily agreed. The group then discussed whether there existed a need for Buzz to enter into a state's witness protection program, to which Superintendent Colden argued that unless Buzz's name came up in court or in official documents accessible by those to be arrested, charged, and convicted that he failed to see a need. The District Attorney cited a new law stemming from gang actions and drug trafficking which allowed for endangered witnesses' names to be withheld from documents that convicted persons could access. It was also agreed that relocation to an undisclosed community could be negotiated.

"Gentlemen, let's hold off talking so I can make a call to the prison," spoke Superintendent Colden. He then used his cellular phone to call the prison and spoke to the Shift Lieutenant in charge, advising him that inmate Brent Galen was being released from the system by court order and that Sergeant Ben Hunt was in possession of a certified copy of the order and was en route to the prison. He then directed the Lieutenant to ensure that all property be removed from the Galen cell, that it be inventoried and bagged, and be placed in his secretary's office. He further directed the Lieutenant to ensure that the staff handling this task use care in accessing the property, and that nothing be destroyed or mishandled. "Lieutenant, do not put me in a position of having to explain to the Judge that our staff were careless in handling that inmate's property! Do you clearly understand?" To which the Lieutenant advised that he would ensure those orders were followed.

Buzz was then moved to an adjoining office, where he was shown writing tablets and pens for his use to write his statement. He was provided coffee and sodas, and was told to bring his statement to the door when done, and if he needed to ask a question or anything else, to knock on the door and they would assist him.

Getting back to their conversations, Captain McLeod spoke that there was surveillance evidence to be introduced that was certainly vital, with the SBI agent adding that the stockpile of notes taken from Ace Tyler's home and his admissions were also significant. Superintendent Colden then asked Captain McLeod to share the surveillance that he had removed from the gym the previous day. Those present watched in disgust as Faye Hondo engaged in having unprotected sex with three different inmates in the equipment storage room during a segment of time where she spent at least ten minutes with each of the inmates, and the inmates gave her monies when they finished. The monies were carried by two of the inmates in their armpits, with cellophane tape used to hold the rolled bills in place. The video showed the third inmate removing the rolled bills from the waistband of his pants. In all three instances, Faye Hondo could be seen placing the rolled bills in the rib-binding of a book, which she carried with her as she left the room. The surveillance video taken using a camera in the gym lighting showed Fran Russell and Jay Dillon exchanging monies as well as Fran Russell giving cell phones to him. Video also showed Fran Russell with Jay Dillon in the equipment storage room where she partially removed clothing and engaged in sex with Jay Dillon. Captain MeLeod then spoke and said that he had several other video tapes showing the same kinds of behaviors with numerous inmates, and in some instances, Faye Hondo provided pills, drugs, and condoms to the inmates she was having sex with. In each instance the inmates gave her money. Other videos with audio involved Jesse Oxenberg providing drugs, tobacco, and cell phones to inmates as well as having conversations with inmates and Jay Dillon on bets to be placed on sports games through a local individual in the community.

Unexpectedly several of the surveillance audio conversations involved Jesse Oxenberg talking with inmates in the gym about getting monies for helping to attain changes in custody grades and for his supposedly helping make contacts for paroles, and in several instances monies were actually passed to Jesse Oxenberg. Captain McLeod spoke up saying this activity had been more hushed until he had heard the 'money for parole' comment in the audio that he had from the light in

Buzz's cell, where Buzz had confided in Chuck that Oxenberg indicated he could help if Buzz could come up with some money.

"Wonder how much extortion has gone on in there?" asked the District Attorney, to which Superintendent Colden commented that he was not quite sure because he had heard little to no complaints from inmate families on that.

"What about the Oxenberg visits to the inmates' wives?" asked the Superintendent Colden. "Did you learn anything more?" directing the question to the individual named Taylor from the State Bureau of Investigation.

Jared Taylor spoke, "We have statements from victims—at least three—in different communities, with supporting statements from individuals who will testify they saw Oxenberg go to these homes, and we are ready to proceed with those charges for rapes, assaults, extortion, and home invasion. In fact, one of the victims went to the local emergency room after his departure from her home, and reported she'd been raped by someone who broke into her home. A rape test kit was done as well as a police report, which we have obtained. Robbery will also apply in one case where he took the money from one's purse when he left, as well as prescriptive medications that the woman had. In fact, he had taken one or two of the pain-killers and on a traffic check en route to his home, was cited for driving while impaired and being in possession of a prescription bottle of pain-killers that belonged to someone else. Our agency is prepared to proceed, and I strongly feel we need to be vigilant in this."

Captain McLeod asked if the police agency had uncovered anything as regards motor vehicle concerns on Faye Hondo. The police Lieutenant sitting in gave an affirmative that he had learned that "Faye Hondo has been working as a stripper at a club on the beach strip for the past year two to three nights a week, generally leaving there around one o'clock at night."

Superintendent Colden and Captain McLeod focused on each other, with Captain McLeod speaking, "That accounts for the speeding tickets late at night, but she's never reported the second job, is not approved for it, and never reported the tickets."

The police Lieutenant further commented, "Well, gentlemen, she is a hot commodity down there! It's an adult night-club called The Babe's Place or something like that."

Seemingly exhausted, Superintendent Colden then stood up to stretch, saying "this is certainly a squall of a mess, and I favor moving on all of this quickly, gentlemen. What do we do now? Why not go on in and confront these folks, and do it now? Let's take a break, please; I've got to go to the men's room—that coffee's hit me!"

As they all stood up to take a few minutes break, a knock came on the door from the room where Buzz had been placed. The District Attorney walked to the door, opened it, and retrieved the pages of paper that Buzz gave him. He asked Buzz to sit down, and he himself began to read the document that Buzz had written. He then passed it to the State Bureau of Investigation agent, who read over it and nodded to the District Attorney that it was acceptable.

"Well, it's lunch time, folks. Mr. Galen, where would you spend the night— have you thought of that?" asked the District Attorney.

"No, sir. I haven't thought that far. I have no money at all. I have a friend— he lives about 100 miles away from here. I'm sure he'd drive here to pick me up. I supposed he'd be at home. I can give him a call, and see," Buzz spoke nervously. "I sure could eat something. And what about my property in my locker at the prison? I really would like to get that stuff—it means a lot to me. It's all I have, really."

He was assured that it would be sent to him with his whereabouts address well protected.

"Let's see. This office could provide you with a meal and have someone on staff drive you to wherever you plan to stay. Use that phone to call your friend and see if he will be around home, and we'll take yon there," said the District Attorney, trying to be helpful.

Buzz called David Simms's home, was delighted that he was there, and told him of his release and of being transported there that afternoon.

The District Attorney then picked up the phone, called an inter-office number, speaking with one of the office investigators on the issue at hand, and arranged for Brent Galen to be taken for a meal and driven to David Simms's residence. Within a minute or two, the investigator left the office with a very nervous but excited Brent Galen aka Buzz beside him. Buzz had provided an address and telephone number with the District Attorney in the event he was needed for anything else, but knew he would never again do anything to cause himself to be placed into prison. Walking outside he looked up to the sky and uttered the words, "Well, Chuck, I'm free, my friend." He looked at the investigator, smiled and said he was ready.

Chapter Eleven

The remaining group of men left the office and traveled to a nearby restaurant for lunch, Returning to the office, the State Bureau of Investigation official, Jared Taylor, was designated to assume the lead position in the investigation team, with travel to the prison the following morning to interview pertinent staff and inmates already identified. Jesse Oxenberg was to be the first individual to be interviewed by Taylor's team, with Faye Hondo to be interviewed thereafter.

Superintendent Colden felt it to be in the best interest of all for the gym to be shut down for the day, with the interview teams to be given a walk- through of the location so they could visibly see the lay-out. It was agreed, as well as Oxenberg, Hondo and Fran Russell to be held in the main office upon their arrival at the workplace to be interviewed; they were not to be allowed to go beyond the foyer of the administration building or interact with inmates or other staff. The element of surprise would serve them well in the investigation he thought.

Returning to the facility that afternoon, Superintendent Colden gave the property bags for Buzz to Captain McLeod, and directed him to personally ensure that the stuff was placed in the U.S. mail to the address that Buzz had given them, and to protect the address. The Captain agreed to personally handle the mail himself, and would develop a fictitious forwarding address for the inmate records section so as to not jeopardize Buzz's protection and whereabouts.

The following morning, Superintendent Colden arrived a bit early and went on into his office. Captain McLeod then arrived shortly thereafter, and stood around in the entrance gatehouse to observe staff perform their duties checking staff and items being brought into the facility. Faye Hondo and Jesse Oxenberg pulled into the parking lot at the same time, and he saw them walking toward the gatehouse together. As they entered the gatehouse, they both acknowledged his presence with, "Good morning, Captain!"

He responded, "Good morning."

They then stood to await the search and walk-through at the metal detector, but Captain McLeod could detect their nervousness and observed Faye Hondo passing her lunch-bag to an Officer standing at the front door. He then advised the Officer to empty the contents of the bag on the table, as another Officer began to frisk Faye Hondo. Seeing three frozen food meals and several items of fruit, Captain McLeod asked why so much food.

Snickering, she said, "Why Captain, I eat two or three times a day."

Captain McLeod spoke up and said, "Well, today, we'll open those packets and check it out," and he nodded to the Officer to open the packets. "And if it is as you say, I personally will reimburse you for the foods."

The Officer started to pull the strip, when he noticed small pieces of cellophane tape on the boxes, and showed it to the Captain, who told him to pull it off. Opening the packets, the Officer emptied the contents onto the table, and readily found a cellular phone, and several small plastic bags of leafy-green substances. Looking at Faye Hondo, who had turned a beet-red and was quite shaken up, the Captain asked, "What is that, Ms. Hondo?" pointing to the bags.

"I don't know anything about that, sir!" she said, raising her voice.

The Captain then had the Officer to put the items in a clear plastic bag, and stand with her at the door. He then had another Officer call inside the facility for additional staff to come to the gatehouse to work. "Move on up, Mr. Oxenberg, please," the Captain spoke, and watched as Jesse Oxenberg stepped forward. Jesse Oxenberg laid his thermos, newspaper, and clear lunch box on the table, and stood to be frisked. Upon opening the thermos, the Officer could smell the coffee but the

Captain reminded him of the policy on clear beverage containers as the only beverage containers allowed to be brought in. It was disallowed. The lunch box held one sandwich and an apple. The Officer opened the newspaper and several pieces of paper fell out on the table. The Captain asked Oxenberg what they were.

"Just notes I need, sir," Oxenberg said.

The Officer spoke up saying they were more like numbers, and Jesse Oxenberg told the Officer to shut his mouth, that "You don't know numbers from letters!"

The Captain told the Officer to bag it all, and saw the Lieutenant enter the gatehouse. He then told the Lieutenant to escort both Mr. Oxenberg and Ms. Hondo to the Superintendent's Office, and to give the two plastic bags to Superintendent Colden.

At that time, Captain McLeod saw several vehicles pulling into the parking lot, which could be staff as well as the investigative teams coming in for the day. He had his mind on ensuring that Fran Russell got into the facility before the investigative teams, and he had fears that she might see strangers and abruptly drive back out of the parking lot and not report back to work. He was a bit relieved to see her walking toward the gatehouse with several other staff, and felt that maybe the investigative teams would be delayed as he had suggested to ensure that work staff got in before they arrived. He greeted all the staff as they came in, and went through the searches and metal detector checks. As Ms. Russell was cleared, he advised that he'd walk with her into the administrative building, and as he did so, she chatted casually about spring coming. Opening the main door, he directed her to go to Superintendent Colden's office, and sit in the waiting area. Seeing Faye Hondo and Jesse Oxenberg, she rather quickly asked what was going on.

"Just have a seat, Ms. Russell, and let's withhold the conversation, please," Captain McLeod spoke. He then directed the Officers standing at bay to ensure there was no conversation among them. He further pointed to a restroom and indicated that they could only use that particular restroom if need be. He had the water cut-off in that restroom earlier that morning, in anticipation, so that nothing could be flushed away, just in case they were carrying contraband that had not been discovered. Captain McLeod then entered the Superintendent's office and called the gatehouse to give instructions that he was expecting visitors, and if any staff came to work but left abruptly that he was to be notified immediately.

Sometime around 8:30 that morning, the lead investigators arrived with other staff accompanying them. Jared Taylor of the state's bureau of investigation carried two attaché cases, as did another agent. The police Lieutenant was carrying a camera case, additional rolls of film in his coat pocket, and a notebook. Captain McLeod was summoned to the gatehouse because of questions surrounding the Officers searching the cases and possibly discovering the documents in the cases relevant to the case under investigation. Upon his entry to the gatehouse, the Officers questioned checking the individuals and their possessions.

"Gentlemen, if you have any weapons on you, please return them to our vehicles. Everything else, I will check for you if you'll open the cases here on the table," said Captain McLeod. None of the visitors carried weapons. Speaking to his own staff, he said, "You officers stand over by the entry door, and I'll handle this, please."

The briefcases were opened for visual inspection and closed, with the six individuals presenting identifications, being given visitor badges, and escorted out toward the administration building. Speaking to the lead Officer, Captain McLeod advised that the gatehouse shift log indicate that six individuals were in the facility with the Superintendent and Captain McLeod for investigation purposes, and to list their names and work agencies, as well as a notation that Captain McLeod had performed visual inspections of attaché cases and a camera case. They left the gatehouse and went on to the administration building, and entered the conference room, meeting with Superintendent Colden. Coffee, refreshments, ham sandwiches and donuts, and soda had been set up. After a brief discussion on the day's planned schedule, Superintendent Colden left but re-entered to provide the personnel files on the three staff to be interviewed. Arrangements had been made for them to conduct a walkthrough of the gym, a housing pod, and to be given a presentation on the inmate orientation program with focus on the federal prison rape and elimination law, inmate-to-staff boundaries, contraband rules, and this presentation would include the new hire orientation for employees. Since staff were being held for interviews, it was decided to proceed with the first three interviews, have a break, then conduct the facility tour followed with the presentation series.

Jared Taylor and the others with him set up audio equipment to record the conversations with the staff: the first to be interviewed was Faye Hondo. Captain McLeod escorted her into the room, introduced her to the group, and directed her to have a seat. Jared Taylor began by advising her of two essential facts: that she had been mentioned in Ace Tyler's notes, with some details as to her supposed involvement with inmates, and that they were in possession of video surveillance, Too, they made her aware of written statements that had been provided by individuals associated with the nightclub called *The Babe's Place* where she allegedly had been working as a dancer or stripper in the club.

"Ms. Hondo, have you ever engaged in any illegal activity with any inmate or inmates in this prison facility?"

"I have not, and I don't know what Ace Tyler said about me. I have not been involved with any inmate, other than work here and offer counseling to inmates on their cases."

Jared Taylor asked what her relationship had been with Ace Tyler. She reported that they simply worked together, and had socialized a bit away from the facility, and that he had on occasion had gone to the club where she worked at the beach. She then asked what he had said in those notes about her, and was advised that the notes implied sexual activity, her supplying cell phones to inmates as well as occasional marijuana and cigarettes. She denied everything that Ace Tyler had written. "I've never brought anything into this prison for an inmate until today. I did have a cell phone and some small bags of marijuana with me today, that Captain McLeod has that was taken from me in the gatehouse this morning. That's it! You said sexual activity—that's a lie! You said video surveillance—of what?"

"Alright, I'll cut to the point. Video surveillance taken in the gym, from the equipment storage room. Now do you want to regroup and go back on this?" asked Jared.

"Can I see what you're talking about?" she asked.

"Gentlemen, start the tape and let Ms. Hondo see what we've seen, please. Ms. Hondo, you can say stop at any time," spoke Taylor.

One of Taylor's co-workers started showing the video, which showed Faye Hondo in black slacks and a bright green pullover sweater entering the storage room with a tall white inmate with a crew-cut style haircut, and she stood as the inmate loosened his pants and sat down to straddle the weight bench. Then the video shows her dropping her pants, and begin to straddle the inmate. She then spoke up, saying, "Stop it!"

"Well, Ms. Hondo?" asked Jared Taylor.

"Okay, so I did get involved with that guy. But it was a one time deal!"

"No, Ms. Hondo, we have many of these scenes, different inmates, on different days and at varying times," said Jared Taylor quite sharp and pointedly. "I will only say this one time—tell the truth!"

"Okay, okay then! Yes, I've had sex with guys in that room." She stammered. "And my working at the club is not illegal. So what next?" she asked. "I want a lawyer—I ain't talking no more to you!" She jumped from the chair, and turned to walk out, when the police Lieutenant stopped her by placing his hand on her arm, and turning her to face the others. Jared Taylor then advised her of her rights, and told Faye Hondo she was being charged with several crimes, the first of which was sexual activity with inmates in a prison facility possession and providing drugs and cell phones to inmates in a prison facility, bartering with inmates for money in a state prison facility, and state cigarette and tobacco violations as regards prison facilities. He also advised her that the revenue services would also be looking at her for unpaid tax on monies she received in exchange for sex with inmates, as well as looking into her true ownership of an Escalade vehicle, and the method of payment for it, and that it might be confiscated as ill-gotten gain.

Angrily, she stared at Superintendent Colden and Captain McLeod, and said to them both, "You did this! It ain't over by a long shot, and you'll get yours!"

The police Lieutenant handcuffed her, helped her to stand and read her, her rights under the Miranda laws. Captain McLeod handed her purse to her, and demanded that she hand him any keys to the prison property as well as her work identification. She produced both and gave them to him. The police Lieutenant then escorted her from the room, out of the prison and into a police cruiser that was sitting in the parking lot. He gave the Officer instructions to take her to the Jail and turn her over to the police Sergeant at the command desk. He then called the police Sergeant on his cellular phone and advised him as to charges to be lodged against Faye Hondo. He then returned to the conference room to further their work, but decided to get some coffee and a donut before starting up with the next interview session.

Looking at the others in the room, he said to them without hesitation, "A cobra has less venom than that one! Evil! I'm ready for the next one, folks."

Superintendent Colden went to the waiting room, and asked Jesse Oxenberg to come with him, and upon entering the conference room did the introductions. "Mr. Taylor, we're ready," he said to Jared Taylor, who was laying documents in front of him on the table.

Taylor opened the floor by asking Oxenberg how long he had been employed at the prison and in what capacity. Oxenberg supplied the answers, and was asked what his relationship had been with Ace Tyler who had been employee at the prison. The relationship was one of working together, and on occasion Oxenberg had employed Tyler to do repairs at his home but had paid him in cash for those services.

"Did you socialize with him away from work, other than when he did work at your home?" asked the police Lieutenant.

"Sometimes, but not much. Once or twice he and I went to the beach to a club or two," responded Oxenberg, who constantly twisted in the chair. Noticing this, the police Lieutenant asked if Oxenberg wanted to use the restroom or have some coffee, but Oxenberg indicated with a flat 'no.'

Jared Taylor then asked, "Have you had occasion to talk with Mr. Tyler about his involvements with inmates and going anything that might have been seen as illegal or wrong?"

"No, sir! Never heard anything on him. Never discussed anything like that with him—had no reason to. He seemed like a straight-up guy to me, with a family and all. I didn't see him as doing anything like what I've read in the paper," Oxenberg spoke.

"Let's talk about you, Mr. Oxenberg. Have you ever done anything in the prison that would be illegal?" asked Jared Taylor. "And I'll cut to the point and tell you right now that we have Mr. Tyler's notes, where he mentions you, and we have some surveillance video with you in them as well as statements on incidents we want to ask about."

Suddenly panicky, he started pulling on the knot at the neck of his tie to loosen it, asking, "What did Tyler say about me, if I can ask?"

"Did you make bets with inmates on sports games and handle bets with a bookie agent in the community on behalf of inmates?" asked Jared Taylor.

"That's stretching it a bit; I did talk with inmates about the games and my betting on games on my own time, but I didn't involve any inmate in that. It doesn't make it illegal to talk with inmates about it. If Tyler said that, he was way off base and misunderstood what I said," snapped Oxenberg.

"Did any inmate ever give you monies to place bets for him on games," Jared Taylor asked, and Oxenberg loudly spoke to deny the remark made. "Okay, let's move on. Are you or have you ever been aware of staff involved with inmates in sexual activity in the prison?"

"No, I have not been privy to that at all!"

"Are you aware of it going on in the gym? I believe yon were the person in charge of the recreation section to include the gym, is this right?" asked Jared Taylor. "And to cut to the point, we may have surveillance taken from that area of the prison."

Stammering, with beads of sweat building on his brow, Oxenberg said, "Surveillance? That's a surprise. I was over the gym inmates but other staff went in there all the time."

Superintendent Colden then spoke up, and told Oxenberg to breathe deeply, and go back over in his mind, and rethink. Oxenberg was sweating; he repeatedly wiped his brow, while his eyes moved from one to another of those sitting in front of him. He stammered, "Let me back up. I have heard of some sex stuff going on in there, but it didn't involve me and I didn't ask. If I'm going to come clean let me say that

I have on a few occasions taken monies from a couple of the guys -the inmates- to place bets on some games. Faye Hondo was the one having the sex; I had told her to be careful one time, but she didn't listen. She has a thing about men; she even had a thing for Ace Tyler at one time." Looking at the floor, and around the room, Oxenberg was quite fidgety with his voice breaking up as he talked. "Can I go to the restroom?"

"You can," said Jared Taylor, directing a co-worker to escort him there and back.

Standing up, Oxenberg tried to turn the door knob but was having difficulty, when the police Lieutenant stepped in front of him and turned the knob to open the door.

"You, okay, Mr. Oxenberg?" the Lieutenant noting how red-faced Oxenberg had become.

"Yeah. I'll be okay in a minute." said Oxenberg.

Once in the restroom, he used the facility, washed his hands and took a wet paper-towel with cold water to his face. After a moment, he and the Lieutenant returned to the conference room.

Jared Taylor asked if he was okay, to which Oxenberg responded in the affirmative.

"Want a cup of coffee?" Captain McLeod asked, but Oxenberg rejected the offer, sat down and looked at Jared Taylor.

"Mr. Oxenberg, have you ever talked with any inmate about getting money from him in exchange for making some calls about his getting parole considerations?" asked Jared Taylor.

Quiet for a moment, Oxenberg then spoke: "I have a time or two, but the money was for a lawyer to get involved in the case to help out."

"Did you accept the money, and what did you do with it?" asked Jared Taylor.

"I kept it, sir. I made a call or two to the parole offices to ask about the cases I was dealing with, and talked with the inmates. Not much money— maybe a couple of thousand dollars. I don't recall right off. But the inmates did get paroled. I kept the money. That was wrong of me, but I guess I was desperate and knew they could get their hands on the money," Oxenberg stated.

"Have you ever talked with or visited with inmates' wives for any reasons to include picking up monies for parole work or whatever? I suggest you think long and hard before you answer this question, Mr. Oxenberg," spoke Jared Taylor in a hard stare at Oxenberg.

Shaking his head nervously, Oxenberg said that he had done so.

"Did you have sex with any of them?"

Looking straight ahead, Oxenberg mumbled, "I did—they came on to me, I guess."

"Came on to you? Or did you rape them?" asked Jared Taylor. "And let me say again, that we have written statements from them and their neighbors who can put you in those yards, at those houses, of those women. It would be better for you to stop lying! We also have a police record with emergency room records relevant a rape test done on a victim which has your DNA on it, so you'll face a rape charge."

Dropping his head, Oxenberg muttered, "I raped them. I'm so ashamed. Let's stop this right now. You've got me. I'll cooperate, but I don't want to go to prison. I'm a dead man in a place like this. Please help me. My nerves just won't take it. Can I get a lawyer? I can't talk no more," he stammered, and became so emotional that he began crying as a child, mumbling, "I am so sorry, so sorry."

The police Lieutenant then handcuffed Jesse Oxenberg, helped him to stand, and read him his rights under the Miranda law, and told him he was being charged with several counts of rape, home invasion, several counts of extortion, one count of robbery theft of one's prescription controlled drugs, and violation of gambling laws. Captain McLeod demanded that he hand over his work identification and any keys that might belong to the prison.

Jesse Oxenberg pulled the keys from his pocket and handed them over, and fished the work identification from his wallet, tearing it accidentally. Looking at the Superintendent, he begged for forgiveness, in that he knew he had disappointed him.

Sternly facing Oxenberg, Superintendent Colden commented for him to, "ask those victims for forgiveness—not me."

The police Lieutenant escorted him from the administration building, through the gatehouse, to a police vehicle waiting in the parking lot. Instructions were given to the police Officer to turn him over to the Command Sergeant at the police headquarters. The Lieutenant re-entered the administration building, calling the police Sergeant on his cell phone while walking back into the building.

"Well, let's finish with this other one out there, and go take a look at the place," said Jared Taylor. "Mr. Colden, would you please that person on in, sir."

Superintendent Colden went out of the room, and momentarily returned with Faye Russell. He told her to "have a seat right there, please. Do you want a coffee or something?" And he then made introductions of those in the room.

She whispered, "Nothing, Mr. Colden. I've had too much coffee already in the waiting room."

Jared Taylor, sat quietly staring at her for a moment or two before speaking, such that she perceived his look as one of disbelief, disgust, and perhaps anger. He then spoke, asking her what her job was and how long she had been employed at the prison. "But before you respond, Ms. Russell, let me say a number of things. First, we have some videotapes with you in them, as well as some audiotapes, and of course Ace Tyler, a former employee here, mentioned you in his book of notes. So, let me caution you against saying things that we can construe as perjury. Now, you may proceed."

Shaking her head she seemed somewhat reluctant to believe video and audio tapes of her existed, and asked "Video tapes of what, where? With whom?"

"Do you want to watch one of them, Ms. Russell?" ask Mr. Taylor. And with that said, he signaled for the accompanying investigator to show one of the tapes. As the video began to play, it became evident to her that surveillance had been conducted in the facility gym, without their knowledge, and she quickly surmised that they had been under suspicion. The video clearly showed her walking into the gym, uttering profanities at Buzz about an inventory, and a short time later kissing Jay Dillon, with her hands rubbing his backside.

Fran Russell had her hands in her lap rubbing them together, and those present could see she was becoming more exasperated as the video progressed. "You can stop this! It's clear that this lousy job isn't worth the hassles, and being set up. I want a lawyer right now! Yeah, I've cursed the devils; everybody here curses. So what? Get me out of here," she shouted, jumping up from the chair, so abruptly that the chair fell over backwards. She then pointed her right hand at Superintendent Colden, shakily, and told him, "Keep this sorry ass job. I'II find another one and probably make more money!"

The police Lieutenant in a high tone of voice, quite irritated with her demeanor, spoke saying, "Ms. Russell, you need to calm down, and sit back down. We are not done with you yet!" He leaned over and set the chair back upward, and pointed to it, with his green eyes solidly fixed on her, and his stare unwavering. She hesitated but continued to stare back at him and sat down as she had been told to do. "Are you quite sure you no longer wish to talk with us—that you wish to forego this opportunity? This is your one time to help us set the record straight, Ms. Russell," he said to her.

"I'll take my chances with a lawyer," she said.

Jared Taylor then advised her of her rights under the Miranda law, telling her that she would be charged with taking undue liberties with a state prison inmate, uttering and directing obscenities and vulgar remarks to a state prison inmate against state law, providing contraband to state prison inmates because they did have that on video, as well as having sexual activity with at least one state prison inmate, and receiving monies from that inmate. He also added that the revenue service agencies would probably get involved because of the monies involving unpaid tax.

The police Lieutenant directed that she stand, he handcuffed her and escorted her from the building to a police vehicle waiting in the parking lot, with orders given to the driver to take her into headquarters. On his return, the notified the police headquarters Command Sergeant, and returned to the conference room. Speaking to Superintendent Colden, he chided him for hiring vicious women but stated, "Maybe that's what you need in here. I don't know, but those two are mean! Maybe a criminal element in staff to match that of the inmates in order for them to get along, but then all staff aren't bad, are they? Some are the exception, I have learned."

The group gathered and closed their belongings, placing them to one side and exited the room, but stood in the hall while Captain McLeod locked the door. They then moved to look at the gym to get a visual on the room, and the equipment storage room. The group was met with glances that ran from friendly smiles, to mumblings, to comments that were almost threatening, and outright comments of anger. In fact, Captain McLeod had a couple of inmates removed from the hall and placed in segregation holding cells for disrespect and foul language.

As they entered the gym, which had been locked down until further notice, to ensure that the investigative teams could study the location to see how it is possible for inmates and staff to get together since there are no staff assigned full-time to the gym. They saw the lighting, the interior of the equipment storage room, taking note of the hidden surveillance with transmitters. Speaking up, Captain McLeod indicated that the system in place was some of the most advanced surveillance technology in place, and that federal agencies had utilized the same equipment. Yes, it was extremely expensive but necessary to combat unlawful activities in the facility. Jared Taylor and his coworkers were very complimentary of the Captain, and Superintendent Colden to employ the measures taken, and for having the straight-forward desire to strive to manage a prison where rules would be adhered to, where inmates could serve their prison sentences without added suffering and abuses or harassment and cruelty and where honest hard- working employees could work in a job with self-respect without undue pressures from coworkers. Jared Taylor had seen corruption in a number of agencies, and knew of several instances where inmates in jails and prisons still tried to manipulate staff and conduct illegal business using money as a tool. Following the tour and the presentation, they decided to end the day but to return first thing in the morning to talk with inmate Jay Dillon and several others to be identified through the videotapes. Captain McLeod volunteered to sit with the police Lieutenant for the remainder of the day and evening to watch the videos in order to name the inmates, so that he could have their prison files on hand for the next day's work. They completed this project around ten o'clock that evening and had identified fifteen inmates with large rolls of money seen and being passed with Faye Hondo, and another five in what appeared negotiations on games with Jesse Oxenberg, and some eleven others in the storage room having sex with Faye Hondo.

Chapter Twelve

Early the next morning, Jared Taylor, two of his co-workers, the police Lieutenant, Captain McLeod, and Superintendent Colden had set up to conduct inmate interrogations in the small visitation room. Jay Dillon, handcuffed, had been brought in and was seated at a small table.

Jared Taylor introduced himself, and quickly advised Jay Dillon that he had been implicated in a number of written statements, and conversations with folks as to a number of things, such as drug trafficking in the prison, arranging for and selling of sex to other inmates, illegal sports betting, selling of cell phones, loan-sharking, as well as communicating threats. "And we have you on video and audio tape as well," he said, further explaining that he (Jay) needed to talk with them or things could get a lot tougher on him in that they could place him in a long-term lockup setting, and that he was facing a number of criminal charges such that he could well forget any parole eligibility. Hearing this with silent concentration on what Jared Taylor had said, Jay Dillon's facial coloring paled quite considerably, and he felt the hair stand on his neck, with such an itch that he began to scratch. He felt less and less like the big man on the block. Over and over he heard this conversation in his head, suddenly looking at Jared Taylor, asking, "What is it you want to know?"

"Start at the bottom, and tell us how the selling of sex began and when. Who initiated the idea behind it?" asked Mr. Taylor, keeping his eyes on Jay Dillon in order to keep him pinned down.

Jay Dillon told about Jesse Oxenberg telling him that Faye Hondo worked as a stripper at a nightclub on the beach, even before she began work at the prison. Oxenberg even discussed having spent a night or two in a motel with her near the club, saying that she slept with men purely for the money because it took lots of money for her to live as she wanted. As that had been a recurring topic of conversation between them, Jay Dillon had suggested to Oxenberg that he could help get her some money if she'd have sex with some inmates, that Oxenberg had discussed it with Faye Hondo, who was resistant at first but realized that quite a bit of money could be made. Too, Oxenberg and Jay Dillon had schemed, and convinced her that they could shield her, that no one would be the wiser, or talk, and that Jay Dillon 'ran' what went on in the gym. Oxenberg persuaded her to watch the gym for a while and let him know, and after a while she realized that the custody management rarely made visits into the gym, that Jay Dillon had observers in place most of time to forewarn of incoming traffic to the gym, and that she could make a ton of money. That had been approximately one year ago. He surmised that she may have taken out some eighty thousand dollars for sex alone, and she mostly supplied the condoms to the men. He went on to comment that a nurse in the medical area would discuss certain inmates' health status with Oxenberg if he asked, because Faye Hondo worried about AIDS, HIV, and "stuff like that," said Jay Dillon. Sometimes the money got left in a can somewhere outside the prison, with a note, for Ace Tyler to pick and get it to her. To her it was nothing more than a job, a good paying job.

"What about the drugs?" asked Jared Taylor.

Jay Dillon said that Jesse Oxenberg, Ace Tyler, Faye Hondo, and two Officers, one being Officer Penelope Payne, had over the past year kept him supplied with marijuana, cigarettes, and an occasional crack cocaine, and he discussed the various ways and means they employed to bring it in. Jay Dillon had a tenacious memory, and in time past, had supplied information to law enforcement officials when it served to help him. He guessed that in the year that he had shared in about seventy-five thousand dollars for drugs, with his take being about fifteen or twenty thousand dollars and some marijuana for personal use. With the inmates he had involved most of them had some easy access to money, that came in off the streets and they carried money on them, generally suitcased in the butt, stuck in their inkpen barrels, hidden in clothing, in watches or other places. "Concealment is easy, especially when these folks pass you off and don't take the time to look," Jay Dillon said with a rather strange look that somewhat contorted his face. He spent several hours talking with the investigative team, and prison management, having a deep-seated hope that leniency would come his way, but also realizing he was a major player in this whole ugly picture.

Over the intercom all of them clearly heard "Count time!" and they realized a need for a break. Jay Dillon sat thinking for a minute, until Captain McLeod told him to stand and stretch his legs, and walk into the hallway with him. Once outside in the hallway, Jay Dillon spoke, asking the Captain if thought there was any way he could be spared long term lock-Up. The Captain certainly could not make a promise of any kind, and said those decisions would be left up to other people, depending on the final outcome of this investigation. "But," spoke Captain McLeod, "you've sure gotten yourself into a barrel of mess this time, and you may never live to hit the streets. And, you may have spend your days on protective lock-up for a long time. I just don't know!"

"I've been thinking that, sir. But it just seemed to be going so good. How did you catch on?" asked Jay Dillon.

"Inmates talking, too much going on in that gym, and your smirk on your face every time I went in there," spoke Captain McLeod. "Made me wonder and start checking."

They were summoned back into the room to finish the session, which ended just past noontime. Jared Taylor advised Jay Dillon that they would be discussing the case, his information— which was being dictated by electronic equipment, and he would be advised of felonious charges in the very near future. Superintendent Colden then told Jay Dillon that he would be placed in segregation status pending final disposition, effective immediately, with possible relocation to another facility. Captain McLeod was then directed to have Jay Dillon moved to segregation, with close observation measures employed. During the interviews other staff discussed intense pressures from inmates to bring in cell phones and cigarettes mostly, and of having been threatened with physical harm, and even harm to their families. One muscular burly officer, newly recruited, admitted being threatened if he failed to bring in two cell phones and he'd dealt with it by using his fist. He'd hit the inmate in his face, causing a busted nose, and the inmate stumbled against a cabinet in the bathroom foyer, fell to the concrete floor and had advised medical staff of that to account for his nose injury. A couple of Officers did break down and admit to doing some bartering and trading with Jay Dillon's prison buddies, like bringing in some pastries and donuts in exchange for jewelry which they had learned was stolen from inmates. Strong-arming of the weaker, smaller inmates was common, but few complaints were made because of fear and intimidation by Jay Dillon's followers. Titus Hawks's name came up because he had done some tattooing on two officers, and they let him escape disciplinary actions for a number of prison violations, to include his having been caught with a cell phone and no action taken. Two officers scheduled to be interviewed had called in to the Sergeant with verbal resignations, but the police Lieutenant sent after them and had them interviewed at the police headquarters.

After lunch that afternoon, the investigative team conducted interviews with several other inmates, and staff named by Jay Dillon and the other inmates who had been interviewed already. The same continued for two more days, until the team thought they had exhaustively completed all the interviews, and left the prison facility. In the next week, on Tuesday, all information was shared with the District Attorney's office, and final decisions were reached as to charges and handling of the inmates. Charges were written up and appropriately lodged against the former staff, as well as several inmates, on Wednesday. Prison actions against inmates were taken by Superintendent Colden and his staff.

On Friday, it seemed there was an absolute air of silence within the facility, with looks of disbelief on many employee faces, yet some inmates laughed and talked as if a terror had been dealt with and removed from the place. The morning counts had gone without incident, breakfast had progressed well with inmates mingling with one another in laughter, and inmates going to work assignments and to classes as well as meetings with case workers. At approximately eleven o'clock, there sounded an intercom alarm for assistance needed in red segregation, and several staff were seen running in that direction to include several medical personnel. Shift command staff ran to red segregation as well, speaking into their lapel microphones. An Officer was seen scrambling to a telephone in an office to contact the local emergency medical services in Glen Cove, and within a few minutes, one could hear the sirens of an ambulance entering the grounds of the prison. The halls were secured and all inmates removed to allow staff to rush by with a litter carrying a person covered by a green woolen blanket with a breathing mask on his face and staff carrying a portable oxygen tank. He was taken into the medical station, with curtains pulled into place in a manner to shield folks from seeing what was going on. Those nearby could see the gurney with EMS staff come into the station, and the EMS staff leave with the person on the gurney almost in a run. The sounds of the ambulance vehicle leaving the grounds, and staff running about made others sit and wonder what had happened.

Within minutes, hearsay began to spread about the inmate who had hanged himself in red segregation. By the end of the day, word had spread throughout the entire facility that Jay Dillon had hanged himself. A tee shirt stripped into pieces. An overhead light fixture. Staff shortage. Staff involved with meal trays. Prison managers were looking at work schedules, hoping to explain the shortage of staff working segregation. Superintendent Colden had asked if Jay Dillon had history of suicidal thoughts or had he said anything to indicate possible suicide. Agency division management had been notified, with no direct questioning. Contact with the District Attorney and Jared Taylor was made, with no unusual comments made in turn. Public information contact notification was made with a rather short statement to indicate death of an inmate by suicide.

The local newspaper contained a small paragraph on page two the next morning.

> *Glen Cove Correctional Institution management reports that an inmate was found hanged in his cell. After finding him and cutting him down; medical staff and local EMS were unable to revive him; he was declared dead on arrival at local hospital. Pending notifications to next of kin identity is being withheld.*

The inmate grapevine for the day carried talk of Jay's fear of having to face a lifetime behind bars and of having to remain in segregation, as a number of those who knew Jay rather well knew of his growing claustrophobia, and his constant fear of inmates turning on him with such a viciousness that the scrubbing of inmate Murphy would look like a prank. Jay had known that if this ever happened, the shanks would be pulled out and used on him, and he cringed at the thought; so he surrounded himself with so-called friends that he had the goods on.

Chapter Thirteen

"Count time!" intercoms occurred twice that afternoon, and it appeared to shift supervisors that staff had been so absorbed in the gossip, that their concentration was not up to par. Captain McLeod spoke with the shift Lieutenant at shift lineups about how the staff needed to focus on facility operations, security measures and business at hand, and not get caught up or distracted. He hoped that all facility staff would cease dwelling on recent activities, and spoke of this in a hastily called meeting with his line officers—the Lieutenants, and Sergeants, and he included Maintenance Supervisor Marcus Torn. At this meeting Marcus Torn announced the upcoming arrival of the accreditations standards coordinator, and asked that everyone stay on their toes and to bring to his attention those items that needed to be addressed.

Superintendent Colden came in at the last minute to address the group, thanking them for their cooperation, support and due diligence at maintaining security within the facility. He was very complimentary of both Captain McLeod and Marcus Torn for their recent workmanship at helping uncover wrongdoings and handling of the perpetrators. He went on to comment that he and his chain of command supervisors were working on a plan to increase the staffing at the facility, as well as to recruit staff to fill the vacancies, and he encouraged those present to help in the efforts to locate and recruit correctional staff. Sgt. Ben Hunt spoke up expressing relief on behalf of others for the regards to quickly bringing new Officers on board and increasing the staffing, and received a round of applause. Ending the meeting, Captain McLeod stated, "The supervisor need to work on accuracy in our counts, so talk with your staff and get out on the housing pods with them, please, and I thank you."

Over the next few weeks, Officer Mariel Gaben was promoted to Shift Sergeant and moved to first shift and was given a special task of working with new officers on conducting inmate counts and monitoring inmate movements within the facility. She had proposed an idea of a suggestion box for officers to submit their thoughts and recommendations, and this was fully supported. She had also spoken with officers to interact more professionally with inmates, and was seeing improvements. Inmates seemed less intimidated than in the past, and seemed more satisfied with seeing more supervisory personnel in the housing pods and more frequent unannounced appearances on the housing pods especially at count times. Even Superintendent Colden seemed to spend more than half of his time in the housing pods.

"Young man, how are you doing?" Colden asked, speaking to an inmate who seemed new to the facility.

"Just killing time, sir," responded the young man.

"What's your name?" asked Colden, learning to hear that the inmate's name was Maxwell, and that he was newly sentenced to prison.

"What are you assigned to do here?" Colden asked of Maxwell, who said he was waiting for orientation and hoped to get a job. He spoke of a like for sports but also wanted to go to school to learn a trade so he could get a job when he was paroled. But he also needed to get his GED. "Can you help me get into school, sir?" asked the young Maxwell.

Superintendent Colden focusing on the young man thought of Brent Galen, and said "I sure will. You can do more than just kill time, young man. You need your GED first and foremost, and you can learn several trades here by going to school. Just stay out of trouble and maybe things will work out for you in the long run. I will have someone make contact with you." Superintendent Colden walked off engaging in conversations with other inmates in the housing pod.

Young Maxwell spoke to an older inmate standing nearby, asking,

"Do you know who that white-haired man is?"

"Oh, yeah, he's the Superintendent, and you need to walk the white line with him, and stay out of trouble," said the older inmate.

"Imagine that!" whistled Maxwell, as he sat down on the chair in his cell Glancing up at the wall he noted 'Cell 40' painted on the wall, and spoke softly, "More than just killing time in here."

For the next few months, Glen Cove Correctional Institution's staffing increased, positions seemed to stay filled, and staff absenteeism was almost non-existent. Counts occurred without delay and incident. Captain McLeod and Superintendent McLeod were both relieved that they had received accreditation at the facility, with media recognition, and that the sex and drug scandal was over. Faye Hondo had been sentenced to a term of life in prison and was held in a facility on the west coast but had learned she was HIV positive and had lung cancer; Jesse Oxenberg was in prison for two life terms, housed in a northwestern location; Fran Russell was serving thirty years, somewhere in the Midwest; and several other staff involved were serving prison terms in other states. All the inmates convicted of involvement were housed at locations away from Glen Cove Correctional, and notes had been placed in their files that they never be returned to Glen Cove Correctional Institution. Superintendent Colden was sitting at his office desk, staring out the window, giving thought to Matt Ranham's submittal of retirement papers, and mulling over his own anticipation of retirement. A knock came from his door.

"Come in," he said, raising his voice. Seeing Captain McLeod, he said, "What are you up to, Captain?"

"Thought I'd go check out the parking lot, sir, and wanted to let you know I'd planned to take time off this afternoon afterward, sir."

"Well, that's good, Captain. Just got Matt Ranham's retirement papers; you should apply for the job of Assistant Superintendent."

Captain McLeod smiled, saying, "I may do that, sir. Good afternoon."

Superintendent Colden thanked McLeod for all his work, and raised two fingers waving him on his way. He picked up his phone, called Vanis Goodson in personnel, and advised her of Ranham's paperwork on his desk. A short time later she walked in, bringing him a fresh cup of coffee and a stack of forms for his signature.

"What are you doing, Mr. Colden, just sitting in here staring out the window?" she asked with liveliness in her voice.

"Oh, just killing time, Ms. Goodsn. Just killing time!"

"Well, enjoy it, sir. Oh, by the way, I just hung up the phone with a Mrs. Eva Bond in the state's EEO officer. There have been two major complaints lodged against the facility for sexual harassment, not related to the investigation just completed, but it can wait until tomorrow. She's going to fax us a copy of the complaints in the morning. We have nothing on these two cases at all, and personnel has no clues on them either. I have the complainants' names in my office, if you'd like for me to go get them. I assumed it could wait another day, sir."

"Yes, it can wait another day," he said, as he leaned back. He propped his feet on the right hand corner of his desk, and told her, "Take off and go on home early, Ms. Goodson. You've earned it. Good night. Oh, by the way, remind me to write letters of appreciation to those folks who helped us with the investigation. And I want to especially thank the District Attorney for keeping his word to look into someone's conviction." He leaned back in his chair, thinking of Brent Galen and remembering that teary-eyed young man with the biggest smile ever leaving that office who was possibly close to being a prison tragedy had inmates found out he had talked. And a prosecution casualty had the District Attorney not duly investigated the crime and corrected a grievous error before the young man lost his faith in the criminal justice system.

Smiling, she thanked him and walked toward the door, saying, "Good night."

Chapter Fourteen

Standing on the driveway that morning, J.T. Colden waved at his neighbor across the street, who had gone out to pick up his morning newspaper, and he opened his truck door to get in. Backing out of the drive, he thought what a pretty day it was. But it was back to work. He had taken a few days off from work and had gone fishing over the past week; he left word with his wife not to disclose his whereabouts, but that she could take a message and relay it to him by phone. He badly needed some personal time to regroup, and certainly needed the time off from the everyday problems and staff issues that he had been dealing with. He and his wife of thirty-seven years did talk every day at least twice by phone, and at night; she did not mention the prison one time. Darby Jane Colden, a retired elementary school teacher, knew her husband all too well, and had seen to it that he took a week off to go to their cabin on Lake Manito in eastern Virginia. With no interruptions, she promised him. In the weeks before his vacation, the telephone seemed to ring non-stop, and he was called back to the prison so much that she wondered why he even bothered to go home at night. He had been so irritable or ill-tempered that she didn't think she could live in the same house with him; she gave him an ultimatum—take time off work and go somewhere, or go ahead and retire from the job. She had known he was contemplating retirement for some time, but knew he loved his work and the work family. It had been three years since he had taken time from work and that was so he could accompany their oldest son, on two weeks of vacation leave from his law firm, and a brother on a hunting trip to Minnesota that they had talked about for two years. Driving along the road, he snickered, thinking about Darby and her way of getting things done. She was a caring but feisty little woman, but when she spoke, he listened! He thought back to the days when he had envisioned that a prison warden's job was a piece of cake; was he so wrong!

As he turned his pickup truck off the main highway, onto the asphalt entrance road, he slowed down, glancing over to his right, and stopped, looking at the facility sign sitting in the corner. He felt a sense of pride especially seeing his name on the silver-colored metal-plate affixed to the stone and brick structure which read GLEN COVE CORRECTIONAL INSTITUTION, with the second line reading also in bold print J.T. COLDEN, FACILITY ADMINISTRATOR. Oh, yes, he thought, that's what he had worked for and it had taken a number of years, but he felt good about his overall accomplishments. Oh, there were many issues, and he wondered what new problems had arisen since he had left for a much- needed break. He was aware of the sexual harassment complaints that had been filed because Ms. Vanis Goodson, personnel specialist, had advised him of such before he left but he had yet to see the actual complaints that had been sent to the headquarters office, and was not aware of the name or names of the complainants or the substance of the allegations made. Before pulling into his assigned parking space, he decided to ride through the parking lot to see what he might find. He did take note that the spaces designated for the disabled needed to be repainted, and highlighted with a special color, but he'd check with Marcus Torn in maintenance and let him handle that task.

Pulling into his reserved space, with the nameplate on a metal pole for Facility Administrator, he cut the ignition switch off, put his keys in his right coat pocket, and retrieved his work identification from his glove compartment where he had placed it on the last day at work. He sat there watching employees who were arriving for work and were going into the gatehouse entry doors to be frisk-searched and have IDs checked before they were allowed to go into the prison facility. He watched several interacting with each while they walked together, some shaking hands, some hugging each other, laughing and talking, while others walked alone, heads dropped or held high, with most carrying small clear see-through lunch containers. Superintendent Colden thought to himself that the idea of requiring only lunch containers of clear see-through plastic or mesh was an excellent idea, and he needed to ensure that a commendation letter was sent to Captain Buddy McLeod, with a copy to his personnel file, as well as the Division Director. Staff who propose new innovative ideas needed this, and it wouldn't hurt to give them a little money if the Division Director would find the guts to go forward in pursuit of it. It sure helped to control contraband from entering the prison, and was a time-saver for gatehouse staff in checking containers being brought in. Opening his truck door, he stepped out, locked his door, grabbed his portfolio case and started walking to the gatehouse.

As he walked inside, officers and others present greeted him, "Good morning, Mr. Colden. Good to have you back with us."

Smiling at them, he responded, "It's good to be back, and I hope all is well." He emptied his pockets into a clear plastic box on a table, placed his portfolio beside it, and walked through the metal detector to his left and on clearing it, presented his identification to an officer who checked it against the computer bank, with his photo appearing on the computer monitor. The officer quickly flipped through the portfolio, and cleared him for entry into the facility. He retrieved his personal effects from the plastic box and pocketed them. As he exited the gate-house, he stopped to look across the front grounds, taking note of the spring flowers beginning to open, and the neatly manicured lawn. He smiled and walked the sidewalk to the front door, greeting several employees along the way and standing on the front patio. He took note of the general mood, which was a good sign, for he had hoped there were no animosities prevailing from the Jay Dillon-Faye Hondo investigation, one of the most regrettable experiences he had ever endured in his career. After that ordeal, he needed that time off. Stepping into his office, he surveyed his surroundings, walked over to open his window blinds, took in a deep breath, and sat down at his desk. Momentarily, his executive secretary, Marley Brooks, walked in, smiling and carrying a cup of coffee.

"Good morning, sir. Glad to have you back. Did you enjoy your time off?"

"Thank you, Ms. Brooks. I did enjoy the time away. I hope things have been going well. Do you know if Captain McLeod is in yet?" he asked.

"He is here somewhere. I saw him down the hall with Ms. Goodson a few minutes ago. I will locate him and let him know you need to see him. Ms. Goodson also wants to talk with you when you get the time." He asked her to get both of them to come to his office, and leaned back taking a sip of his coffee, looking out his front window in the direction of the gatehouse. "It is good to be back," he murmured. Shortly thereafter, a knock on his door caused him to turn.

"Come in," he stated as both Vanis Goodson and Captain McLeod walked in.

"Good morning, sir. Glad you're back." They spoke simultaneously, with smiles.

"Well, the desk is not piled as I thought it might be. Guess you've taken care of things while I was out? Anything happen regarding the Jay Dillon- Faye Hondo case during my absence?" he asked, staring at Captain McLeod.

"I would surmise that business is over, sir. We did have a couple of inmates running their mouths about Dillon and Titus Hawks catching more time, but they're now on administrative segregation over at LongView Correctional, and it's been quiet since they were moved. We had three new officers submit their resignations because they were being pressured by inmates to bring in cell phones, and felt they couldn't handle it. Scared to tell the names of the inmates, and scared to go to the housing pods to deal with inmates. Otherwise, it's been business as usual," spoke Captain McLeod.

Vanis Goodson then spoke about the officer recruitments that were on- going, as well as the approval received on the retirement for Assistant Superintendent Matt Ranham, who had been out of work on sick leave for some time. Interviews were scheduled for Officer positions and the plan was to fill six positions that week. She then mentioned the sexual harassment complaints that had been filed against the facility just prior to Colden's time off. "We need to talk about the EEO— equal employment opportunity office concerns that I told you about before you left. There are two complaints filed, and Eva Bond in the state office faxed me a copy. I'm still waiting for hard copies to come in through the mail service. I will give the faxes to you for your reading, and we can get back together after you've reviewed those. Ms. Bond's office is supposed to conduct the investigations into those, but I have no clue when that might be."

Superintendent Colden asked, "who specifically are they lodged against?"

She looked at Superintendent Colden with no change in facial expression and said, "Lt. Peter Gibbs."

"Oh, boy! This may be the end of his career if it rings true. He does have quite a bit of baggage regarding women," spoke Captain McLeod.

"We'll see once the EEO office investigates," said Superintendent Colden. "Meanwhile, let's keep this ourselves, and move on. We do need to move him from second shift to the Operations Office so you, Captain McLeod, can watch him. Let's get that reassignment notice done today, and issued to him. I assume he is scheduled to work?"

Captain McLeod advised that he would check and get the assignment handled. He left the office.

Superintendent Colden, looking at Ms. Goodson, asked if the recruitment notice or the posting for the Assistant Superintendent position had been done, and she indicated that it was on the web. He asked if she had received Captain McLeod's application, to which she indicated that she had. Dismissing her, he asked her for the faxes on the allegations as well as the personnel file for Lt. Gibbs. Ms. Goodson left the office and returned to give him the materials he had asked for. He locked them in his desk, and advised his secretary that he was going for a walk-through in the facility and would return before the noon hour. On entering the general population housing pod, he spoke to several inmates who were lounging in the dayroom, some watching television, some on the telephones, and several were sitting at the stainless tables playing dominoes and card games. He was concerned with the inmate idleness numbers, and had given lots of thought to ensuring that every able-bodied inmate was given an assignment to a meaningful job, or had been offered the opportunity to attend academic and/or vocational schooling. But, realistically, there just weren't enough jobs to place every inmate who wanted to work, in a facility where 1500 inmates were competing for 640 jobs, and there were 432 school positions. He spotted a young man sitting near a window with his feet propped on the concrete window seal, and walked over to him, frowning.

"Young man, take your feet off that window ledge and put them on the floor. There are inmates who try to keep this place looking decent, but it is difficult to clean those smudge marks. What is your name?" Colden asked.

Looking up, the young man, chewing on bubble gum blew a bubble, asked, "And who might you be?"

"I am Superintendent Colden, and again, what is your name?"

Sitting upright in his plastic chair, and removing the bubble gum from his mouth, the young man advised that his name was Greg Elliot, and that he had been on the facility for two weeks. They engaged in conversation, with Superintendent Colden learning that he had arrived with several detainers for pending charges, both in-state and in Tennessee, as well as a court hearing on a breaking and entering charge for the following week. He relayed to the Superintendent that he had been told that he would not be assigned to a job until the court hearing. So, the inmate said he was sitting around just killing time like everyone else.

Moving to another inmate who was much older, Colden realized that he knew the inmate from other prison locations over the years past. "Gus Burke? Is this you?" asked Colden, standing off to the left side of the inmate, studying him, taking note that his hair was considerably thinned, gray and uncombed, his hands shaking uncontrollably.

"It's me, Captain. I hear you're the Superintendent here now. It's been a long time since I saw you at River Birch camp; you were the Captain there. I got paroled out but didn't do well out there, you know. Me and the licker still buddies. It makes me do things, and this time they say I killed a boy; run over him. But I don't remember it," he spoke, repeatedly moving his hands, weaving his fingers, while having difficulty maintaining eye contact with Colden.

"How old are you now?" Colden asked.

"About sixty—not sure; I don't think so well anymore. I guess they won't let me out no more, huh?" commented Gus.

Making observations and recollecting the earlier years when he first got to know Gus Burke, Colden suspected that the inmate had spent the majority of his life in and out of prisons, and at one time had spent considerable time on lock-up for he had earned a reputation for carrying a shank, and on two occasions had cut other inmates rather severely. Alcohol had been a primary factor to the man's downfall, as well as inabilities to manage his temper for he remembered that Gus Burke was quick to anger and lash out at those in disagreement with him over even the most petty things. If memory served, Colden could recall at least two prior manslaughter or murder charges against Gus Burke, and that all his family had ceased having contact or anything to do with him. Colden wondered how much of a sentence Gus had received this time around, and pulling out a notepad, wrote down the name with a note to check sentence and medical status.

"Well, Gus, I've got to move on. You take care of yourself." spoke Colden, as he walked off to exit the housing pod and enter the adjoining pod. Superintendent Colden completed his rounds of the general population, and went to the segregation housing area. He spoke to inmates in their cells, and staff manning the area. Checking the shift log he was pleased to see that staff shortage had not affected post assignments. He had walked out of the segregation area, en route to the maintenance warehouse when the intercom screeched, 'Count time.' Smiling to himself, he decided to re-enter the segregation housing to observe staff and the count procedures, and was pleased with the staff's adherence to policy and procedures that were in place. He then proceeded to walk to the maintenance area, where he spoke with staff, and entered Marcus Torn's office.

"Hello, Mr. Colden. Have a good vacation?" spoke Torn.

"I did indeed. You might want to take one too. I wanted to have you take a look at the painting of the lines for the handicapped parking spaces, and to determine if there is a dedicated color for those as well. I saw them driving in this morning, and they could use some sprucing up. I sure would appreciate it," Colden advised Torn.

"I'll have someone get right on it this afternoon. We just purchased a stencil for the disabled van accessible parking spaces, and I believe we received some blue powder paint for those designated spaces, but I'll get some on it, sir."

"I hear it's been relatively quiet while I was gone. That's good, and supposedly our accreditation inspections went well?" Colden commented.

"That's what Captain McLeod told me. By the way, the additional surveillance equipment came in, and the extra fence fabric we needed for that area adjacent to the wooded area where folks are throwing contraband over the outer perimeter. Captain McLeod wants a security camera over there with a thirty-day tape; we might get lucky and see who's throwing that stuff over, and I can handle that," Marcus Torn stated, with a tone that resonated energy and enthusiasm for his work.

"Proceed on; keep me posted on developments. And, thanks," Colden spoke, as he stood to leave. As he walked up the corridor, he heard the 'count time' blast from the intercom.

Re-entering his office, around noon time, he summoned his secretary, asking her to pull an inmate record on Gus Burke for him to review, and to please get him a fresh cup of coffee. He then unlocked his desk and retracted the materials that Ms. Goodson had given to him earlier. He studied the faxed report of allegations, taking note of the checkmark that was in the box for uninvestigated. The complainants were two of the evening shift Officers, who had filed separate and individual complaints against Lieutenant Peter Gibbs alleging that he had made unwelcomed comments to them on the job. Interestingly, the complaints were a day apart in the filings, and both had been called in by telephone from the facility to the state EEO office. The statements were not very detailed but one simply stated that Gibbs had offered to help in her studying for an upcoming promotional examination in exchange for sex, and the other alleged that he made references to her as being a strumpet. Laying the documents aside, Colden wondered about the merits to both, if any, and thought that maybe he needed to spend a little more time in the facility around the staff in the evenings and learn more on what has been going on, without asking too many questions that might impact the upcoming investigation into these allegations. He knew that Lieutenant Gibbs had a history of involvement with females at other locations, which resulted in his being relocated by the Division headquarters to the Glen

Cove facility. Granted, there had been no formal complaints filed, but the gossip and the fact that his second ex-wife alluded to his affairs with females working at the facility in her divorce complaint and cited alienation of affection with no actions being taken by prison managers. The divorce complaint with innuendos had been hot fodder for the news media, and folks naturally believed what they read.

One citizen had sent copies of the newspaper article to corrections officials in the state office, to the Governor's office, and to the public information office under anonymous cover. During the court hearing on the divorce action, Gibbs had stated in open court that he had had affairs with several staff that he worked with, and that two of them had been subordinates that he directly supervised. The two ladies later had resigned their positions, and did not file complaints against Gibbs for improprieties on the job. The correctional headquarters officials made an inquiry and when contacted, the two ladies in question refused to discuss the case with them. To save further embarrassment and ease tensions, an agency directive was provided to the facility manager to reassign Lt. Peter Gibbs to Glen Cove Correctional Institution for the betterment of the agency and for duty. Gibbs thought it best not to argue the point, but to relocate altogether to the Village of Glen Cove. His ex-wives had left him broke, but he had acquired mechanical skills over the years such that he was able to secure a mechanic's job at a local garage to supplement his state job. Colden could recall that upon Gibbs's arrival that he had sat down and talked with him at great length, to have Gibbs reassure him that such incidents were not reoccur. Colden had known that Gibbs was not overly happy working on second shift but he had a knack for moving about among the staff and inmates and nosing out who was doing what, and had an exceptional knowledge of surveillance equipment. Besides, when Gibbs arrived at Glen Cove he had in some twenty-seven years, and with his time at Glen Cove, he should be nearing his thirty year mark. Well, with Gibbs now moved to day shift, working under the watchful eye of Captain McLeod, he'd visit the evening shift and learn what he could. He put the file back into his desk drawer, and began going through a pile of incoming mail stacked on his desk. Shortly thereafter, his intercom rang and Captain McLeod on the other end asked if he could come to talk with him.

"Sure, come on," he said, "and bring Lieutenant Gibbs with you."

"Yes, sir," responded Captain McLeod. Hanging up the phone, he wondered, why did the Superintendent need to see Lieutenant Gibbs? Captain McLeod walked into the adjoining room and advised Lieutenant Gibbs that they needed to report to the Superintendent's office. While walking up the hallway, one could see the nervousness in Gibbs; he stammered when he spoke and constantly shook his arms.

"Captain, did he say why me?" asked Lieutenant Gibbs.

"He did not, but we'll find out in a minute. Just calm yourself down. Mr. Colden doesn't bite, you know."

"Yeah, but he's a bit hard-nosed at times, and doesn't give you much rope. His expectations are so rigid; always expecting you to walk a white line, and that's tough nowadays," said the Lieutenant.

"That may be, but it's reasonable to expect your staff to be on the up-and- up, and to conduct themselves professionally on and off the job. It's tough having to constantly check behind staff and defend them in actions they should never have gotten themselves into. Besides, we don't know what it is that he wants anyway, so let's just wait and see," spoke Captain McLeod. "You might be sweating and worrying over nothing."

They arrived at Superintendent Colden's office door, knocked, and walked inside when advised to. "Good afternoon, gentlemen. Have a seat, please."

"Well, it's been a busy morning. I've asked both of you in here to discuss inmates and cell phones, and a facility shakedown we need to have. It's been quite a while since our last shakedown, and if my records are accurate, we've found a number of cell phones over the past six months. Too many. Lieutenant, I do know that you've been stressing to staff on the evening shift to keep their eyes open and to talk with inmates to see what they could tell us. Is there any word on that end?" spoke Superintendent Colden. Looking at his desk calendar, he glanced at the lower right corner notation of 31 cell phones for the month, and 87 for the previous month.

"We've had 118 cell phones confiscated in the past two months, gentlemen. We cleared that Dillon crowd out, impressed upon folks adhering to the entry policy at the gatehouse, and we are checking incoming supplies better, aren't we, Captain? So, what are we missing?"

"Well, that is exactly what I wanted to talk with you, sir," said Captain McLeod. "I've been watching the numbers of confiscations, watching the gatehouse checks and searches, and we've been walking the perimeters more to seize what might have been thrown over. In fact, we've changed the schedules so we can walk the yards before letting the inmates go out for yard privileges, and we're still missing some that get inside. We can't locate all of them. We need to try to obtain a cell phone sniffing canine, or at least give it our best shot. I've been doing some research and there are plenty of grant monies out there for us to apply for, so we can acquire at least one or maybe two dogs. Too, there are a couple of states that are training their own dogs to sniff out cell phones."

"Are you versed in writing grants, Captain?" asked Superintendent Colden.

"No, but the agency has staff who do research and write applications for grants, so why not pursue this through the agency channels? It's long overdue, if you ask me. These cell phones are a major problem in prisons, as you well know, and legislation needs to be enacted to make it a crime to possess a cell phone in a correctional facility, a jail, or any type of institutional confinement setting. In my research, I've seen where California prisons had discovered well over fourteen hundred cell phones in 2007, and the number grew ten times that in just four years. We saw how much money was being funneled with cell phones through Jay Dillon, and a forty-nine dollar phone can sell for up to eight hundred dollars. That's big! We need a special team of staff who can deal with cell phone sniffing dogs, special searches around the seven-day clock, and work with local law enforcement on this. Maybe Lieutenant Gibbs could help in this? What do you think, Lieutenant?" spoke Captain McLeod.

Lieutenant Gibbs responded slowly, saying "Captain, that's a big problem all over the nation, and it'll take a lot of money, and specially trained, committed staff. It would be a major undertaking, and I'd be willing to help, but I'm only one person. But the dogs would be a major tool to help combat cell phones on the housing pods and elsewhere. Meanwhile, we could ask the local law enforcement agencies to come in from time with their canines and do walk-throughs."

Superintendent Colden then spoke up asking if either of them were familiar with local agencies that were using cell phone-sniffing dogs, and both responded that they did. He then assigned them the task of working together to seek out these agencies and develop a schedule for the dogs to be brought in for walk-throughs. He advised that he would follow chain-of-command to determine how to go about a proposal for grant applications on acquiring the sniffing dogs, as well as his composing a letter seeking agency support for legislation on criminal laws as regards possession of cell phones by inmates, and much stronger law on criminal actions against employees or civilians who provide cell phones to inmates. The current laws made this a misdemeanor, which had no real impact on persons. He also wanted to see state policy put into place that denied state employment to civilians who were found guilty of such actions, as well as a requirement that employees be terminated with no appeal rights and that they have to forfeit retirement earnings if they were found guilty of same, regardless of their term of employment.

"Let's move on and discuss a shakedown, if you will," said Superintendent Colden. "I would prefer it be an early morning surprise, say around two o'clock a.m., with cell phone sniffing dogs, our facility emergency response team, extra staff to facilitate observances of inmates in holding areas while others are checking the housing areas, dayrooms, all school areas, the gym, and other areas. Personal effects in lockers need to be checked thoroughly, because cell phones can well be concealed in hygiene items containers, like powders, deodorant, and all colored containers. I seem to recall a deodorant canister holding a cell phone a while back that a new officer located. So, the two of you need to work on setting this up, and get those programs and classification staff involved. They have ownership in this facility just as much as we do, as well as the maintenance staff. Captain, get back to me in the next two days and lay it out for me."

"Yes, sir." spoke both the Captain and Lieutenant.

Superintendent Colden then dropped his head, and entwined his fingers before looking at Lieutenant Gibbs. Pursing his lips, he spoke, "Lieutenant, you are herein advised that there have been two complaints filed with the state EEO office against you, that have yet to be investigated. I would surmise that you received your letters of notification from the state office by now. I expect the investigators to come in at any time to delve into the allegations and talk with staff. The complainants work on the evening shift, so I arranged for you to be reassigned to the day shift to work under Captain McLeod, pending the investigation and final resolutions. Until that time, you are to have absolutely no contact, no communications with anyone on that evening shift. You are not to discuss the allegations and you are not to discuss the two complainants with anyone, other than the assigned investigators. Do I make myself clear?"

"Yes, sir, I fully understand, and I have received my notices," spoke Lieutenant Gibbs.

"Do you also understand that if you hear anything, from anyone on this, that you are to immediately contact Captain McLeod and inform him; if he is out of place, call me. Is this clear?" said Superintendent Colden.

Yes, sir." Said Lieutenant Gibbs.

"Good. Go do your work, and Captain, get back to me pretty quick." Both Lieutenant Gibbs and Captain McLeod departed the office, going back to the Operations section.

Superintendent Colden tackled a stack of inmate classification actions changing custody from close, lockup to close regular population housing, and handled a half-dozen correspondence letters he had received from inmate family members. Generally, he delegated much of the classification work but he often handled some as it helped him stay on track with what his staff were observing with inmates and what they were recommending; sometimes he had to override actions to help move inmates onward due to some semblance of lack of case subjectivity. He thought that objectivity had its place, but a human element needed to be imposed as well. He was well aware that some of his staff despised child molesters and repeatedly rejected them for changes in custody, even when the inmate's sentence was set to expire and he be released to the community. After devoting several hours to this work, he decided to go home. Besides, it was 5:30 in the evening already, so it was time to go. He had called the Operations Center to question the count having been completed; it had been completed, taking about forty minutes. Colden asked why it had taken so long, with the response being 'inexperienced staff.' He proceeded to exit the facility and go home.

Chapter Fifteen

The following morning on his arrival, Ms. Brooks gave him the files on inmate Gus Burke, with his usual cup of decaffeinated coffee. Smiling, he thanked her, asked that she hold his calls for an hour or so, and proceeded to his office to peruse the record. Sitting at his executive desk, he pulled out the left leaf and laid the inmate's medical file on it. Turning to the main desk he then opened the thick inmate record, and quickly determined that this was a cumulative file on the inmate's total prison confinement. He thought that he'd only seen a few of these type files in his career where there were several folders affixed together; it required both hands to handle the file that was about eight inches thick. Rather quickly, he learned that Gus Burke was sixty-five years of age, and had been in and out of confinement facilities for the past forty-nine years, having first been institutionalized at age sixteen in a juvenile facility for repeatedly stealing cars to go on joy rides. Gus had graduated to bank robbery by the time he reached his twenty-first birthday and was paroled at age twenty-five. On day three of his parole, he robbed a liquor store and killed the store clerk; fleeing the store, his vehicle failed to start, and he had fled on foot. He stole a vehicle that same day a few miles from the liquor store, and drove for three days, stopping only for fuel and edibles, which were cold sandwiches, bags of chips, and soda.

Over the three days, Burke had crossed into the state of Oklahoma, where he stopped at a flea-bag motel in the evening hours to get some sleep. He awoke early the next morning just before daybreak with a rifle being pointed at him, and on the other end of that rifle was a thirty-year Oklahoma state patrolman who told him to turn over onto his belly. Burke was handcuffed, and on escort outside the motel room, he found that various law enforcement officials had the motel surrounded. He was jailed until he could be extradited back to North Carolina which took about 2 days. Charges for murder, robbery, and vehicle theft led to conviction with a forty-five year sentence in the North Carolina state department of correction, and incarceration at the penitentiary in Raleigh. Early on during that term, Gus Burke was violent with his inmate peers and extremely bull- headed when prison officials tried to talk with him; he spent a lot of time in segregation, which at that time, according to Colden's memory of stories he had been told, was an eight by eight unheated cinder block structure with a steel door that had a small opening with steel vertical bars, and an opening in one wall big enough for a tin plate of food to be passed through. On the cement floor was a mattress, with a wool blanket, on which he slept, and sat. A metal bucket in the far corner served for relieving himself, with it being emptied on alternating days.

The record indicated that Burke spent two years in such housing in the first three years, and later had been moved to work on a mountain prison farm, where he stayed for eleven years. He had worked on highway squads beating on big rocks or boulders with sledge hammers for days on end, to produce road gravel used to build roads. He wore chains with solid steel ten-pound balls attached to his ankles, so there was little worry that he would escape. He'd had few family and friends, and by the time he turned thirty-eight, there were no visitors. No mail came for him. His attitude worsened. He had severely beaten two different prisoners and had struck an officer with a handle he had broken from a work tool. He was moved to various prisons across the state for several years, mostly for lock-up, after which he was placed on work crews for hard labor on highway squads, cutting right of ways, digging ditches, building bridges over swamps and lowland areas. He was paroled again, with a job working with a road construction company, but was revoked within the month, as he stole a company truck, committed another robbery, burglarized a hardware store and stole several weapons. A few days after the burglary, he was caught sleeping in the truck, parked in the edge of a wooded area just off Highway 74 near Wilmington. Once re-incarcerated, he had spent considerable time on lock-up in isolation, and had worked on prison farm labor crews, until his health began to deteriorate, mentally and physically. Colden saw references to mental instability in several reports, with the word 'institutionalized,' as well as comments about unworthiness for parole considerations. The inmate's medical folder noted some early dementia, with several medical issues of diabetes, high blood pressure, bursitis, gout, and there had been signs of heart ailments. Colden wondered why a move to Glen Cove Correctional had been made, when relocation to a geriatric facility would have been the most preferred option for Gus Burke.

Closing the folders, he sat them atop each other and placed them on a corner table in his office, thinking he would summon someone in the population movement sector and have them seek to have Burke moved elsewhere, more suitable.

He was responding to e-mails on his computer when Ms. Marley Brooks rang him on the phone's intercom, to inform him that one Charles Frederick in the local District Attorney's office had called, wishing him to return his call that afternoon around two o'clock. Superintendent Colden advised Ms. Brooks to remind him of that when she returned from her lunch.

"By the way, Ms. Brooks, contact Mitch Steele and tell him I want to see him in the next half-hour, in my office, please."

"Yes, sir," she responded, hanging up the phone. Mitch Steele was the Assistant Superintendent for Correctional Programs and Support Services, and had been working in the facility for five years; he had transferred on promotion from another facility. His father and two uncles had served in the correctional work force for the Federal Bureau of Prisons in the mid- western part of the country. Steele had attended college in North Carolina on football scholarships, and after graduation had sought employment, and had taken a position with the department some sixteen years before, but worked hard and had promoted through several positions rather quickly. He was very computer literate, well versed with policy and procedures, security, minded, and had been thought of as one of the most brilliant programs and classification employees in the agency for some time. Some persons saw him as being prepped for movement to the agency headquarters because he was a talented visionary, of extremely high intelligence, with loyalty to the agency, who had developed proposals and shared his ideas on the future of managing inmate populations.

Ringing his office, Ms. Brooks advised him, "Superintendent Colden asked that I contact you, for he would like to see you in his office in the next half-hour."

"Yes, Ma'am, Ms. Brooks. I'll come right on up to the office. But do you have any idea what it might be in reference to? Is there anything I might need to bring?" Steele asked.

"I don't think so. I do know he has studied the file of an inmate Gus Burke. In fact, that file is in his office, now," she advised Steele. Hanging up, she dialed back to Colden's office and advised him that Mitch Steele was en route to his office. He thanked her and hung up the phone.

Mitch Steele knocked on the door, to which Superintendent Colden spoke, "Come on in, please."

"You asked to see me, sir?" asked Steele.

"I did, and thank you. We've got an inmate here that I would very much like to see get moved, preferably to a geriatric facility. I don't know what the purpose was in sending him here, but I've read the file on him, and he has a number of health issues that could be given more attention if he were elsewhere. I spoke to him yesterday on the housing pod; in fact, on my rounds, I thought I recognized him, and spoke to him. Some years ago, he was housed where I worked at two different locations, but he's aged considerably, both mentally and physically. Gus Burke is his name. Got quite a history." Superintendent Colden stood to retrieve the files, and handing them to Steele, said, "Poor guy's been paroled a couple of times, but re-offended and came back each time with more time on him. Old with no family, it seems. Please see if you can get anything done for him to go where he can get some attention. Also take a close look at his custody level and see if his classification is accurate. And I'd like to see our numbers for the idle reduced. When I talk with some and ask what they do, I hear them say they are just killing time. I thank you so much."

Steele took the files, stood to leave, and commented, "We've been getting a number shipped into us that should never have come to Glen Cove. We've moved a dozen or so already. But I'll look at this one and see what we can do. I'll keep you posted, sir." He left the office. As he left the office, Captain McLeod had come to the door and came in on Steele's exit.

"Mr. Colden, it's rather urgent that we speak," he spoke, with being told to come on inside and speak whatever was on his mind. One could tell he was anxious to share what he knew, as he looked like he was in emotional distress with shaking in his arms; he needed to sit down a minute and get his thoughts together before speaking. Looking at his wall clock, Superintendent Colden felt hunger pains in his gut, realizing he had not eaten solid foods since lunch the day before. He spoke and asked Captain McLeod if he wanted to go out for lunch, as it would give him a chance to talk at length, to which he agreed and he even welcomed a chance to have lunch away from the facility.

"We'll take my old truck," spoke Colden, who picked up his intercom and spoke to his secretary advising her of his lunch plans. Turning back to Captain McLeod, he said, "We'll need to get back here before 1:45, as I have to make a rather important phone call."

En route to a local family-owned diner, Colden asked Captain McLeod, "What's up?"

"Sir, we've got some problems, serious problems. I've spent most all morning on the compound and out on the rec yard. Two of my snitches, been here for a couple of years, tell me there's been a hit put out on Jesse Oxenberg. Not sure of the source or who put it out, or how it's to be done. Word is someone, maybe a worker, inside here is talking about those rapes of the inmates' wives. There's supposed to be big bucks put on this with backing from one of the gangs. I spoke with a couple of other guys on the yard, and they know nothing about any such hit, but one of them did say that he heard that Titus Hawks's friends with the Hell's Angels want revenge for Hawks's troubles, and they think Oxenberg ratted him out. You know Oxenberg had little real guts; he was always the sneak in the back door, who'd do most anything to save his own skin. With these darned computers, he could be found if someone was looking real hard because he's not under identity protection. None of them are. What do we need to do?"

asked Captain McLeod. "The rascal did wrong, got caught and is being punished, but to be killed is not right."

Picking his words carefully, Superintendent Colden said, "I want you to keep gathering intel off the yard, and let me handle the rest. I'm speaking with the District Attorney today, and I'll notify the chain of command, and even make contact with the officials at Oxenberg's location to forewarn them. We'll need to alert the State Bureau of Investigation on this. We really need to get those cell phone dogs in here. If a hit's been made, you can bet a cell phone is the weapon. Did you locate local dogs?"

"I did, and have them set up to come in on Friday morning early, around daybreak. I'd like to do a shakedown on Saturday morning, starting at 2:00 in the morning, using the state canines and check the place good. I figure to use the dogs on Friday might help locate the phones and get them, and what we miss we hope to get on Saturday. And then come back on Sunday evening with the dogs again. Using four to six dogs at one time would be good. The local sheriff will be happy to help us out, and has agreed to do whatever it takes, and has offered a dozen of his best team to work with us. What do you think?" spoke Captain McLeod.

"Sounds like a plan, Captain, we can move on with. Set it in motion. Let Lieutenant Gibbs spend his time on the yard gathering as much intel as he can; we desperately need to jump on this word of a hit. Have him call other prisons around and see if anyone is hearing about a hit among their gangs. But ensure he knows to keep this close to his vest pocket."

On approach to the diner, Colden studied the old cinder-block building, built in the 1950's with its white paint long faded and mismatched shingles on its roof. The black asphalt parking lot boasted potholes filled with clay and dirt and had needed repaving for quite some time; the sign on the side of the road cried out being in desperate need of refurbishing or replacement. Most of the customers were locals, and there had been a number of construction workers frequenting the eatery since the retirement housing had been on the upstart for several months as of late. Entering the diner, he continued to wonder why the owners didn't make some effort to renovate and replace some of the furnishings. The bar stools were the old fashioned round seats clad with red and black vinyl that was badly worn, and had been taped with colored duct tape. Several still had the stainless steel rings around the seat. He still preferred to sit in one of the wooden booths in a corner with a window to the side. The floor tiles were worn, and in some places busted or completely missing. Surely, enough money was being made to do some remodeling, he thought. It surprised him some time back when he had seen the county health department's food service rating of 97% with an 'A' certificate on the wall, at the entrance to the cooking area. Maybe the rumors were true that count, workers ate there with a discount on their meals, and this may have attributed to the courtesy extended to the owners. Could be family owned, as he had learned was prevalent in the rural areas around Glen Cove.

Nevertheless, an overhaul in the diner's appearance, inside and out, certainly wouldn't damage the reputation, for the food was the best Colden had eaten, aside from Ms. Darby's, since he had relocated to this part of the state. The hospitality of the diner's workers was and had always been cordial and generous. Very friendly. Taking his usual seat in a booth, they proceeded to order from the hand-written menu on the overhead chalkboard; the diner served home cooked foods daily, Monday through Saturday, and Colden enjoyed the flavor of the meals right down to the cornbread and hushpuppies. Sometimes he could make a meal off hushpuppies and a cup of coffee, sitting right in his office, and he thought he was in heaven if he could get a bowl of lima beans as well. And then there were times when he wanted nothing more than a Styrofoam bowl filled with black-eyed peas and rice, and a piece of fried corn bread. Over the years, he'd grown to love local foods, especially vegetables, and wished that little Miss Darby would take lessons from the local ladies in several eating establishments. Darby was born and raised in Boston, and could prepare pasta meals five days a week, reserving Sunday as a day for dining out, and Fridays for fried chicken with mashed potatoes. Thanking the waitress, after placing their order, they continued to talk about the rumors on the prison yard, and Captain McLeod had learned that Titus Hawks had been assaulted and stabbed repeatedly two days prior. They wondered if that was the information to be gained from talking with the District Attorney.

"Well, in all my years, the money being funneled through those people was unbelievable! But the drug dealers operate from prisons with cell phones, gang members manage gang activities using cellphones, and the list goes on and on. Large amounts of money exist, and employees can certainly be bought off to play in their games. Set aside self-respect, integrity, personal safety, commitment to the job, and go after the almighty dollar. That's what Oxenberg, Faye Hondo, and the others did and it cost them. Lost everything they had.

"A high price to pay to live in a prison cell for the rest of their lives! And those inmates' wives are probably still scared to open their doors to strangers. One of them, I understand, is so worried over her husband's reaction that she's filing for divorce to spare him the pain and anger, and is planning to move to parts unknown, or at least that is what I gathered from the Chaplain. He told me that she said if her husband finds out, he'll be out for Oxenberg's blood and end up in prison for the rest of his life, probably. I need to revisit this case, come to think of it, because that might a factor in this," said Colden, pulling a table napkin to scribble notes on, and stuff into his coat pocket.

"We need to look at everything remotely attached to that investigation, and turn over rocks to determine if we left something loose. We do need to make contact with the Interstate Inmate Housing Program on this quickly; maybe Oxenberg needs relocating again?" said Captain McLeod, looking at Colden for a response. At that time, a waitress brought over their plates of food and beverages. Thanking her, Superintendent Colden dropped his head in prayer with thankfulness for the food, friendships, and their multitude of blessings.

"Captain, I've been eating here a long time, and it just seems to get better!"

Captain McLeod, smiling, fully agreed. His weight gain had begun to show in recent months, and he had cut back in his food intake, opting for healthier foods to include steamed veggies, and water with lemon instead of soda.

"Let me say something about the Assistant's position, Captain. I plan to have a team from the headquarters conduct the interviews next week, and I want you to do your best. That's all I ask. Oh, I'll have input but I won't monopolize the interviews. So, get in there and make us proud!" said Colden. "Enough said."

Chapter Sixteen

Colden listened to the ringtones and greeted District Attorney Charles Frederick with courtesies and pleasantries extended, as two professionals would, especially after having worked together as long as they had. Fredrick's office had indeed been contacted by the news media inquiring into hearsay about inmate Titus Hawks having been stabbed severely because of his testimony against prison staff in a recent corruption investigation. Frederick had, in turn, contacted the state director of prisons for the state of Nebraska, where Titus Hawks was housed, and had learned that Hawks had been stabbed with a home-made shank in his upper backside while in the library and was in critical condition in a state prison hospital under double security. Supposedly there were two differing accounts for the assault, with one being his bragging about helping to bring down corrupt prison staff in North Carolina, and the second being his bragging about his old escapades while running with the Hell's Angels on the east coast. Colden then proceeded to advise Fredrick of the inmate gossip being circulated that Jesse Oxenberg had been targeted for a hit for his role in the downfall and additional convictions of Titus Hawks as well as the death, although by suicide, of Jay Dillon, with implications that Oxenberg turned state's evidence.

"How in the world did that start?" yelled DA Frederick, startled and angry. "That had to get out of the courthouse records! We cut a deal so a lot of that wouldn't be openly discussed in the courtroom, and he did talk, but that was behind closed doors. My, my, this is bad! Have you spoken with Jared Taylor of the state bureau on this?" Colden advised in the negative, and Frederick quickly said he'd get on that right away and get back with Colden soon, and hung up.

Charles Frederick and Jared Taylor were in communication with each other that afternoon, and Taylor agreed to make contact with the Oregon correctional management to inquire into Jesse Oxenberg's status, and to request that he be placed under watch on protective custody. He also made contact with the Oregon state Office of Intelligence and Gang Management, to forewarn them as to a possible gang hit, and further questioned the official on information relevant to any Hells' Angels group in the state. That official wanted to alert his chain of command, seek out the information being requested, and would contact Frederick within the next twenty-four hours.

Meanwhile, Superintendent Colden was on the phone with his supervisor, Region Director Polk. They were pleased with agency support for the expedient pursuit of the grants for the cell phone-sniffing dogs, and it had been learned that an emergency expenditure had been approved for the purchase of two puppies to be used in cell phone detection operations, with the puppies and two officers as handlers being trained in the state of Virginia over the next six months. For the immediate needs, the state offices had worked out a mutual agreement for Virginia Department of Correction to loan two trained Officers and two cell phone-sniffing canines to North Carolina with stationing at the Glen Cove Correctional Institution. Colden was ecstatically happy! Polk encouraged Colden and his staff to continue to monitor the yard and compound intelligence, and urged him to stay in daily communication with the District Attorney's office. Before leaving his office at the end of the day, Superintendent Colden contacted Captain McLeod for word on any latest developments; there had been nothing, and the Captain had planned to work into the night walking around talking with inmates. That evening he was standing in the corridor outside the dining hall, watching the inmates as they left following their evening meal. He had spotted an inmate with a shaved head moving about several tables in the chow hall, talking to inmates, and it appeared that he was being accompanied by two broad shouldered, beefy guys; the two stayed just behind him and carried themselves as bodyguards would an important person, but the Captain thought he'd seen one with the lion tattoo on his right arm in recent months on the compound, and it seemed that the guy had been on a maintenance work squad. The Captain walked over to an Officer on dining hall observation duty, and asked who the inmates were. He learned the inmate with the bald head was one Adam Law, who had a reputation for strong arming at his previous location—River Birch Correctional—in the western part of the state, and rumors were now circulating that he was controlling the cell phone rackets at Glen Cove Correctional. The other two were Sid Pullem and Mark Burns. Pullem, he was told, had been on the compound for a while, and had worked for Ace Tyler for some months, until he was removed from his job for bad- mouthing Tyler after the man had died. Pullem had just recently started fooling around with Law and Burns. Adam Law and his two followers exited the dining hall, and Captain McLeod called Law aside to speak to him. The two followers stayed on Law's heels, and had to be given direct orders to go on about their business. The nod rendered by Adam Law to them was duly noted by Captain McLeod, who struggled to maintain his composure.

"Tell me, just what are your dealings with those two, Law?" asked Captain McLeod.

"They're good friends of mine; that's all. Is that a problem? What's it to you, or is this just your way of harassing me?" spoke Law, with a deep- booming voice, and constant waving of his arms. Realizing his loud tone of voice, he quickly apologized for speaking so loud.

"Let's say I'm making it my business to know what is going on here. And don't stand there speaking in that tone of voice with me. What are their names?" Captain McLeod asked of Law.

"Ok, I'm sorry, man. They are just good friends. Mark Burns and Sid Pullem. Is that it, and can I go to my housing pod?" Law stated, turning to locate the two who had moved on into the corridor that led to the general population housing pod, and were waiting on him. Captain McLeod saw that as well, and made a mental observation that these guys needed to be looked at. He talked with Adam Law to learn that he was serving time for a drug trafficking offense, had served time in other states, was a military veteran, and had been in Iraq but got busted trying to move some drugs at Ft. Bragg and in the Fayetteberg communities in the months after his return to the USA. Captain McLeod took note of the tattoos on his arms and neck. He dismissed Adam Law, and decided he needed to speak with the Pod Officers on his assigned housing pod. He walked around in the housing pods that evening until about ten o'clock, deciding to go on home.

Captain McLeod arranged to get the files on Adam Law, Mark Burns, and Sid Pullem early the next morning and spent the morning perusing the folders and studying the computerized files on them as well to include all case management notes and classification records. Once done, he quickly made a mental observation that Adam Law was trouble anywhere in the system, because he preyed on the weak, sold his services as a problem solver, and always managed to be involved in getting cell phones and with drugs. It seemed that Mark Burns had been with Law in other prisons, because the files carried references to them as a 'pair of thugs' with Burns doing things commanded by Law, although no hard evidence could be secured to prove them guilty of things which prison officials had suspected them of, such as locker thefts, the beating of one inmate rumored as owing money to another. Clearly they needed to be separated with computers flagged to indicate that they should not be housed in the same prison locations. Sid Pullem had grown up in the same community of New Jersey that Adam Law had been raised; they had been in the same street gang; they were in the military together, and were co-defendants in crime. Pullem had been at Glen Cove Correctional for less than a year, but was housed on the same pod as Burns and Law. He had been on Jesse Oxenberg's case load during that time. He had electrician training, which was the reason behind his being placed on the maintenance assignment; the record had been documented to show that he had gathered inmates together in the maintenance shop and had spoken in a loud tone of voice against Ace Tyler on the day that the newspaper article appeared about Ace Tyler having committed suicide, and he repeatedly pointed his fingers at Marcus Torn and others in that section while yelling that they knew that Tyler was dirty and did nothing about it Captain McLeod thought that maybe Pullem had joined forces with Law to be more controlling, but the Captain intended to rectify some things with them to save troubles down the road. He intended to see to it that they didn't run or control a darn thing at Glen Cove Correctional, except a push broom! Until he could get them separated with movements elsewhere. And he'd get with Mitch Steele to have their records flagged for housing separation for the duration of their prison confinement.

Later that day, Captain McLeod and Lieutenant Gibbs had worked out the cell phone- sniffing dogs coming the next day, with the shakedown following the morning after, on Friday, instead of Saturday, and a succession of days for the canines to come back to conduct walk-throughs of the housing pods. They had sat down with Superintendent Colden, who helped finalize the schedule of events. They had also discussed selecting two officers to work full-time assigned to the two officers with canines that would be arriving from Virginia early the next week. Superintendent Colden was still waiting on a call-back from Charles Frederick on the Oregon information they were seeking.

Before going home for the day, Captain McLeod summoned Mitch Steele to come see him, on his way out. Steele came in, and they chatted briefly about things going on with the population. They both had concerns about the amount of inmate idleness, and had been working on a plan to create more work assignments with crews to clean windows during the day, and the development of a plastics recycling center to employ inmates handling the recyclables. Mitch Steele was still working on the implementation of the pilot program with the aid of the local county recycling center management, which had procured and loaned the storage bins constructed of heavy gauge mesh wire, and the baler machine. He was still awaiting the shredding vat in which plastics containers would be crushed, chopped into flakes, and pressed into bales. He had chosen the dozen or fifteen inmates to work the site, and they were in a classroom setting being taught the safety aspects of the recycling processes and machine operations. The materials would be baled, with the county center hauling the bales to their site for pick-up by a major recycling company truck. The prison would supply a dozen inmates to work the county site, as a cooperative exchange program.

"You've done a good job, Mitch, getting that project off the ground. I am thrilled with the initiative you've undertaken. If I can help, let me know. What I wanted to talk with you about is the flagging of records to separate three inmates that we are housing, and to get them moved. Are you familiar with Sid Pullem, Mark Burns, and Adam Law? I hear Adam Law was into some strong-arming at River Birch," spoke Captain McLeod.

"You've hit on some big dogs, Captain. They're controlling cell phones in here and trying to set up rackets with dope. Come to think of it, that Sid Pullem tries to be a slick one; he's been asking a lot of questions about Jesse Oxenberg, and generally trying to found out where he is. Oxenberg was his case manager the whole time, and I heard Oxenberg say once that Pullem had a load of money stashed, and had offered to pay several thousand dollars to hire help on getting paroled. I found Pullem's residence address in Oxenberg's rolodex after his arrest, and wondered. But then he had several inmates' residence addresses in his rolodex. Pullem had schooling in welding, plumbing and electrical works, so he had been assigned to work in the maintenance sector. Come to think of it, he worked with Ace Tyler but he and Tyler weren't crazy about each other. He tried to incite a riot back there in maintenance the day after Tyler's death was in the papers. So, he was removed, and we hated to put him on another job assignment. He then started hanging around that Adam Law. Pullem's wife has filed for a divorce; wrote him and sent him the papers. She is a gorgeous little black-haired beauty—Jennifer Lopez lookalike. I saw her at visitation one day. I hear he's holding out on signing them papers until he can find out what's going on. She has access to his money, and word is that he left a ton of it somewhere in some banks. He had a visitor last week who is a neighbor to the wife; the neighbor generally tries to keep an eye on the wife and kids for Pullem. An inmate told me today that Pullem's hired some street goons to put the word out that he wants to know where Oxenberg is and to locate his family to see what they have to say. He's pretty desperate; thinks Oxenberg is behind his wife wanting this divorce. That's trouble, Captain. You might want to pass this on to Superintendent Colden."

"What about Burns; hearing anything on him?"

"Nothing other than he does whatever Law tells him to do. He used to lift weights on the streets and worked as security and as a bouncer at a nightclub. Did a little drug running too. Some of the guys here knew him on the streets. As for Adam Law, he's the brains behind those two, and I've heard that he's telling Pullem every step he needs to make on this thing with his wife, even to the point of helping contract those street goons. Law is vengeful, Captain. Know what I mean?"

"Yeah, I do. On second thought, Mitch, hold off moving those three until I can get back to you," Captain McLeod spoke, thinking that additional information could be gained through yard intel on their activities and Pullem's efforts to locate Oxenberg.

"Will do, Captain. If that's all, I'll say goodnight. I've got PTA at my son's school," said Steele, who stood up and left.

Sitting in his office, giving thought to what he'd just learned, Captain McLeod pondered putting Pullem in cell 40, where the hidden surveillance technology was in the overhead light fixture. He stood up, locked his office door, and went on home, thinking he'd give that idea more thought and discuss it with Colden the following morning.

The next morning, Captain McLeod went by the Superintendent's office on his way inside, and discussed his conversation with Mitch Steele. Colden was glad that the two of them had sat down the evening before and talked, because it enabled them to share information gained from inmate talk, and this was much needed. The idea of putting Pullem in cell 40 was discussed, but Colden thought it better to put Law in cell 40 because he could visualize Burns and Pullem at Law's cell and not the opposite. Too, if Law was controlling cell phones, chances are that he had one and would use it in his cell, with surveillance being able to detect it. He authorized the move of Law to cell 40, to occur that day; in fact he directed that a number of inmates in that housing pod be moved around so as not to cause question with the single move of Adam Law.

The cell changes occurred with no incident, as did head counts. Inmate programs, school, and other activities went as planned. Gus Burke was moved out of the housing pod and into the receiving area to await the evening transfer bus that would take him to a geriatric facility in the northern part of the state. Lieutenant Stanley Deeker was making rounds in the facility, and came to observe counts being made, standing alongside Sergeant Mariel Gaben.

"Lately, Sergeant Gaben, the counts process has improved, and I suppose the reduction in staff turnover has attributed to that," Lieutenant Deeker spoke. "Keep up the good work."

"Thank you, sir. How are you adjusting to second shift?" Sergeant Gaben asked.

"It's okay. I suppose Lieutenant Gibbs made rounds routinely? I do see that staff make sure inmates clean up before going to bed at night, and that's a plus," stated Lieutenant Deeker, who saluted her and walked off. He had a gut-feeling that Sergeant Gaben was not one to confide in or say too much around about other staff.

Friday morning

Some time around 4:30a.m. Captain McLeod arrived at the facility, and once he cleared the gatehouse, he entered the main building and ordered the master control center to turn off the facility phones for calls being made, but the leave the system so that incoming calls come continue. At 5:00 A.M.. the first shift Officers came in and were told to go into the staff line-up room for discussion, with the facility emergency response teams, programs staff and employee maintenance workers. The local county sheriff's canine teams, of four dogs and four trained canine handlers, also came in assist. Captain McLeod went in and advised all supervisors and staff in the room that a facility shakedown of general population was to take place, and that they would be working jointly with most of the night shift staff who would be held over for several hours, unless they needed to go on home because of childcare issues and other concerns deemed of special concern and were authorized to leave by a supervisor. The inmates were gathered in the dayrooms adjoining their housing pods, with night shift Officers handling the supervision in the dayrooms while other staff conducted searches of the cells, lockers, bathrooms and storage closets.

Superintendent Colden had arrived within a few minutes of the commencement of the shakedown, and walked around in observation of the work being done by staff. He watched the Officers going in cells, taking only the assigned inmates, removing all items from lockers and examining the contents, as well as examining all books, magazines, and other paperwork, with especial checks made of the envelopes, book bindings, and cardboard items. Even the bars of soap were checked. Shoes were checked with flashlights, and the heels were examined to ensure that no false bottoms existed. Clothing was checked for concealment. Maintenance staff were checking cell fixtures such as plumbing works, light fixtures, and water faucets. He took pleasure in the fact that Maintenance Supervisor Marcus Torn was taking part, and had personally checked those cells where he had surveillance equipment installed, in order to not have other staff locate the equipment, which would jeopardize the security program in place. Torn did not trust other staff to keep their mouths closed if they had detected the equipment.

As contraband was found staff carefully recorded it by description, noting the cell and inmate's name. Several tattoo paraphernalia, accumulated medicines, cigarettes, and excessive clothing were found in the first housing pod cleared. Several inmates who became rowdy and agitated were placed in segregation. As the other housing pods for general population were cleared, it seemed that the shakedown was becoming more and more successful, in that a dozen cell phones, several hundred dollars in cash, and a large amount of tobacco with cigarette rolling papers, were being found. Two new cell phones and three hundred dollars were found in Mark Burns's cell. He became extremely mouthy, claiming the items had been planted in his cell, and spat at an officer, causing Sergeant Ben Jacobi to place him in a segregation holding cell Superintendent Colden was well pleased at the discovery made, and with staff's work, because it was dedication and commitment in their work to have made the finds, almost as if no rock was left in place, so to speak. The visiting cell phone sniffing canines were wonderful, and both Captain McLeod and Colden repeatedly thanked the canine handlers for their assistance at making this shakedown so successful. The shakedown was complete by nine o'clock in the morning, to the relief of the staff who had been held over. They were happy to be released to go home, as it had indeed been a long night!

Superintendent Colden and Captain McLeod sat down in the conference room with the shift supervisors to debrief on the morning's work. Everyone was excited, because the shakedown had been the most successful one conducted in the past year. And they all knew the inmates were getting the message that Glen Cove Correctional is not the place to possess contraband, and that corrupt inmates and/or staff would not be tolerated. The local Glen Cove police department had sent in two staff, a Lieutenant and a Sergeant, to sit in at the debriefing; they appreciated the work of the staff at the prison, although it meant work for them to process the charges against the inmates for the contraband, but they were totally supportive of efforts being made to disallow the illegal items, as well as other unauthorized things, and operate the prison in such a manner as to make it a safe working environment for staff and a safe housing for inmates. Again, the assistance provided by the canine handlers from the sheriff's department was noted with sincere appreciation. At the close of the debriefing, Captain McLeod and two Officers handled the taking of the seized monies in the amount of fifteen hundred dollars in large bills to the accounting office with chain of custody forms, for handling in accordance with agency policy. The other items were photographed and attached to disciplinary forms for processing on the inmates determined responsible, as were the cell phones, and tobacco and cigarettes. The cell phones were turned over to the Glen Cove police officials present for criminal charges to be filed, along with the tobacco and cigarettes, for those were criminal possessions as well.

The shakedown was the talk about the facility for the remainder of the day. Captain McLeod had received an intercom phone call that several of the inmates locked up stemming from the shakedown wanted to speak with him; one of those was Mark Burns. Captain McLeod went to the segregation housing to speak him later that day.

"Burns, I was told you wanted to see me," spoke Captain McLeod.

"Captain, you got to help me on this. That stuff was planted in my cell. Those phones were not mine. That's more felon time on me, and I don't need that. And where that three hundred dollars came from, I don't know. Help me on this, and I'll help you," pleaded Burns, with his hands on the bar work of the doors so tight that his knuckles were turning white.

"Why should I help you, Burns? What can you offer me?" asked the Captain, studying Burns.

"I can give up the guy bringing in most of the phones. And how he's doing it. But you got to get me off this camp, or I'm dead. Can we deal?" pleaded Burns. "Please, Captain. I know you'll think about it?"

Captain McLeod shrugged, but then told Burns that he would see what and if he could deal with him, and would get back to him the following day. Walking off, the thought of Mark Burns' safety weighed heavy on his mind, and he needed to consult with Colden before going further, but they needed the source behind those phones. Burns might offer up other information as well, but they'd have to talk and see what he would give up. He decided to go on home and revisit this matter the next morning.

On arrival the following day, the canine handlers were immediately taken inside with their dogs. Captain McLeod and several staff guided them through the general population housing pods, the clothing warehouse, the commissary stockroom, the laundry area, and gym. Only two cell phones were located, stuffed inside a plastic container of clothes detergent that had been placed inside a washing machine. A plastic ziplock bag was found stuffed inside the exhaust vent pipe of a dryer; it contained two one-hundred dollar bills. The day's use of the canines was another positive measure, and the Captain was remarkably happy. On the way escorting the handlers and their dogs outside of the facility, arrangements were made for them to return the following day, which was Sunday. They were to arrive before the visitors were allowed inside, but would also be accompanied by two other handlers with drug-sniffing canines who were to be stationed outside the gatehouse. If visitors were bringing drugs or cell phones into the facility, the canines would alert on them, and it was felt they'd drive on away once they saw the dogs in position.

Inmate counts, and all other routine work, went as good as hoped that day. Being a Saturday, not much happened other than scheduled religious programs and some special recreation activities like bingo games, or maybe the showing of a video movie.

Lieutenant Gibbs arrived to work the morning session of visitation, and had greeted the canine handlers with their dogs, with freshly made coffee, and bowls of fresh water for the animals, for it was late spring and the weather was warmer than usual. Several deputies from the local sheriff's department were stationed in the parking lot in unmarked vehicles, with a plan to give chase to vehicles that arrived and came into the parking lot, but drove out. The thinking behind this move was that perhaps the drivers had seen the canines and decided not to stop, particularly if they had something on the vehicle that might have been illegal. The drivers of the unmarked vehicles did in fact stay busy that morning, for they ended up arresting a half-dozen men and women for having drugs in their vehicles and on their persons. The cell phone sniffing dogs were responsible for the arrests of three men who tried to enter with cell phones hidden on them, in socks and one had two cell phones hidden in a plastic boot being worn because of a broken leg. He admitted having them when he was directed to remove the boot for inspection, as staff could see that it was one that could be taken off. A successful morning for law enforcement and the prison staff.

Captain McLeod arrived after lunch time to supervise the afternoon session of visitation, and was thrilled on hearing Lieutenant Gibbs's report from the morning's events. Their plan was working! The afternoon visitors were not as corrupt-minded as the morning visitors, for there was only one visitor caught and charged for trying to bring in a cell phone inside her high-topped leather boots. Lo and behold she was Adam Law's girlfriend; arrested and charged, she was advised that she would be permanently suspended from visiting privileges with him. At the end of the day, the staff working at the gatehouse were relieved, and expressed appreciation to the Captain and Lieutenant for their being present, to see what they had to deal with each weekend at visitation time. They made various type comments about the need to repeat the presence of the canines, which Captain McLeod heard loud and clear.
The next edition of the local newspaper two days later carried a small article that was pulled from the police blotter.

Glen Cove Police Blotter Tidbits:

With the use of canines from the local sheriff's department, trained in sniffing out cell phones and drugs, several people were arrested and charged with trying to smuggle in illegal items at the local prison this past Sunday. Good cooperation between the agencies.

During the course of the next few days, the inmate grapevine carried the word that cell phones were dried up on the compound, as were cigarettes, and the cash that had been stashed in various places. Inmates were asking questions about how often the canines would come inside, and were canines going to be stationed at the gatehouse at visitations in the future. In fact, on Tuesday evening, Adam Law and Sid Pullem were sitting on the threshold of Adam's cell 40 talking. Adam had lost quite a bit of money, and had promised three inmates that he would get them phones.

"Man, I got to find a break here, to get those three phones in. You may have to loan me your phone, Sid, for a while. Have you located Oxenberg? You've called your buddies at the court house; don't they know anything, yet?"

"Nope. They're still checking. And the wife wants me to sign those divorce papers now, but I ain't doing it. She ain't getting my money, man! I want Oxenberg dead. He did go to see her 'cause the man at the courthouse said so, and he told me she did go to the emergency room for being assaulted. That's all I know so far. I got to hang onto my phone right now. It's hid good."

"I got my notice today that MaryAnn's been suspended from visiting me; she's in jail; they arrested her on Sunday out front 'cause she was trying to bring me a phone. That Captain's a real smart-ass; thinks he's a real cowboy, and if he ain't sharp, I'll see he gets him a piece of a gun. Messing with me. My phone's messing up, and I really needed that new one MaryAnn had," admitted Law.

They talked about a number of things, to include Pullem's efforts at getting a work assignment, because he wanted to earn the sentence reduction credits, and also knew that his being constructively occupied would aid with a parole review. Law knew that prisons officials all over the state had no trust in him and would never give him a job unless it was one working on a road squad just to humiliate him. Besides, he had to do the bulk of his sentence before he could get out, and regardless of how much he worked, the time credits wouldn't help. The Officers working the pod had to tell Pullem to go to his cell, because count was getting ready to commence, so he left the cell, telling Law he'd speak to him the next day.

On Thursday afternoon, two incidents happened that required the full attention of Superintendent Colden and Captain McLeod. Two persons arrived at the gatehouse identifying themselves to be investigators from the state's EEO section, and were directed to go to the Superintendent's office with escort of an Officer. And, two

Officers from the state of Virginia security offices of the Department of Correction with cell phone-sniffing dogs had arrived at the gatehouse. Too, they were directed to be escorted to the Superintendent's office, where Marley Brooks, Colden's executive secretary, talked with them and showed them to the conference room to await Captain McLeod, who was coming out to speak with them. She gathered information from them, so that she could make arrangements for hotel accommodations for them as well as enabling them to obtain vehicle fuel and meals. Captain McLeod came into the conference room momentarily, introduced himself, and expressed the pleasantries that could be expected given the need to have them at Glen Cove and the cooperative gesture rendered by the Virginia agency.

Meanwhile, Superintendent Colden, in his meeting with the two EEO investigators, learned that they would begin their investigation with inquiries of the two plaintiffs the next morning, and would proceed to interview named witnesses and others picked at random, whom they felt might warrant questioning. They planned to question or interrogate Lieutenant Peter Gibbs last, and then would talk with persons he might name, and would requestion the plaintiffs if they determined that it warranted. Any documents that they would need to review would be made available as they needed them. They were advised that Lieutenant Gibbs had been temporarily reassigned to work in operations with the Captain; that he was not supervising any shift, and that he had been made aware of the complaints and given a direct order not to discuss the matter with anyone other than said investigators. The lead investigator, Ken Sharpe, had worked in the Federal prison system for ten years in the states of Colorado and Texas, before relocating to North Carolina to be near his spouse's family, and had been working in employee relations for the EEO office for the past ten years. A personable individual, Sharpe asked several questions about the facility, concerns that were generally posed from night shift workers, and he inquired into Lieutenant Gibbs's background. Of course, Colden possessed Gibbs's personnel file, and indicated that it could be reviewed when they desired. The accompanying investigator was one Cassi Munn, who had been working in employee relations in the EEO office for some twelve years, and also served as a mediator at state hearings. Her questions focused on the character of the complainants and their work history; she also mentioned being able to review performance appraisals at some point during the investigation. With the conclusion of the introductory session, Ken Sharpe asked if someone on Colden's staff could make hotel accommodations for them; Ms. Marley Brooks was called in and asked to handle this task. The two of them nodded, and declared that they would like for the next hour, to review the personnel records for the two complainants: Officer Erica Dorne and Officer Pam Cox. Superintendent Colden asked Ms. Brooks to show them to the smaller conference room and get the files they needed, which she was expeditious about. Colden explained he was needed at another meeting, but for them to ask Ms. Brooks's help as needed, and he walked away. Sharpe and Munn thanked him, and Ms. Brooks, and sat down with the two files.

Officer Erica Dorne, the record showed, had been working at the facility for two years and five months. Her work history had been that of a secretary in a high school, and a bank teller. She supposedly quit both jobs of her own volition, according to notes on her application when she had sought the correctional position. The file indicated she was five feet, three inches tall, weighing two hundred fourteen, with hypertension, aged thirty-three.

Following graduation from high school, she had attended a business college for secretarial sciences for two years. She had gone to work in the high school, staying there for nine years, with nothing documented as to account for why she quit that job. She landed the job at the bank some four months after her resignation at the high school, and stayed there for eighteen months before resigning. She heard about the prison recruitment efforts at a job fair and subsequently applied, landing a position after her third interview. She had been on night shift since her employment.

On reviewing the file for Pam Cox, both investigators raised eyebrows at seeing that she had worked at the beach in nightclubs for eight years, barely finished the required correctional training, and had submitted two resignations but had withdrawn both the following day after submittal, and had been allowed to stay on the job. She had been on the job less than a year. She was raised in the Midwest, left home following high school graduation and had migrated to the coast to Myrtle Beach, South Carolina. She was twenty-seven years of age, with height registering five feet six inches, weight of one hundred thirty seven pounds, and with blondish hair. The application for employment indicated that she had written in the name of one Faye Hondo, prison employee, as a reference. Investigator Mann spoke up saying that this Faye Hondo is probably one to talk to, that it was odd for her to seek employment given her history of work and no education or training focusing on correctional work. Ken Sharpe wholeheartedly agreed, and that he had questions as to why her resignations were set aside. Closing the records, they stood up to stretch; they both appeared to each other to be tired, and needed to start early the next morning, so they needed to eat the evening and check in at their hotel. The took the records to Ms. Marley Brooks' office, gave them to her, and inquired about hotel accommodations.

Ms. Brooks gave them a piece of paper with information on it about the hotel, to include a confirmation number, with direct billing to be made to the agency, and directions for travel to reach the hotel, which she advised them was only ten minutes away. They thanked her, but advised that they would like to begin conducting interviews with staff as early as nine o'clock in the morning. Ms. Brook acknowledged that comment, indicating that full cooperation would be given by the facility; they retrieved their briefcases, and left the facility.

Superintendent Colden had gone into the meeting, being held by Captain McLeod with the two Virginia canine handlers. Walking in, hand outstretched, he shook hands with the both of them, expressing his gratitude for their willingness to come to North Carolina to help them. He sat down and let the two Officers talk about the use of the cell phone sniffing canines in their state, and was incredibly impressed. It seemed that Virginia was at the forefront of using the canines in prison operations, and had been doing so for several years. The two officers, Trey White and Laird Posenn, were both military veterans who had worked with canines in the military, and in fact, had been training their agency puppies for three years, and were helping other jurisdictions, law enforcement included, with training of puppies and staff in managing effective cell phone detection programs. Officer White had trained with his assigned canine at a Federal Bureau of Prisons training facility. As he explained the basics he felt the need to reiterate that the canines' sense of smell is so sharp that they could detect cell phones even if hidden in things such as radios, televisions, in bed mattresses, or other concealment agents. He took especial care to talk about the chemicals used in the manufacture of cell phone batteries, and canine training with some focus on detection of that chemical. But he also indicated that scent tracking in the training of the animals also entails detecting items like marijuana, cocaine, and other drugs. He spoke about the varying concerns posed by law enforcement, chemical agencies, legislators, and prisons as to the most preferred kinds of canines used in such programs, admitting that while his favored and assigned canine was the Labrador retriever, pointing to his animal, Ranger, lying on the floor beside him. As he continued to talk, he referenced the second canine, Betsy, a Belgian malinois. The canines once trained can be quite expensive, which he admitted was why the state of Virginia had begun to train their own. The canines were quite effective, and documentation on finds, he explained, supported the continued use, and had been sufficient enough for the state legislature to continue funding the correctional program. Officer Posenn spoke on the many years that the military had been dependent on the canines' olfactory sense because it was so sensitive. The two Officers referenced a number of cases and incidences where cell phone-sniffing canines made headlines in major crime cases. Cell phones were linked to planned prisoner escapes, assassinations, major drug deals, witness tampering, and many other situations, and once the cell phones were located, they were examined closely and many were used as evidence. Superintendent Colden continued to nod as the two officers talked at length; he could detect that two officers thoroughly enjoyed their work, which told him that the program's success was attributable to staff commitment such as was exhibited by White and Posenn.

Looking at his watch, Colden knew it was getting late, and knew they were a bit tired after their long drive and had things they needed to do, especially with caring for their animals. Ms. Brooks had handled their hotel accommodations, arranged for billing to be made to the North Carolina correctional agency, and had given them several suggestions as to restaurants. He again thanked them for coming to work with his staff, and alluded to Captain McLeod being their point of contact. They all stood up, shook hands, and Officers White and Posenn were escorted outside with their animals by Captain McLeod, and through the gatehouse. They stood in the parking lot briefly talking, and left shortly thereafter, looking forward to returning the next day.

Chapter Seventeen

Driving in to work the following morning, Superintendent Colden pondered the things going on at the prison and really wanted to get an Assistant Superintendent in place quickly. The interviews were scheduled for the following day, and there had been more applicants than he thought might apply. The screening process had reduced the number to seven for interviews. He had invited two superintendents to come in from other locations across the state, making sure that he had diversity well covered, with one of them being a male minority and the other being a female minority. He had met with Vanis Goodson earlier in the week on selecting the interview questions, so he thought everything was in order to finish that process and try to expedite bringing an Assistant on board. The ongoing investigation as regards the alleged 'hit' on Oxenberg, the EEO inquiry, and the visiting canine handlers on top of everything else meant a rather heavy, intense workload. He had hoped that Charles Frederick would communicate with him rather quickly; it had been several days since their last telephone conversation, and his anxiety was growing. Maybe he'd go ahead and contact Charles Frederick today and find out what was taking place with protective custody for Oxenberg, and what the status of Titus Hawks was.

Stepping out of his old truck, Colden saw Captain McLeod and Marcus Torn standing together in conversation in the parking lot, some fifteen feet away from the gatehouse. Captain McLeod saw him, and motioned for him to join them. Walking over to where they were standing, Colden was also watching the vehicles pulling into the parking lot; he'd seen several new automobiles in the lot over the past few weeks. Torn noticed his observations of the vehicles, and thought he'd get in a jab about the old truck Colden was still driving.

He'd kept it in good mechanical condition, and the paint was badly oxidized, and in some spots it had flaked off. He kept it pretty clean as well.

"Say, boss, it's about time you got a new truck, isn't it?"

"Well, I'll tell you, Mr. Torn. That's a 1993 Chevrolet Silverado sportside. I bought it new, and have been driving it ever since. It's paid for! And I don't see any sense at all to go in debt for a vehicle right now. It runs good, and to me, it looks good. The AC is cold in the summer, and the heater works just fine. Why do you know I've had a dozen or so offers from youngsters to buy it! Only thing I've done to it is have the interior seats recovered. I'm not embarrassed driving it like some would be driving a vehicle that is older than five years. Why, just look at the debt sitting in this parking lot!"

"I see your point, boss. Why, some of these folks out here trade every two or three years; never get one paid off! Mine is nine years old, but I'll drive it another few years," commented Marcus Torn.

"Say, what was it that you two called me over here for?" asked Colden, as he eyed Captain McLeod. "Surely my old truck sitting on the front line doesn't embarrass you!"

Marcus Torn spoke up, saying that he had pulled the audio surveillance from cell 40 in the general population housing pod. He had listened to it, found it to be mighty interesting, and thought that the Captain and Superintendent both would be interested as well in sitting down to hear what was being said. He made mention of the talk about cell phones. "It looks like there are some cell phones still in the place that we didn't get our hands on. And I heard Jesse Oxenberg's name."

"Well, that's a start for our day, isn't it? How about bringing it to my office first thing, and I'll rustle us up some coffee. See you both in a few minutes," Colden said, as he started to walk off, but stopped and asked the Captain if the canine handlers had arrived yet.

"No, sir. I thought I'd wait on them out here, if that's okay with you. And I had forgotten that I needed to speak again with that Mark Burns in lock-up. He wants to make a deal. Maybe he'll talk about cell phones. Is it okay with you for me to make some sort of deal with him, if I can get him to talk?"

"That's just fine. Y'all come to the office as soon as you can." Colden turned to walk into the gatehouse, greeting the staff, and unloaded his pockets to walk through the metal detector. He completed the entry process and said "have a good day" as he walked out and toward the main building.

On entering his office, he inquired of Ms. Brooks as to whether she had received any calls for him; she had not. She had a fresh pot of coffee brewing, and commented that it would be ready in a minute or two and that she'd bring him a cup. He proceeded to go into his office, where he saw his sticky note on the face of his computer reminding him to call Charles Frederick at the District Attorney's office and follow-up to see if he had heard anything from the Oregon office of Intelligence and Gang Management, and whether he had learned anything on Oxenberg's status regarding protective custody. He also wanted to check on Titus Hawks's situation as well. Sitting down at his desk, he turned on his desktop computer to scan his e-mails, and try to deal with those he felt were more urgent than others, before the EEO investigators came in, as he felt sure they might want to talk before they began questioning with any of his staff. And there was the matter of listening to that audio tape that Torn had, as well as those interviews which were to commence at 10:00 a.m. Time management would be a must for the day. After about fifteen minutes, he had gone through his e-mails from his supervisor, and responded, and stood up to go get a second cup of coffee from Ms. Brooks's office. He saw the two investigators walk by her office, en route to his, and he proceeded to open his door for them to come in. Greeting them, he offered them a cup of coffee, which they accepted. Shortly thereafter, they sat down in front of his desk, opened their portfolios, with writing tablet, and wanted to ask some questions about the two employees who had filed the complaints.

"First, let me assure you that we will cooperate with you, and of course, I'll entertain whatever questions or concerns you might have.

Right now, I can spend about an hour with you. I have a rather urgent matter to attend to afterward, and then I have interviews scheduled to begin at ten o'clock this morning, which will last about six hours or until two o'clock. After those are done, Ms. Brooks can let you know in case you want to come back in and talk. So, let's go ahead and you can start," Colden stated. "By the way, the two complainants have been held over to talk with you this morning, as they worked last night. And we do plan for them to take tonight off given that we didn't know how long you would need to talk with them. We will make adjustments to their work schedules."

Cass Munn began, asking him, "How well do you know an Officer Pam Cox?"

"I don't know her at all, and don't recall the name."

"Do you know the name Faye Hondo, Mr. Colden?" she asked, noting the change of facial expression on the Superintendent.

Looking puzzled, Colden asked where she came across that name, to which she again asked him if he knew the name Faye Hondo, and he answered in the affirmative, adding that Faye Hondo had been employed until her termination in recent weeks. He then asked again where she had come across the name.

"Well, on Ms. Cox's application, the name Faye Hondo was written in as a reference."

"Really!" he commented.

"Can I ask what were the circumstances regarding Ms. Hondo's termination, and do you know if it had anything to do with Ms. Cox filing this complaint?" the question posed by Ken Sharpe.

"I wouldn't think so. Ms. Hondo had been engaging in criminal activities with inmates, was caught, charged and convicted, and is serving a prison term out-of-state. It was a rather lengthy internal and subsequently criminal investigation involving a number of employees and inmates with a number of elements involved, to even include deaths by suicide of a staff person and one inmate."

"Were you ever aware that Pam Cox had submitted resignations on two different occasions?"

"I have never been informed of that. That is interesting."

"Both were allowed to be withdrawn or set aside, and the name Matt Ranham was shown in the file as the individual who allowed her to withdraw them. Who is he?"

Colden again had a puzzled look on his face, stating, "Matt was the former Assistant Superintendent over the Custody sector, but he retired a little over a month ago. Obviously he never made me aware of this case."

Ken Sharpe then made a comment that if Mr. Colden did not know Ms. Cox, then he probably did not have any idea about her past employment, to which Colden nodded in agreement. Ken Sharpe then remarked, "You would be surprised to learn she had no work history other than that as a worker in nightclubs at the beach." Colden also agreed that he was somewhat surprised, but not surprised given her ties to Faye Hondo.

"Are you familiar with Officer Erica Dorne, Mr. Colden?" asked Ken Sharpe, looking down at his notes.

"I don't know her, never heard the name either."

Cass Munn then proceeded to ask if Superintendent Colden studied employment applications of candidates seeking employment, to which he responded that he generally designated that task to the Personnel Specialist, and persons who usually sat as members of the interview teams. He further spoke on the staff selection process, mentioning that on occasions when the former Matt Ranham did not sit as the interview chairperson, that he handled the employment approvals and signed the appropriate paperwork for new hires for correctional officers. Otherwise, he (Colden) handled the approvals and sign-offs for in-house staff promotions, lateral transfers of incoming supervisory personnel, and all other staff positions. Ken Sharpe, glimpsing his wristwatch, noted the time, and said that they would go ahead and talk with Ms. Cox. He and Cass Munn gathered their belongings and went across the hall to the smaller conference room that they were to use during their stay at Glen Cove Correctional.

Superintendent Colden asked Marcus Torn and Captain McLeod to come on into his office, as they had been sitting in the lobby for the past half-hour, exercising the art of having patience. For the next twenty minutes, they listened to the audio tape, and could clearly believe that there were still some cell phones, at least two, hidden in the facility. It was also clear that someone perhaps in the District Attorney's office was working with Sid Pullem, and the term 'buddies' implied that there was more than one person involved. Then there was the threat made against Captain McLeod. Colden looked at Captain McLeod and advised him that he needed to be extra cautious because of that comment about a 'piece of a gun.'

Colden asked Marcus Torn if the audio equipment was still on, and Torn replied that it was. "But, you know, I'd love to get some video in that cell. If he's got a phone, we could get a better lead on it."

McLeod spoke, saying that he intended to have the visiting cell phone canines and their handlers to patrol the general housing area over the next few days quite heavily, in and out of the cells.

"They're the pros at this, and I believe if one is hidden in that cell, they will locate it. And, Torn, have one of your men take those water fountains apart and check them, and those telephones. Check those vents as well."

"Do you have surveillance hidden in the cell of that Pullem, and if not, could you get some installed? He's one with the buddies at the courthouse, and we could probably get a lead on who they might be if we could listen in at his cell, especially if he's got a cell hidden and he wants Oxenberg dead," stated Colden.

"Oh, getting one installed is not a problem. Let me check and see what I've got; I had ordered a few extras that I've tried to hang onto. We need him on tape, that's for dang sure," responded Torn, who was anxious to leave the meeting and check on his stash of equipment.

"Thanks, fellas, for all your work. You keep surprising me with your abilities and eagerness," spoke Colden. "Right now, I need to get ready for my interviews coming up over the next few hours." Looking over at McLeod, he pointed his finger, saying "and I'll see you later."

Captain McLeod and Marcus Torn left the office, and Ms. Brooks came in with the two facility superintendents from other locations who had agreed to help conduct the interviews. For the next three hours, they sat and talked with the candidates vying for the position of Assistant Superintendent of Operations and Security at Glen Cove Correctional. The applicants had been advised to bring with them their last two performance appraisals, and they were given a hypothetical case scenario to read upon leaving the interview, and were asked to take a few minutes to draft a hand-written statement on the actions they would take to resolve the matter in question on the case. For the next hour, Colden and his cohorts reviewed the appraisals and the case scenario responses. Then the superintendent spoke about Glen Cove, the staffing, recent incidents and what he envisioned an Assistant Superintendent doing to manage the facility and the inmate population. He expected someone who was aggressive, with no qualms or reservations about taking the 'bull by the horns' and essentially get the job by policy irregardless of what someone thought. He wanted the facility operations to be managed by the book, but for the individual to be a visionary, exercise good judgment, and have a sense of humor. In his guesstimate, Captain Buddy McLeod was that individual. Coincidentally, the other two superintendents had already written their notes on the individual they thought would best suit the facility, and were both unanimous in the recommendation that Captain McLeod be placed in that position. In their notes, it was determined that McLeod's response to the case scenario took a lot of factors into play and his response was far more detailed and extensive than that of the other candidates. He covered all the bases, when three of the other candidates only noted a singular aspect of the case scenario. Two applicants failed to even address the scenario or provide any feedback. On the basis of performance appraisals, McLeod outranked all other candidates; he did an outstanding job on responding to the interview questions with thorough replies provided. The necessary documents were filled out, recommending Captain Buddy McLeod; Colden thanked each of them for their assistance, and they parted ways promising to reciprocate as the need arose.

Colden took the position materials to Vanis Goodson and asked that she go through the package and get the necessary processes completed as soon as practicable. He had already briefed his supervisor, who concurred with the recommendation of McLeod. In fact, the supervisor in the headquarters office was satisfied that McLeod was the right man for the job, so to speak, as he had been acquainted with him for some few years and well pleased with his work.

Going into Ms. Brooks' office, Superintendent Colden asked her to inform the EEO investigators that he was free when they wanted to speak with him, if necessary. And he asked her to try to get Charles Frederick in the District Attorney's office on the phone for him when she could. He then poured himself a cup of coffee, and sat down for a few minutes break. Ms. Brooks called on the intercom to inform him that Mr. Fredrick was out of the office but she left word for him to call back once he returned. He then turned to his desktop computer to send e-mails to the two fellow superintendents who had driven over to assist him with the interviews, and to inform them that he would be available to return the favor in reciprocity if they ever needed his assistance. He copied his supervisor in the agency headquarters. The supervisor was always complimentary of his staff, who cooperated and assisted each other, because folks knew it was not an easy thing to leave the Raleigh headquarters office and travel out to the field to help with job or promotional interviews. He finished the work he needed to do on some supervisory performance appraisals, and lay them aside for Ms. Brooks to deliver to Ms. Goodson's office. He noticed that Ms. Brooks had placed out appeared to be a stack of letters in his stack-box labeled 'inmate letters;' he generally delegated these to other staff to review and respond, but he usually read the letters before he sent to the other staff in the programs sector. He then commenced going through the mail that had arrived for him; the first two letters were in-house and he sent them to Mitch Steele. The third letter was a surprise; for it was a letter from one Brent Galen, marked personal and confidential. Glancing at the return address, he mused to himself that the boy is covering his tracks well with a fictitious address, because the address was that of the local courthouse. And it had borne a Glen Cove postmark. Sitting back in his chair, he slid his letter opener under the closure flap, sliding it to the opposite end, and opened the envelope.

Dear Mr. Superintendent Colden:

First, be advised that I am not in trouble. I just wanted to write you a note to say thank you for all that you did for me while I was there. I do so appreciate your belief in me, that maybe I did get railroaded on that crime and being sent to prison. In all honesty, I was so afraid that I would be stabbed or kilt over all that stuff going on with Jay Dillon. But you know what, when you listen to folks you sorta hear a lot of things that maybe you ain't supposed to hear. I also heard that from the man who drive me home that day; he talked a lot too; he knows another guy out there by the name of Sid Galileo or something like that, and he sounded like he and Galileo might be sorta tight. He asked me if I knew the inmate, and I said that I had met him but we didn't hang out with each other. Galileo scared me, Mr. Colden. He handled cell phones all the time with another guy named Law or something. They sit back and laught at pulling the wool over your eyes with hiding places. They put cell phones in the wall phones box all the time. As for me I am doing good. Mr. David and me, we are doing okay. Again, thank you. May God bless you all the time.

B. Galen

The letter was a welcomed prize! Galen may not have known it but he might be a wizard after all, sending the right word when we so needed it. Interesting that the driver from the District Attorney's talked to Galen— talked a little too much! And the wall phone box? What an ingenious concealment location. He placed the letter back into the envelope and locked it in his desk, hoping to be able to let Captain McLeod read it before going home.

Somewhere around 4:00 P.M. the two EEO investigators knocked and were called in. They reviewed their notes and began the task of asking questions focusing on Lieutenant Gibbs.

Ken Sharpe started by asking how long Mr. Colden had known the Lieutenant, to which he replied somewhere around two to three years, or thereabouts. "In that time, Mr. Colden, have you heard rumors on him focusing on complaints that female staff would probably have had?"

"No, Mr. Sharpe, there have been no complaints or innuendos

brought to my attention. Since he came here, nothing negative. And I've heard nothing negative on him within the Glen Cove community, and I'm out there quite a bit."

"How did he get to Glen Cove? I understand he worked elsewhere and there had been complaints made," asked Cass Munn.

"You said complaints made? I've never been made aware of complaints filed against him. It was always my understanding that while going through a divorce action in court, that his wife stated in open court that she was frustrated or angry, or something like that, over his affairs with his coworkers on the job. That was while he was employed elsewhere. The news media picked up on that, from a scandal point of view, and made it appear that agency management was sweeping it under the rug and taking no action against him. But no one, I was told, had ever filed any complaint against Lieutenant Gibbs. The two ladies with whom he had been involved filed no complaints, and did resign their jobs. Even when contacted by someone, I don't know whom, they refused to lodge any complaints. The headquarters contacted me and asked if I would transfer him into Glen Cove. I had no reason not to. Since he's been here, he's done a good job, and I've had no complaints." With an afterthought, Colden went to say, "I have heard that he tries to encourage folks to study for promotional exams, and monitors poor performers with continued counseling to get them on the right track as regards their jobs. We've had poor performers turn around their work ethics and are some of our better workers, and I've heard folks credit that to Lieutenant Gibbs."

"Have you ever heard Lt. Gibbs berate, belittle staff or shout at them," asked Ken Sharpe.

"I don't recall that ever happening in my presence. Never heard anything like that either."

Ken Sharpe then spoke about having talked with the two complainants, and he had come away with more questions for them, and would revisit his talks with them. The next day, he and Ms. Munn planned to talk with Lieutenant Gibbs, and then move forward to interview other persons that the complainants had named. They were interested in talking with Matt Ranham by telephone to inquire into the resignations that had been submitted, and subsequently withdrawn, by Pam Cox. Superintendent Colden thumbed through his personal rolodex and pulled his data card for Ranham, and handed that to them. Cass Munn copied the data onto her writing tablet, and returned the card to Colden. Ken Sharpe and Cass Munn thanked Colden for the continuing hospitality, retrieved their briefcases, stood up and indicated they would call it a day, and return the next week on Monday morning.

As they left the office, Colden's telephone rang and Ms. Brooks advised that Charles Frederick had returned his call but given that he was in with the EEO investigators, she had told Mr. Frederick that she would apprise Mr. Colden and he would call as quick as he could. He glanced at his watch, and seeing that it was 5:00, thought maybe he'd just wait til the following morning. Thanking Ms. Brooks, he told her to go on home and call it a day, that they'd try to reach Mr. Frederick the next Monday morning.

Chapter Eighteen

En route to work Monday morning, his old truck started to stall as he turned off the main highway onto the secondary road that ran in front of the correctional facility. Checking his fuel gauge and his instrument panel, he couldn't imagine what was going on. It jerked forward, with a sputtering that he had never heard, before cutting off. He managed to pull off on the right road shoulder about one hundred yards from the facility turn-in; he kept trying to crank the vehicle but it wouldn't start. Smiling, he thought back to his morning conversation with Marcus Torn over his old truck, and knew this break down would make Tom's day! As he stepped out of the truck, Captain McLeod drove up, letting his window down to speak, and said he'd give the Superintendent a lift on into work.

"Boy, Marcus Torn will rib you good this morning! Any idea what's wrong with it?" asked the Captain.

"I'd suspect I've gotten some bad fuel with trash in it, from the way it was sputtering and jerking. I'll call a mechanic once I get inside to come out and check it, but I appreciate you picking me up out there," spoke Superintendent Colden.

"You could have Lieutenant Gibbs look at it for you. He'd be glad to. You know he's a mechanic in the village," commented Captain McLeod.

"No, no. That could be taken as conflict of interest, and especially when the EEO investigators are here. Anyone would perceive that as a conflict, and I don't want accusations of anyone trying to influence me or those folks one way or another, and that's what would happen if he repaired my vehicle, and was declared innocent of wrongdoings. There are mechanics around I can call, and I'll do just that. But, thanks, again," Colden spoke good- naturedly. "By the way, I received a very interesting letter yesterday, from Brent Galen. Yes, I said the name right—Brent Galen. He certainly provided some thought-provoking information. Even he might not realize the prize he has tossed into our laps. Come on into the office and read it, this morning." He stepped out of the red pickup truck, and stood there smiling as he took a good look at the vehicle, as the Captain pulled off to go park. Mumbling to himself, he thought that maybe he did need to upgrade his vehicle. Maybe Darby wouldn't worry about him taking his fishing trips alone to the lake house. He went on inside the gatehouse and processed through, and went into his office because he expected to have a rather busy day. But the thought crossed his mind that he needed to walk the compound this morning. He always enjoyed the walks, the observations of things going on, and the interaction conversations with staff and inmates. Sitting down, with a cup of coffee, and turning on his desktop computer, he read and responded to his most urgent emails. Within a few minutes, Captain McLeod came in, asking about the mysterious letter.

"Wonder why he wrote to you, Mr. Colden?"

"I gathered just to say thank you for helping him out a bit. Believe he was scared to death, of Jay Dillon, of having seen things he weren't supposed to see, and perhaps others. Young boy, who wanted to get out of prison alive, and got caught up in a system that needs to be revamped, perhaps. It is interesting that he put the courthouse address on it as the return; he's not foolish, by any means." Colden handed the envelope to Captain McLeod, who examined the envelope before removing the letter. As he read it, Colden watched his facial expressions, and could tell that Captain McLeod appreciated the thought behind the letter. The misspelled words didn't matter. They could read it and decipher Galen's words.

"Geez, he does listen, and I figured Galen would go on his way with us never ever hearing a single word of him. He's probably a lot sharper than we realize, very street wise and cautious. I don't recall the man's name who drove him home, but somewhere didn't I hear that he actually dropped Galen off near the Ridgeway post office? Galen didn't want him to know where he actually intended to lay his head down that night; smart man. I suppose after hearing that man mention Sid Pullem that Galen began to distrust the man. This may be the man with the loose lips, huh? And the telephone wall box? That is interesting!" commented McLeod, handing the letter back to Colden.

"Yeah, and the timing was excellent. Let's make sure we get the phone boxes checked."

Captain McLeod left the Superintendent's office. Superintendent Colden retrieved a local telephone directory, flipped over to the yellow pages and began to look for a mechanic. He made several calls to garages, talking to the mechanics before locating one that would come to the prison that day to take a look at his truck, and if it needed to be taken in to the garage, to tow it in for repairs. It was agreed that the mechanic would drive a tow-truck, arriving somewhere before the noon hour, and Colden would be waiting on them inside the main building. Having completed that task, he decided to call his wife, Darby Jane, to make her aware of his vehicular concerns and of the possibility that she might have to come in the evening to pick him up. Upon answering her phone, with a pleasant 'hello,' she listened to him explain about his truck, and his plans for getting it repaired. She very calmly responded that if it couldn't be repaired on site, he needed to call her and she'd be glad to drive to the prison and pick him up around 5:00 p.m. Then with a laugh, she had suggested that he take off the following day and go shopping for a new vehicle, to which he had guffawed and told her that 'there was nothing wrong with his truck!' and then he remembered he had called her to pick him up possibly because his truck was in need of repair. He ended the conversation with a smile, saying, "Well, we will see, my dear. I will call later when I know what's what. Take care, my dear." Hanging up the phone, he smiled, thinking of Darby Jane's suggestion of his getting a new truck.

Knocking on the door, and walking into the office, Ms. Brooks brought him a cup of coffee, and asked if he was doing okay. Other than his truck "wanting to act out," he basically said, he was just fine.

He then proceeded to ask if she would try to reach Charles Frederick in the DA's office for him. She nodded and left. He began to read his e-mails on his desktop, and had finished with a few responses when Ms. Brooks rang him to advise that Charles Frederick was on the line.

Picking up the phone, he spoke, "Good morning, Charles. We've been trying to get up with each for several days now. It's been hectic over here; how are things with you?"

"Oh, busy as usual. More and more crime everyday. We're keeping your agency in business, so it seems. And then there's the stuff we have to deal with in following up on cases like that Jesse Oxenberg. And, I did make some contacts to check on that Titus Hawks character; he was stabbed, still in the hospital on intensive care. Lung damage I've been told, and he's being rather uncooperative with the hospital folks. He's still under prison security with two officers on guard at his hospital door. He's made several wild accusations that prison folks at your facility want him dead, and then there's allegations that someone in an east coast group of Hell's Angels have put a contract hit on him because he's been talking about some the more secretive missions they conducted in which he was a participant. He's been told that his mouth would get him dead, and he needed to refrain from his bragging. The Nebraska state law enforcement agency tends to lean more in the direction that his having been assaulted or stabbed is due to his boasting, and they have determined that there are some former members of Hell's Angels groups in that state's system because of a cooperative gesture with the federal bureau of prisons with scattering them rather than placing them in a singular federal prison. Oh," paused Frederick, flipping through some documents on his desk, "that Oxenberg character, he is in protective custody."

Colden then proceeded to speak, choosing his words carefully because he certainly knew the quickness with which Frederick could become angry, saying, "Remember the mention of Oxenberg's having provided state's evidence? And that it had to come from the courthouse?"

"Yeah. So?" spoke Frederick.

"How well do you know that young man who was to drive Brent Galen home when he was released at the courthouse? What is his name?"

"That was David Autry. He was working as a deputy, and the became a private investigator, before coming to work as an investigator in this office some three years ago. What's up with him?" asked Frederick.

"Well, while driving Galen that day, your man Autry did some talking and mentioned being acquainted with a Sid Pullem who is housed here. By the way, Pullem is believed to be the individual behind that alleged hit put out on Oxenberg. Has something to do with Pullem suspecting that Oxenberg had been involved with his wife, who is asking for a divorce, and probably did assault her. Also, it is my understanding that someone at the courthouse is trying to locate Oxenberg for Pullem. Sounds like our boy Galen did a lot of listening that day! Reckon who the guy at the courthouse could be that is feeding information to Pullem?" asked Colden, who further stated, "oh, almost forgot, they are communicating by cell phone."

"That is interesting, Colden. I'd like to get my hands on that cell phone you say Sid Pullem has. If we could use it to determine that David Autry is in communication with and feeding information to that Sid Pullem, I'd get him charged with interference into criminal actions, and inappropriate contacts with an offender. Can we locate that cell phone, do you?" asked Frederick.

"That is a top priority here as we speak. I do appreciate your support. What about Oxenberg's mail being checked, to determine if he is in communication with anyone from North Carolina?"

Charles Frederick momentarily thought about the idea that Oxenberg had probably written to some of his old friends, and that his address and location could easily be obtained. With his experience as an investigator, he could easily see David Autry learning his whereabouts. Besides, there had been others in the office who felt that Autry had jeopardized some investigations; in fact, one eye witness in a murder-for-hire case had shown up dead, floating in a river just outside the village of Glen Cove, and Autry had been seen talking with the man in a parking lot across from the courthouse. Autry had been questioned intensely, but no evidence to link him to the murder could be found and to terminate his employment based on suspicion would lead to litigation. So, staff in the District Attorney's office were cautious in assignments for him. Frederick then spoke and said he'd make contact with officials to have the mail monitored, as well as phone calls. "Well, Colden, let me get on this matter and make a progress call on these two. I'll call you back over the course of the next few days.

I'm taking off Thursday and Friday, and will touch base when I return. I need some time out."

"Oh, yes, I understand. I took a few days off and went on a fishing trip. Need to get away some times. Enjoy yourself. Call when you return. And, thanks." Superintendent Colden hung up the phone. Standing up, he decided to spend time walking around. He advised Ms. Brooks of his plans, retrieved his handheld walkie talkie, and headed to the Operations Center. He heard the intercom blurt 'count time' as he approached the door leading into the Operations Center. Walking inside, he spoke with Lieutenant Gibbs, Sergeant Ben Hunt, and others who were making changes to the count board for population control. Seeing that some numbers were not filled in, he sat on a desk to await the full count. But the phone rang. Lieutenant Gibbs answered the phone, looked over at Superintendent Colden, and said he'd make him aware that the mechanic was at the gatehouse waiting to see him. J.T. Colden had forgotten that he was to arrive to take a look at his old truck.

"Oh, I had forgotten about him. Please call the gatehouse and let them know I am on the way out. Thanks," as he hurriedly left the Operations Center.

The mechanic checked his truck, determined it needed to be towed into the garage, and worked to load the truck. He advised Colden that he would call him once he determined what the problem was, and they would discuss the parts costs and labor. Colden waved the mechanic off, and re-entered the gatehouse, and went on back into the facility. He headed back to the Operations Center, and asked if the count had cleared. It had not, to everyone's frustration who was standing in the Center.

The Sergeant commented he "was sick and tired of the Officers not getting it right; that this is happening too much."

The Lieutenant then directed Sergeant Hunt to go to the general population pod and determine what was going on. Then, he directed that the shift log summary be noted with a comment that the count had not been cleared after forty-five minutes on G. Pod, that he had sent Sergeant Hunt to investigate.

Overhearing the conversations, Superintendent Colden asked what the problem was, which gave cause for the Lieutenant and an Officer to look at him, and both started to speak, when the Officer stopped and gave a nod to the Lieutenant, who was the senior staff.

"Well, sir. For the past week or so, we have had delays in getting accurate counts in the general population housing pods, and several times we have had the Sergeants directly supervise the counts. Mostly it is some of the Officers just recently hired, and one or two that have been here for several months. It's almost as if they are exhibiting a lackluster attitude about the importance in inmate counts. Basic Prison 101, and they don't get it! They start, and somewhere forget what number they sounded off or counted last." The Lieutenant thought a minute, and continued, "For the past couple of weeks, we have discussed properly making inmate head counts in the shift line-ups. Even this morning, I cautioned one young lady, who's been here for months, who thought it funny for us to continue to talk with them on inmate counts. Why she snickered and asked we kept talking about the same subject, and I told her she'd continue to hear it until they could learn to do head counts with accuracy. Then she said she was tired of hearing it! Can you imagine?"

Colden spoke up, telling the Lieutenant that it sounded like that young lady needed further counseling with documentation in her performance appraisal.

"Mr. Colden, Captain McLeod has talked with her two times, and so have I. And she already has one job performance violation report in her file."

"Well keep doing what you are doing. They have to learn that inmate head counts are as important as them getting a paycheck, if they want to stay in this line work. And we can't tolerate too much of this overtime because the counts aren't clearing. Continue to document this in the shift log narratives as well. Make sure you inform the Captain of this dilemma. I believe he went to talk with an inmate on lock-up." Following his feedback to them, Superintendent Colden left to continue his walk-around.

He visited the staff in the programs and classification section, stopping to chat with several of them. He remembered to call his wife and advise her to pick him up at the prison at 5:00 that evening. Hanging up the phone, he heard the words 'count cleared,' causing him to look at his watch. He mentally noted that it had been twenty minutes since he had left the Operations Center. The staff present noticed his troubling look and pursed lips, and knew he was not happy with the count. Returning to the conversation with the staff present, they aired concerns about the numbers of inmates coming into the facility, with health issues that could not work, attend school programs, and basically needed twenty-four hour medical care. They also talked with him about the increasing numbers of inmates arriving that had been validated as security threat group members. Glen Cove Correctional had not been given extra staff positions to use for work on gangs or security threat groups, or primarily work on gathering inmate intelligence data within the facility and networking with other prisons. Occasionally he had documentations come across his desk for his reviews to validate newer gang members, but as his staff were saying the bulk were already validated. He had delegated this security threat group monitoring to Captain McLeod, but thought that maybe he needed to look at the numbers himself, especially since McLeod was doing the work of two positions, and was working with the two visiting canine handlers. He then proceeded to ask Mitch Steele, Assistant Superintendent for Programs and Support Services, to review the concerns regarding the security threat groups, to include the breakdown of various gang memberships, and to send to him a report outlining the concerns, with a copy to Captain McLeod. Afterward, the staff chatted about the accreditation program, and their satisfaction with the facility operations and things going on. Essentially Mitch Steele's section was progressing, with all positions filled and workloads equal. Superintendent Colden thanked them for all their work and continuing support for the facility, and left en route to the medical section. He desired to speak with the Nurse Supervisor, Pam Heally, about the influx of health care cases.

Entering the medical station, he greeted the nurses, and walked over to speak with the facility dentist and his staff as well. He saw the facility physician and a nurse in an examining room, with an inmate, and waved at them. He walked on down the hall, stopping at Pam

Heally's office, and looked into her office window. Seeing that she was alone, he knocked on the door, and was told to come in. Walking in, he smiled and greeted Ms. Heally and pulled a chair nearer to her desk.

"Well, I've been making rounds and have considerable amount of time with the staff in the programs arena, and they bombarded me with concerns about an influx of sick inmates, many of whom need twenty-four hour health care. I know of one that I reviewed in the past couple of weeks, and had him moved out to a geriatric facility. I wanted to hear your concerns as well, Ms. Heally."

"Mr. Colden, their concerns are well noted. I just don't understand the population management folks sending those inmates here. We can't retain our nurses because of salaries not up to par with those in the community or job market; we have four vacancies and we may lose another one to the county hospital. We just aren't equipped to deal with the wheelchair cases that we've been receiving, and we're down to one psychologist, yet the mental health cases keep coming in. What can we do? I've tried talking with the Regional Nursing Director; she listens, but most of the time she can get nowhere with folks in the headquarters. We've noted our concerns in the monthly reports, and most of the time there's no feedback."

"If you would, please pull your monthly reports and send them to me. Let me get more involved in this problem, and I want you to e-mail Mitch Steele every day, with a copy to me, on the numbers of cases that should not be at Glen Cove. Include the staffing numbers. Otherwise, how are things in this section?" he asked.

"Good, Mr. Colden, but we need help getting fully staffed. It is discouraging trying to give folks time off, when you really can't afford to. I've spoken with the Regional Nurse Director, and she's trying to get approvals to hire some part-time contract nurses, but plans to send us three on loan for thirty days, beginning next week. That'll be a big help."

Mr. Colden relayed his appreciation for all that she was doing to keep things afloat, and voiced his plans to speak with the agency Medical Services Director as well. He stood up to leave, and told her to bring other concerns to him as needed. He pledged his support to her, and again thanked her for doing an amazing job, before opening the door and walking out.

He continued to make his visits to the food services area, to the maintenance section, and on to the gym, the inmate library, and to conduct his observations of the classrooms. As he was finishing his walk-around, he heard his name come across the intercom system, that he was needed at his office for a phone call. He hurriedly proceeded toward his office, stopping by Ms. Brooks's office to check in with her. She advised that Charles Frederick in the District Attorney's office needed to talk with him, rather quickly. Colden asked her to get Frederick on the phone, and transfer the call to his office, which she did.

"Hello," and hearing a lady's voice, he spoke, "this is J.T. Colden speaking, and I am returning a call to Mr. Frederick, please." He waited a moment while the lady transferred the call.

"Colden, I wanted to get back to you rather quickly. We've had a compromise of our confidential files, and it looks like David Autry knows where Oxenberg and Titus Hawks are housed. I'd like to ask for you to do all you can to try to locate those cell phones that you suspect are in the prison. David Autry may be trying to contact that Sid Pullem. Our computer whiz-kid is working to determine if our phones have been used to contact any numbers at the prison, or if a call has come to Autry's office from the prison. I will get back to you when I can."

"Thanks, Frederick. Keep me posted and stay in touch. Now go fishing." Sitting at his desk in thought, Colden wondered if there was a way to determine if any prison phones had been used to call Autry's office number, which he had been given by Frederick that morning and had written down on his calendar. If anyone knew, it had to be Marcus Torn. He picked up the phone and asked Ms. Brooks to locate Marcus Torn and have him come by the office on his way out, for he had looked at his watch and had seen that it was approaching the hour of 5:00 P.M. Ms. Brooks called him back and advised that Mr. Torn had already left for the day, and that Mrs. Colden was waiting on him in the parking lot. Superintendent Colden gathered up his briefcase, stuffing files into it to take home to review, and seconds decided against taking any work home that evening. He lay his briefcase in his desk chair, walked out, locked his office door, and advised Ms. Brooks that he would see her, hopefully, in the morning.

Chapter Nineteen

Driving into work the next morning, around 5:00 A.M., he felt strangely uneasy about being at the wheel of Mrs. Darby Jane's car. Rarely did he operate the sedan, opting to drive his truck, unless it was their attending some special function together. He usually drove his truck to church on Sundays because he always arrived early to help another gentleman open up the sanctuary, check on the heating or air conditioning systems, and conduct a general walk through to ensure that the classrooms were usable. Whereas, Ms. Darby Jane would arrive just before the Sunday School services began. She was peculiar about her vehicle, not happy if anyone left trash, soda cans, or food wrappers in the vehicle, and certainly frowned on shoes with mud being slid across the floor mats. And she did not tolerate smoking in the car! He suddenly recalled that when the boys (their sons) were little, they were allowed to eat and have soda in the car but when the car stopped at home, Mrs. Darby Jane always reminded them to "get the trash out of the car, boys." And if for some reason they climbed into the car with mud caked on their shoes or sneakers, they had to remove the floor mats once they arrived at home, brush them off, and place them back into the car, or else there would be a smell of mud in the vehicle the next morning. Leave it to Mrs. Darby Jane to put old newspaper on the floorboards or floor mats if the boys had ball practice on a rainy day. She kept the house clean, as well as her automobile, and he had been grateful that she had instilled an appreciation for cleanliness in their two sons. Once he arrived at work, he headed on into the building, with two objectives: to attend shift line-up and ensure that staff heard his expectations as regards accurate inmate head counts, and to get an early start on reports he had left last night and to get his e-mails out of the way. Ms. Brooks had grown accustomed to his arrival before she got there, and sometimes found that he had started the coffee. He enjoyed the quietness without the phones ringing, for he sometimes thought that he could complete a half day's work during that hour before the 8:00 start-up.

Going into the shift briefing room, Officers were milling around chatting and catching up with each other's goings on. Many of them spoke to him with 'good morning,' or 'glad to see you,' or 'happy you're joining us this morning' type greetings. He always enjoyed the shift line-ups, and it gave him a chance to observe the staff, as well as to observe the supervisors in their making of post assignments, coverage of important matters and review of policies, and most especially the announcements of special activities. The Shift Lieutenant and Sergeants arrived, along with Mitch Steele, who sometimes came in for observation purposes, and staff were called to attention. The Lieutenant spoke of the presence of Superintendent Colden, making an especial introduction to the newest employees who might not have had the opportunity to get acquainted with him, and then turned the floor over to the Superintendent for remarks that he might have on his mind. Colden thanked the Lieutenant, and commenced to talk about inmate head counts, and the fact that these were basic to working in a prison. He reminded staff to study the policy on inmate counts from time to time. Then he discussed the overtime that had been accruing due to the delays or time elements involved in conducting the inmate head counts, citing one instance in which it took forty-five minutes for the count to be accurately performed in the general population housing pod. Counts in the segregation units were generally done within a few minutes. He then advised the Officers and supervisors therein that he clearly expected everyone at Glen Cove Correctional to adhere to the policies, and if they had a problem they should consult their supervisors. Lastly, he asked the question: "Is this clearly understood by persons in this room?" From the middle of the room, a hand raised, and he saw that the individual was a young lady, chewing bubble gum, who was blond haired, and guessed her to weigh one hundred thirty pounds.

Colden addressed her, asking that she first remove and dispose of the gum, and to ask her question. She removed the gum, mumbling something inaudible, placing it in a piece of paper she pulled from a shirt pocket, and spoke asking why it was necessary to conduct the head counts several times a day, because, "Quite frankly, sir, there is no sense in it, in my way of thinking. If you count in the morning, and three are taken outside the facility all day long, then you should know what you got. Your evening count should confirm this, shouldn't it?"

Colden then asked her name, and she replied Pam Cox. He then asked her how long she had been employed; she replied nine months. Colden then asked if she had ever given thought to prisons escapes; she replied no and commented that she couldn't see anyone escaping from Glen Cove. Colden then stated, "Well, Ms. Cox, it has been tried several times. We are held accountable for knowing how many prisoners are on site regardless of the time of day or night, and knowing where prisoners are that are away on writs, outside assignments, and the like. State law places that responsibility upon us. You are and will be held accountable for following the state agency policy at conducting inmate head counts with accuracy. I would suggest that you review your performance appraisal key responsibilities under the security listing, taking especial note that key responsibility number one is conducting accurate head counts. There will be no discussion on conducting counts as you, Ms. Cox, have indicated. Do you have other questions?"

"No, sir." she said.

He then addressed the group with "anyone else?" No other hands were raised. He then nodded to the Lieutenant who began list of post assignments, as well as making staff aware of the continued presence of the visiting canine handlers. Updates on policies were reviewed, and staff were told to check the bulletin boards for other items of interest. He then dismissed them to go to their assigned posts. Superintendent Colden watched them in their departure, and immediately thereafter inquired of the Lieutenant regarding Ms. Cox.

"She's got a nerve, asking that fool question in this group. The woman has no business here, Mr. Colden, if you don't mind my being so straightforward. She can't count worth a darn, and just can't get it through her thick head that there are some things that must be done regardless of what you think, and doing head counts is a problem with her. She is dense in the head. I'm at my wits end with her, and today you've seen what we have to deal with. A number of Officers do not want to work with her. She was on night shift, with Gibbs, and they were fed up with her, and asked us to take her on first shift and see if she could do any better. What a laugh!"

"I get your meaning, Lieutenant. I can easily see that she is one who can wear on one's patience.

"You need to document her actions of this morning on her appraisal. I would also expect that her supervisor meet with her, and forbid her to appear at shift line-up with gum in her mouth. I do appreciate your handling of this morning's session," spoke Colden, shaking the Lieutenant's hand.

The Lieutenant thanked Superintendent Colden for his appearance at shift line-up, and left the room. Colden went to his office to start on his desk work with some quiet time, hopefully. He had managed to complete quite a bit of work, when Captain McLeod knocked on his door and was told to come in. Good mornings were spoken by each, and Captain McLeod started with telling Colden about his chat with inmate Mark Burns the day before, reminding Colden as to whom Burns was and why he was in lock-up.

It seemed that Burns had figured the points that the disciplinary action for the money found and the two cell phones; he guesstimated that criminal charges for the cell phones alone would net him another four years, and that he'd get substantial loss of his merit time off his sentence as well as loss of visitation and telephone privileges for at least a year. Plus, there was the fact that the money belonged to Adam Law and had been another inmate's payment for a cell phone that he had not received because the cell phone was found on Law's friend at visitation time and confiscated. Burns had told Captain McLeod that he would give up the name of the Officer who was helping Law get some cell phones if criminal charges were disposed of and that he not lose his privileges. Plus he wanted to be relocated elsewhere to do his disciplinary segregation time. Captain McLeod advised that the trade-off was a 'big wish' and that only the Superintendent could render such a decision, and that he would confer with the Superintendent at the earliest opportunity, and render feedback to inmate Burns. Colden then asked the Captain what actions he thought might be appropriate. Captain McLeod sat in thought for a few minutes, and then stated that he could go along with the inmate in exchange for his help at getting rid of a corrupt staff person. Superintendent Colden then spoke saying that he favored not disposing of the criminal charges but working to have the sentences run concurrent, instead of consecutive, with the time that Burns was serving, and would support the privileges not lost as well as movement. He based this on the theory that others, inmates and staff, knew that the cell phones were found and they needed to follow through on the criminal charges to save face and preserve the integrity of the law on cell phones. Captain McLeod agreed and indicated that he would revisit Burns, with the options.

"Well, how are the canines working out?" asked Colden, knowing that the canine handlers had been moving about the facility all week long.

"Oh, they are working out well, sir. In fact, we've searched cell 40 twice— no phones. Marcus Torn added that extra audio surveillance to inmate Sid Pullem's cell, so maybe we'll get lucky on that one. Still finding a lot of nuisance type contraband, and some cigarette tobacco concealed in a deodorant bottle. Nothing in either phone wall-box which is puzzling. Must be moving it around is what I think. Or staff is helping them."

"Find out what Burns will say; that may be the mover in this. And thanks."

Captain McLeod left to go about his business, leaving Colden to continue responding to his desk matters. He worked most of the day on reports, inmate inquiries and requests, and studying the facility reports on inmate urinalyses completed and findings, as well as studying the numbers of inmates associated and involved with gangs. He had worked through lunch, for he'd brought in a ham sandwich and a banana. It also gave him an opportunity to walk down to speak with Vanis Goodson, as regards the progress or actions being taken on the recommendation that had been submitted to promote Captain McLeod. It had gone through the chain of command and was at the state personnel office undergoing an assessment for salary enhancement, and she did expect to receive some word of disposition in the next few days. Going back to his office, he sat for a few minutes break, turning to watch things outside his window.

The week was moving along quickly, as the EEO investigators were still talking with different staff but were planning to take off on Friday, and return the next week. The canine handlers were still walking about the facility, and had spent two days working and training with the canine handlers for the sheriff's department. Colden had caught up reading the shift log narratives, noting that inmate head counts were improving with less time involved, and thus less overtime incurred. The mechanic had contacted him and advised that he expected the truck to be ready for pick- up the following day, on Friday afternoon. He summoned Captain McLeod to his office, wherein he advised that he was taking the afternoon off as well as the next day. In fact, he went on and confided that he was taking Mrs. Darby Jane's car to be washed and cleaned out at a local detail shop, and would be vehicle shopping on Friday, but he would be reachable by cell phone.

Chapter Twenty

Superintendent Colden had gone in to work early, hoping to catch up on things since he had taken the previous Thursday afternoon and Friday off for personal reasons. He had always had a strong penchant for working and getting to work on time; taking time off had never been a common issue with him. He'd worked as a police officer in three municipalities after his honorable discharge from the U.S. Army, for some seven years, but had served four years in the military with the military police. In all that time, he had taken off on three occasions, once to get married and have a short honeymoon with Ms. Darby Jane, and the other two were to spend some time with his family when his two sons were born. He'd worked with prisons for thirty-three years, and had probably taken some half dozen vacations. Work ethics had been drilled into him by his father during his adolescent years, and as a teenager he always had a part-time job after school hours. But in the past few years, his wife had begun to insist on his taking time off from work with the frequency seeming to increase since she had retired from teaching.

On his desk, he found a pile of reports, inmate letters and letters of inquiry from family members of inmates, and the regular run-of-the-mill classification actions to be handled for changes to inmates' security levels. On the very top of the pile were the facility shift log narratives for the past few days. He made a pot of fresh decaf coffee, and sat down to read the narratives because they gave a summary report of activities that had occurred within or at the facility, and that was what he was most interested at the present time. He was pleased to read that improvements had occurred with the inmate head counts, and that his segregation cells had open cells; usually the weekends ended up with rowdy inmates, and they ran out of enough empty cells on lock-up and had to take some inmates out and use the cells for the most assaultive, or others deemed security risks.

Sometimes, it had become necessary to transport inmates to other facilities for lock-up because Glen Cove's segregation was full with no cases that could be removed. He saw that there had been no weekend transport trips, except for one that had to be taken to the nearest emergency room for chest pains. He did see a notation for the Operations Center log where Officer Pam Cox had refused to participate in head counts on Friday, and had been sent home by Captain McLeod. He thought to himself that perhaps she would resign. He continued to work on the pile of work, most of which was delegated to others with his transmittal slips, and he placed a pile of it on Ms. Brooks's desk for her to deal with on her arrival. He started to plow through the pile of letters, managing to read them, circling with his highlighter portions to be focused on, and place his transmittal slips on them in short span of time. He came across two with return addresses that he immediately recognized, addressed to him in a confidential manner; he quickly opened them. The first letter was from the Chief of Security for the Nebraska Department of Corrections, regarding Titus Hawks, informing him of Hawks's assault. Reading on, he learned that Hawks was hospitalized under double security guard, and it had been officially determined that his assault stemmed from his boasting about having been a member of an east coast segment of Hell's Angels and talking about secretive missions of violence he had participated. He was further informed that to reduce the likelihood of continued threats against Hawks, that the Nebraska agency was contemplating placing him into a witness protection program within the Federal Bureau of Prisons, and relocating him. Officials were currently engaged in negotiations with Hawks, and with Federal prisons officials, and it was hoped that a decision would be reached. He and the local District Attorney would be notified by official letter under cover of confidentiality in the next few weeks. Sitting back in his chair, Colden wondered if Titus Hawks realized the position he was putting himself in with his bragging.

Opening the second letter, from the Oregon Department of Adult Correctional Services, he saw that it referenced one Jesse B. Oxenberg. Supposedly, Oxenberg had received letters of threats against his life from parties unknown, with accusations in the letters that the writer was aware that Oxenberg had been convicted of several rapes in North Carolina, and the writer believed one of the rape victims was his wife. Coupled with telephone contacts from Charles Frederick in the local District Attorney's office, the Oregon system had placed Oxenberg on protective custody housing. Additional options for secured housing were being explored, to include prisoner protection placement that was very similar to the Federal government's witness protection program, to include identity alterations in prison files. Colden had read that other correctional agencies were contemplating prisoner protection placements to include name changes, and a series of relocations in differing states, designed to thwart individual searches for an inmate. He could recall that the number of inmates needing this type placement were in the thousands, ranging from witnesses in mobster convictions, gang killings, and drug trafficking cases, as well as former correctional and police officials who had been convicted and sentenced to prison. The Oregon continued to welcome and urged communications on the alleged hits against Oxenberg, but had turned over the threatening letters to the state's bureau of investigation. The agency's director of the inmate management office indicated that they would stay in touch with Superintendent Colden.

Colden placed both in a small locked box in the left hand drawer of his desk, along with other articles that he had accumulated and felt the need to retain under lock and key. He went to refill his coffee cup, and was at the coffee pot when Ms. Brooks entered the office.

"Good morning, sir," she said smiling. "See you got the old truck back on the road! Did you have some good days off?"

"I did, Ms. Brooks, and I see things were quiet around here. I've gone through a pile of work that was on my desk, as you can see. Is there anything I need to know this morning?"

"I received a call from Captain McLeod last night at home. He is very anxious to see you this morning, and wanted me to let you know."

"When he gets here, send him on in, please. I still have some letters to write, and I guess the EEO investigators will return this morning." He sat down in his office chair, near to the plate glass window, with the letters to respond to and his Dictaphone; he sat looking out at the front lawn, thinking what a well-manicured yard. The flowers were blooming, with an abundance of bright and pastel colors, all down the sides of the walk-way, surrounded with pinestraw, and the camellia bushes were budding with bright pinkish mauve blossoms. He watched staff sitting on the front patio area, interacting with each other for a few minutes before entering the building; it was such a beautiful day, and for a moment he thought it would be such a good day to be at home working in his yard, planting new flowers, placing pinestraw around his shrubs and just sitting in the yard enjoying the day's blessings. Shaking his head, he thought it must be spring fever! Glancing back to the letters, he read each one and dictated a response, until he had finished, and stood up to take the materials and Dictaphone into Ms. Brooks. She looked at him and thought 'What's come over him?' because he was smiling, and seemed to be full of wit and enthusiasm. She said, "Mr. Colden, you sure seem to be in an extraordinarily good mood today."

He responded, "It must be spring fever, Ms. Brooks! A good day to be out doing yard work. And if I were home, that's exactly what Darby Jane would have me doing. She constantly talks about putting in another rose bed beside the front patio."

At that moment Captain McLeod came into the office, greeting both with a warm smile and extending 'good mornings' to them. Colden sensed happiness with the Captain, and asked, "To what we do owe for your being so chipper this morning?"

"We should be happy. Spring is upon us, and things are getting so much better, and we found two cell phones over the weekend! That is great news, and we think they are the ones we've been looking so hard to find. Guess where they were hidden?"

Colden gave it a moment's thought, and gave in to the suspense. "Have no idea. You tell me."

The Captain went on to say, "Well, you recall that Ace Tyler installed those stainless steel benches in the dayrooms in the general population pods? We've never really paid them much attention, but the supporting pipe stand for four of those tables have cut-outs with cover plates on them. You have to get on your knees, and look just up under the bracket where the table tops are bolted into place, and you'll see those cover plates. The schematics for the table designs that are in the maintenance do not show the cut outs or cover plates; Marcus Torn recalls that Ace Tyler did have a small welding unit with him during the installation. We believe Tyler deliberately made the cut-outs and placed cover plates over them, and provided a key for the security screws to possibly one or two inmates. Guess what? That Sid Pullem was working with Tyler at that time. I went back to check to see who his team of inmate helpers were; they were Pullem and another inmate who was moved from here some months ago. Those two visiting canine handlers found these with their dogs and have been ecstatic over the find. I have those two phones locked in my office; we need to get law enforcement to look at them, and I sure hope we can get fingerprints off them. What do you think, Sir?"

"Let's do it. A lot of people are hoping these phones will give us some information we badly need. Go ahead and contact the local police and see if they can help, and you may have to go on and contact the state bureau of investigation. It seems that they spoke about having staff on board who could check the phones and pull out data from them. Make this a priority, and Captain, I am very much appreciative of your work on this. I will get with those two canine handlers and personally thank them this morning. How did things go with Burns last time you spoke with him? By the way, have you informed Marcus Torn about those tables?"

The Captain advised that the inmate was thinking over the options given to him. He had been unable to get with Marcus Torn, but would continue to try to reach him. He left to make his contacts to get the cell phones examined. Ms. Brooks spoke up, "Well, it sure is about time that something good came over to our side, Mr. Colden. The Captain's been working hard on some things, and it is good to see him so excited. Do you think his promotion will come through?"

"I hope so, Ms. Brooks. He has earned it, and more. He has been a terrific right-hand person for me to work with," commented Colden, who walked out of the office. He stepped back into Ms. Brooks' office, and advised her that he was walking to the maintenance area to see Marcus Torn and would be back in a little while should anyone call.

Walking into the maintenance plant, he visually scanned the room, and asked where Mr. Torn was. One of the inmate workers said he saw Mr. Torn walk toward the boiler room a few minutes earlier; Colden headed in that direction, finding Torn working on pressure gauges with one of his assistants. Once Torn saw him, he turned the project over to the assistant, stood up and walked toward Colden. "Glad you walked down here, sir. It's been hectic since I walked in. Pressure valves not working, kitchen equipment inoperable, and inmate wall phones shutting down after a minute or two use. Tell me you don't have bad news!"

"Nothing for you to worry with right now. The Captain has more cell phones found, and you'll never guess where? Concealed in the support pipe-stand for the dayroom tables, in cut-outs with cover plates! Word is that Ace Tyler crafted the cut-outs in the stainless steel pipes, made the cover plates, using security screws but may have given special screw keys to an inmate or two.

He has examined the tables, with only four of them having the hidden compartments. He checked the schematics drawings for the tables, and the compartments were not on the designs. We got lucky, or rather I should say that the canine handlers and their dogs got lucky; they found these. In pod B. When you can, please check those support stands, and see that they get welded shut. Check all of them in this place. It's about time we had some good outcomes. What about those surveillance devices; any more word?" spoke Colden.

"Will do, sir. We're looking at quite a bit of money on this project right here if we have to replace gauges. Not to mention having to shut down the hot water for a while. We'll stay on it til we get it fixed. The vendors for the kitchen equipment have been called, and they are en route as those are still under warranty. And I've got staff checking on those wall phones. We'll see what happens, and I'll get back to you, sir," declared Marcus Torn, who needed to get back to work.

Colden waved him off, and returned to his office. He still had enough work to do or last him for several days piled on his desk, especially with some of the personnel investigations that had been landing on his desk in recent days. He had given Ms. Vanis Godson several vehicle license plates to run for him, over the past few weeks, because his curiosity continued to nag him about the new, expensive vehicles he kept spotting sitting in the parking lot. And since his vehicle shopping trip last week, he was shocked at the costs of new vehicles, even the compacts and small model trucks. He generally tried to get his money's worth out of a vehicle, and kept them for fifteen years, and knew that with good care, regular preventive maintenance, oil changes, and other servicing, a vehicle could last for sometime. He certainly couldn't afford to buy a new vehicle every two to three years; he'd always felt the need to save as much money as he could, which is probably why his family referred to him as a tight-wad. But they also admitted that his not being a spendthrift allowed for the ownership of a nice second home on a beautiful lake as well as his help to their sons with the purchase of their homes. And the family knew that he wanted to be able to live a very comfortable life, and do some traveling, whenever he and Mrs. Darby Jane both retired. Tackling that pile of reports, he scanned the subject matter lines, and restacked them in order that he preferred to read them, with the most pressing reports stacked to his immediate left, and those for general reading stacked in another pile. The most pressing reports were those that he knew something about, which were reports of staff misconduct that most often meant terminations, polygraph needs, or referral for more information to be gathered. Colden spent several hours reading the reports, writing his notes of decision and actions to be taken, in order that Ms. Goodson could get with the appropriate supervisors and handle the matters. There were several where she would need to compose letters of terminations, personnel discipline, or make referrals for polygraph examinations to be rendered, and get back with Colden for his signatures. He came across two license plates cases where Ms. Goodson had discovered that the owners' motor vehicle drivers licenses had been suspended, one for a drunken driving offense, and the other for failure to attend court for two speeding tickets. Neither of them had reported this to their supervisors in accordance with policy, but what caught Colden's attention more was the name of the drunken driving case - that of Pam Cox. And she had not even reported the charge for the driving while under the influence of alcoholic beverages.

Even more troubling was what he saw on the driving history record that Ms. Goodson had attached, for it showed a series of motor vehicle violations to include speeding, driving with open containers of alcoholic beverages, non-compliance with court ordered attendance at refresher driving classes, and driving while intoxicated. He determined after the review that termination was in order, and made notes for Ms. Goodson to get the paperwork in order. The second case he determined needed to be talked with, and it appeared this was a first-time matter, but he withheld making a judgment until he could speak with the Officer. He managed to complete the reading of all the case files on his desk, and was reading a draft of a policy that Mitch Steele had submitted to him for the handling of incoming inmates with health issues who needed to be housed elsewhere, when his phone range and he learned that Captain McLeod was en route to his office.

Captain McLeod walked in and sat down, making him aware that he had taken the cell phones down to the sheriff's office, that a set of fingerprints had been successfully pulled from each phone, and that data had been retrieved from the phones. He handed the detective's documented report of findings to Superintendent Colden, who studied the report. One of the phones carried a set of fingerprints belonging to Adam Law, and the other was definitely showing Sid Pullem's prints. The Captain had both inmates on lock-up, being housing in cells on opposite ends of the housing block, but had not spoken with either of them, yet.

"Mr. Colden, let me say this first, that while the detective was examining the phones, he was accompanied by an agent of the state bureau of investigation as well as his supervisor. This detective has had remarkable training in retracting data from used cell phones, as well as being a certified fingerprint analyst. Here is his business card," he said, handling a pocket- sized card to Superintendent Colden, which bore that information. Continuing, he stated, "Detective Barr is pretty much regarded within the law enforcement circles as an expert; very proficient."

Colden re-read the reports on the two cell phones.

SHERIFF'S DEPARTMENT REPORT ON CELLPHONE RETRIEVAL

Source of cell phone: Discovery in table pipe at Glen Cove Correctional Institution

Description: Samsung—serial # 20BC10789001

Date: March 22, 2012   Fingerprint scan: Yes [X] No [ ]

Identified through SBI: Yes [X] No [ ] Number: y2890xy1006-BDL0016

Identified through FBI: Yes [X] No [ ] Filenumber: NC00011234657109

Fingerprints determined to belong to: Adam H. Law, w/m/dob 8-7-61 (NC)

AKA: Doby Law; Adam Howard Lawer; A. H. Law

Data retrieval: Cell phone contained calls placed to sources in NC, Ohio, Nebraska, Louisiana, Texas, New York. List of calls made is attached.

Key words in calls: dollars, contacts, kill, dead, woman, Oxenberg, visits, trac-phones.

1. Inmate soliciting to kill Oxenberg once located.
2. Inmate says Oxenberg in prison in Ohio.
3. Inmate says Oxenberg in prison in Oregon.
4. Inmate soliciting to kill a woman in North Carolina.

Alerts: Yes [X] No [ ] Need to advise NC SBI and FBI.
Dissemination: NC SBI; FBI-Charlotte office; Source agent; Files

He studied this particular report and was pleased that the fingerprints had been checked against those on the files in the state and federal bureaus of investigation, and scanned the attached list that listed the phone numbers in the states to which Adam Law had made the calls. He then studied the second report.

SHERIFF'S DEPARTMENT REPORT ON CELLPHONE RETRIEVAL

Source of cell phone: Discovery in table pipe at Glen Cove Correctional Institution

Description: Samsung—serial # 14WXC0987622

Date: March 22, 2012   Fingerprint scan: Yes [X] No [ ]

Identified through SBI: Yes [X] No [ ] Number:
                                   f343yy105-WXL0023

Identified through FBI: Yes [X] No [ ] File number:
                                   NC000776543092

Fingerprints determined to belong to: Sid Pullem, w/m/dob 7-7-71 (NC)

AKA: Sidney Pullem; Sidney Pull

Data retrieval: Cell phone contained calls placed to sources in NC, Oregon, NY.

List of calls made is attached.

Key words in calls: dollars, contacts, kill, dead, woman, Oxenberg, visits, trac-phones.

1. Inmate soliciting to kill Oxenberg once located.
2. Inmate believes Oxenberg in prison in Oregon or Nebraska
3. Inmate says Oxenberg assaulted wife.

Alerts: Yes [X] No [ ] Need to advise NC SBI and FBI.

Dissemination: NC SBI; FBI-Charlotte office; Source agent; Files

He did take notice that some of the numbers were different from those on Adam Law's sheet, but it was interesting to look at the network of call sites.

After studying them, in addition to looking at the attached pages, he determined that there was sufficient evidence to process disciplinary actions against both inmates. The Captain was authorized to proceed with charging both inmates with possession of the cell phones.

Too, he made it clear that he wanted them to remain separated until law enforcement officials could interview them, and he felt strongly that criminal charges would be forthcoming on the supposed hits against Jesse Oxenberg, and conspiracy to commit murder. He continued to study the attachment sheet with the listing of the phone calls that had been made by Pullem. He came across three phone calls that brought a smile to his face; those were to a number that he thought might be to the county courthouse, because he readily recognized the prefix and the group of numbers following that three-digit number. The District Attorney's office would certainly be interested in this information, and he thought he needed to personally deliver the document to Charles Frederick. He rang Ms. Brooks and asked if she would reach Mr. Frederick for him quickly. In a few moments, she rang back and stated that Mr. Frederick was on the line.

Colden picked up the phone and began to speak, saying "Frederick, we had the two cell phones checked, and we may have hit pay-dirt. I want to bring these reports to you in the next few minute if you plan to be around?"

"Oh, yes, I'm rather anxious to see what you have. Come on over. I'll be waiting."

Colden stood up and advised the Captain to go ahead with the paperwork on Pullem and Law, and that he'd be back shortly. He then left the facility and drove over to the courthouse. When walking through the front door, he saw a young man standing off to the side wall talking with two uniformed officers, and the young man glanced at him as if he wondered about his being at the courthouse. Colden thought he recognized the man as being David Autry, said hello and kept walking, certain that the young man was watching him. As Colden turned the corner to travel another hallway, he turned around and saw the young man standing at the corner watching him. Colden proceeded on into the Office of the District Attorney, shaking hands with Charles Frederick, and taking a seat. He handed the envelope with the documents to Frederick, who sat perusing the documents. At one point, he lifted his head and made a comment, "This is what I've wanted for a long time!"

Colden spoke and asked about the phone numbers to the courthouse, and if Frederick recognized those numbers.

"Oh, those numbers are to David Autry's office. And our computer and phone technician has checked those phones with the computer scans, and it turns out that David Autry has called the prison inmate phones on two occasions, as I've had those numbers checked as well. This shows he had received calls from the cell phone listed here."

Without hesitation, Colden spoke up telling Frederick that he thought he saw David Autry in the foyer at the courthouse entrance, and as he turned the corner of the hallway leading the office, he saw the same man standing at the corner watching him with interest. "I remembered that he looked like the man who supposedly took Brent Galen home."

Frederick spoke up, "I want to get with this Detective Barr and get him over here; I want to listen to these three calls. I need absolute proof that David Autry told the inmate where Jesse Oxenberg is housed, and it would be good if I could hear that he told that inmate that his wife had been assaulted and/or hospitalized." Frederick picked up his phone and asked his secretary to locate this detective so he could speak to him, and it was rather urgent. In just a few moments, Detective Barr was on the phone, and they arranged for Frederick and Colden to come right on over to his office, as he already had the appropriate equipment set up to listen to the calls data. They would be able to listen to what the inmate was hearing and saying thanks to the highly sophisticated equipment. On the drive over, they chatted about the whereabouts of the two inmates, and Colden made Fredrick aware of the two letters he had received; he learned that Frederick had received copies in the mail as well. Both thought that placing both Titus Hawks and Jesse Oxenberg in the protection programs noted were good plans, but as to whether there might be long-term success with it, they had doubts. Colden still needed to share and discuss that avenue with his supervisor in the agency headquarters, before giving final support. On arrival at the sheriff's offices, Detective Barr greeted them and escorted them down a long hallway, entering a large equipment room full of what appeared to be computers, monitors, and many other pieces of equipment. There were two men inside at tables with an assortment of cell phones, small computer tablets or notebooks, and other items. Detective Barr introduced them, and told them to proceed with two cell phones that he removed from a locked cabinet, which were in clearly marked evidence bags with chain-of-custody worksheets inside. Both Colden and Frederick were then asked to sign the data transmission portions of the worksheets, to indicate that they had been privileged to listening to data taken from the cell phones. Sitting down, the two technicians began to play back the calls through some of the equipment.

After some time of listening to the calls, Frederick sat up in his seat, saying "That's Autry's voice! Can you turn up the volume a tad?"

They continued to listen. It could be clearly heard that Autry spoke the name Oxenberg, and used the words 'prison in Oregon.' Further, Frederick clearly heard Autry's voice when he told Sid Pullem that he owed him fifteen hundred dollars for the information, and that he expected Pullem to get his dough to him in the next ninety-six hours. Upon hearing that, Frederick advised the Detective that he wanted a clear statement on the content of these transmissions, signed by him and the two technicians. Arrangements were made for this to happen within the next twenty-four hours with personal delivery to him the next afternoon.

En route back to the courthouse, Charles Frederick verbalized his plans to contact the state's Attorney General's office as well as the state's bureau of investigation, while Colden would talk with those in his chain of command. They wanted to get this matter handled swiftly, and proceed with getting both inmates charged with criminal actions as well. Another piece to the puzzle was to resolve the matter of Mark Burns and the name of the Officer who had been helping the inmates with the cell phones.

As they talked in the courthouse parking lot, Colden advised Charles Frederick about the Officer being named, hopefully that day, and stated that he'd be calling him with that information. They parted ways, and Colden drove back to the prison. On arrival, he looked for the Captain's vehicle and saw it was still in its parking space. He hurriedly went back inside, and asked Ms. Brooks to let the Captain know he was back and wanted to speak with him. He sat down at his chair, picked up the phone, and dialed his supervisor's number, and was pleased that the man was still in the office, for usually his supervisor was gone or tied up in a meeting. Extending a pleasant greeting, Colden advised Region Director Polk about the events of the day, but found himself having to keep clarifying pieces of the case;

he spoke to his supervisor every day and would enlighten him on the case progress, but oftentimes found that Polk's recall on the case was not that great. Polk expressed his satisfaction with the handling of the case, and rendered his support of the actions being considered on both the Hawks and Oxenberg cases. Copies of the letters that Colden had received had been disseminated to Polk's office and that of the agency legal staff, and Polk advised that a letter of response was being drafted to both states on the agency support position. Colden was pleased that the agency had undertaken that task already. Once he hung the phone up, the Captain entered the office and sat down.

"Captain, has inmate Burns given you a name or names of the Officer involved in helping get the phones into the facility?"

Captain McLeod spoke up and stated that Burns had taken the options given to him, and had stated that an Officer Larry Brown had been the culprit. The Captain continued to talk, saying that Burns said, "When Brown takes an inmate out to the hospital and brings him back, he brings in his gear as well. He carries a big block flashlight, and puts cell phones in that flashlight, 'cause no one ever checks him when he returns. He passes the cell phones off to the inmate janitor in the receiving ward, who takes them to the general population pod. Nobody checks him either; he's a trusty, sort-of, and they all know him. That Brown, he's been doing this for a while now; gets a lot of money for sticking his neck out, so says Burns. You know, Mr. Colden, that inmate is right! When staff come in through the front gate they get checked. But when these Officers take inmates out for trips or whatever, out through the receiving area, and come back through receiving, they are not checked again. That's our fault, and I plan to rectify that today."

Superintendent Colden asked where Officer Brown was, and the Captain advised that he had already left for the day, but the plan was to have him brought in the next morning, checked, and questioned in detail. And if need be, have him polygraphed. Superintendent Colden agreed, and thanked the Captain for the work. He then spoke about his afternoon meeting with Charles Frederick and his conversation with Region Director Polk.

"Well, this Oxenberg and Hawks mess—I hope it is over. Wonder what the EEO folks are finding? Have you seen them? They ought to be winding their talks up," spoke Colden, who stood up and put on his suit coat… "I am going home. It has been a busy day. See you tomorrow."

Colden went by Ms. Brooks's office and advised that he was going home. "Good night, sir," she stated. Exiting the gatehouse, Colden sat down in his old truck, put the key into the ignition and cranked the vehicle. He sat there for a minute or two, listening to the purr of the old motor and studying his surroundings. Other employees had begun to exit the building, some laughing, some standing around chatting with each other, and others just waving as they entered their vehicles. A few waved at him as they passed. He thought to himself that Glen Cove Correctional was a good place to work, with lots of good people, and lots of things to do. Backing out of the space, and putting his truck into drive, he pulled out of the parking lot, and felt good about being able to go home at a decent hour. With a couple of hours of daylight left, maybe he would be able to get out in the yard and help Mrs. Darby Jane in her garden.

Chapter Twenty-One

As Marcus Torn pulled into the parking lot the next morning, he saw the turquoise colored Chevrolet with a white Z71 on its side parked in the Superintendent's parking space. Exiting his truck, he walked over to take a look at it, in surprise that the famed tight-wad, as others fondly referred to Colden, had actually bought a new truck. He smiled, thinking it was about time, and he was happy for the guy. Torn actually had a lot of respect and appreciation for the Superintendent Colden, and truly enjoyed working with him, and knew of no one else who was totally loyal to his agency. Torn walked through the gatehouse and into the main building, going to Colden's office, where he knocked and entered, only to tell the Superintendent that he liked the new truck.

"Well, thank you, Mr. Torn. It is not totally new; it's used, last year's model but has less than twenty thousand miles on it. Clean inside and out. Serviced right. Got it at a great price, with a little negotiating. But I'm satisfied. How are things with you?"

"Things are great, Mr. Colden. By the way, the kitchen equipment is all operational, with warranties in place for getting them back on line. We came out better than I thought we would on the boiler; had to replace one pressure gauge. And those inmate phones are working just fine; the lightning had run in on some lines, but the phone company did the repairs. So, right now, we are in good shape. Well, just stopped in to speak. I need to get on to work and see what's going on. See you later."

"Have a good day, Mr. Torn," spoke Superintendent Colden, smiling.

Sometime later that morning, Colden met with Mitch Steele and Captain McLeod to discuss the handling of classification actions for Sid Pullem and Adam Law and Mark Burns. Disciplinary actions for prison violations were being processed. Captain McLeod had received a call from the sheriff's office about warrants to be issued on Pullem and Law, for conspiracy to commit murder charges, and for violations of state cell phones in prison laws. They were to be retained on lock-up until the court actions were handled, after which they would be relocated appropriately and dependent on their sentences. Records were to be flagged indicating that they were never to be considered for future housing at Glen Cove Correctional. Captain McLeod had confronted Officer Larry Brown on his arrival, whom admitted to the charges; the local law enforcement agency Lieutenant came and charged him with smuggling of cell phones into a state prison, and of bartering and trading with inmates in exchange for money. Officer Brown was taken to jail. He was also advised that notices were being provided to the federal and state revenue agencies, and that he could expect them to penalize him as regards the untaxed monies involved. Too, his notice to staff had been posted; it was an advisement that all staff taking inmates out of the prison for any reasons would be searched when returning, as well as their property items, in the same manner as they would be on entering the gatehouse. Superintendent Colden was well pleased with the interactions between Steele and Captain McLeod, as well as their management skills. He and the two of them walked around the facility that day, with Steele breaking off at intervals to chat with inmates, and it was gratifying to see him pull his little notebook out and make notes as he spoke to inmates, something that Colden had always done when he walked the housing pods and inmates asked questions. He made notes and ensured that some feedback was sent to the inmates he had spoken with, and oftentimes he referred the matters to other staff who knew that he expected them to get back to the inmates in question. He wanted to remember this so he could place a note into Steele's performance appraisal progress sheet when he returned to the office. He'd often gone to the housing pods once the 'count time' intercom signal was heard to observe the staff perform the head counts, and found Steele and the Captain doing the same thing.

Superintendent Colden heard his name come across the intercom, that he was needed at his office. He said to Steele and the Captain that they could continue making their rounds, and he walked back to his office, to find Ms. Vanis Goodson standing at his office door.

"Ms. Goodson, you wanted to see me? Sounded urgent! Come on in, and have a seat, please."

"Well, Mr. Colden, I knew you'd want to hear what I have to tell you. First, the final approvals were faxed to me on Captain McLeod's promotion to Assistant Superintendent, and we got his pay raise that was requested. I am surprised that we got all of it, instead of it being broken down and part of it delayed. It is effective yesterday! Hold on to your chair for this next one! That Officer Pam Cox—remember her? She has submitted her resignation this morning, giving a one week notice. How do you want to handle that? Lastly, we have a fax authorization to go ahead with selecting the two canine handlers and submit the names to the agency headquarters within the next two weeks. So, I figured you'd want to move on these today before you left work, sir."

"Why, Ms. Goodson, you are indeed a godsend. Thank you so much, and yes, I want these matters handled today. In fact, get on the intercom and advise Captain McLeod to come to my office immediately. Please." He walked into Ms. Brooks's office to speak to her. Ms. Goodson could see that Colden was happier than she had seen him in some time, for most of the time in the past year, he appeared to have looked empty and exhausted, or rather drained by the pressures of the job. She quickly summoned the Captain, and she then went to Ms. Brooks' office to advise the Superintendent that the Captain was on his way. Both ladies were elated with the news of the day. As Captain McLeod approached the doorway to Ms. Brooks's office, Superintendent Colden spoke telling him to come into Ms. Brooks's office, and close the door behind him. Colden then extended his right hand to the Captain, with a wide grin.

"Congratulations, Mr. Assistant Superintendent! We are glad to have you on board," declared Colden, still shaking McLeod's hand.

Echoing congratulatory sentiments, both ladies shook McLeod's hand. In fact, they both hugged him, making remarks about it being such a well- deserved promotion.

Catching his breath, McLeod became a bit emotional, in extending his appreciation for the support for the promotion, first to Superintendent Colden, then to both Ms. Goodson and Ms. Brooks. "Mr. Colden, you've certainly taught me a number of things in prison management, and I hope to continue learning. This means an awful lot to me, sir, and I thank you so much. Ladies, you've supported me for so long, and that means the world to me. I thank you and look forward to working with you more and more. This is so overwhelming for me."

"Well that's not all of it," spoke Colden. "Officer Pam Cox submitted her resignation. I will be issuing a letter to her that we have accepted and acknowledged her resignation. Also, we have the go sign to select the two canine handlers, and it needs to be done within the next two weeks. No, let's get it done within the next six working days, please. And, I'd like to get the letters of rejection completed today and mailed out to those candidates who were not selected, Ms. Goodson. I will compose a notice advising all staff of your promotion, and will post it day after tomorrow late afternoon. Anyone have a question?"

Those present shook their heads. Superintendent Colden then asked that Ms. Goodson take Mr. McLeod to her office and review the promotion package with salary concerns with him. He then asked Ms. Brooks for a fresh cup of coffee, saying that he "needed to sit down with a cup of coffee and enjoy the moment of the day." He then went to his office.

He spent the most of the day reviewing materials that had been placed on his desk. He read and responded to the e-mails on his computer, and spoke by telephone with his supervisor. Once he hung up the phone, Ms. Brooks advised him that the EEO investigators wanted to speak to him, to which he responded for them to come on in. In a few minutes, Ken Sharpe and Cass Munn came into the office, sat down their briefcases on the floor, taking out writing tablets, and asked if this would be an appropriate time to review their findings with Mr. Colden. He advised them to proceed on, that he was in no hurry to go anywhere. He then said that he needed to make them aware that Officer Pam Cox, one of the complainants, had submitted her resignation; neither of them was surprised.

Ken Sharpe spoke up, "We're not all surprised by that, Mr. Colden. In fact, that is or probably is to her benefit. We spoke with her again, yesterday, and she admitted that the Lieutenant never made references to her as being a strumpet. When we first spoke with her, she was adamant that it happened, because he was upset over her previous employment as a dancer at a night club, her friendship with one Faye Hondo, and the fact that she was having difficulty learning her job as an Officer. Other employees stated that she was very argumentative, had difficulty following policy, she spent too much time talking with inmates, and no one had ever heard the Lieutenant speak to in a loud tone or use non-professional language to her. Certainly no one has ever heard him use the word 'strumpet.' The Lieutenant admitted that he had been surprised that she had been hired, when he learned of her background work, but he was told by her that Faye Hondo went to bat for her to get the job, and he said that bothered him. But, he never mistreated her, even in speaking with her, and never used the word 'strumpet.' When we spoke to her yesterday, she commented that she'd probably resign, and that the job just doesn't appeal to her."

Colden thanked Mr. Sharpe for sharing that with him. "And the other case?" he asked.

Cass Munn began to speak, while looking at her notes. "Officer Erica Dorn. Another allegation with no merit. In fact, she was angry because Lieutenant Gibbs refused to help her study for the promotional exam. Told us she didn't know why he would not help or tutor her. When we spoke with the Lieutenant, he refused to waste the time because he felt she was just not ready for advancement or be placed in a position of supervising others. He qualified that on the grounds that Sergeants and others have had to counsel her on several occasions about bypassing policy, of spending too much time chit-chatting with inmates, of leaving her posts several times without authorization. We checked her performance appraisal and there have been performance and conduct concerns, which she had acknowledged in writing. We confronted her about this and she felt this was wrong for Lieutenant Gibbs to base his refusal on these notes or actions. She even admitted at one point that she propositioned him—that she'd have sex with him if he did tutor her. He said this happened, and he just ignored her. There were two other Officers that overheard Ms. Dorn make that proposition; they spoke to us as well and provided written statements. I believe she will resign as well, because she knows her credibility is questionable."

Ken Sharpe then spoke up, "Would be drafting the investigation report to show that nothing was found to have merit as regards the allegations made, and that in conclusion both complainants had lied and/or misconstrued the facts. Further, that upon re-interviews, both the complainants remarked about resignations being imminent. Upon interviewing numerous other Officers, it appears that Lieutenant Peter Gibbs is very supportive of those officers who work in accord with the job description, who are committed to doing the best work possible, following policy and demonstrating good work ethics. Many of them have a great deal of respect for him. On talking with him, he acknowledged his problems of the past but has strived to make improvements and is enjoying his work at Glen Cove Correctional. That's the summary report, Mr. Colden. My office will fax to you a brief summary report tomorrow, because I know you'll want to share our findings with Lieutenant Gibbs. The final written report should be sent out in two to three weeks. We have appreciated the hospitality and professionalism extended during our stay. Thank you." Both Sharpe and Cass Munn gathered their possessions, stood up, and shook hands, turning to depart the office. Colden walked with them to the front exit, waving them off; he then sat down on the patio bench next to the building, thinking over their conversation. He was well pleased with their report. As he sat there, employees exiting the building spoke to him as they left for the day, and he responded with 'have a good evening' or similar remarks. Several sat down just to chit-chat with him, and he smiled when a few of them even commented about the new truck he was driving. They noticed things too, he thought, with a smile. He glanced at his watch, and decided to close his office and go home; another day he'd get home at a decent hour.

Chapter Twenty-Two

The next few days at the prison were without any new incidents. The notice of advisement as to Buddy McLeod being the new Assistant Superintendent for Operations and Custody was well received by the facility employees. Superintendent Colden began having both McLeod, Mitch Steele, and Marcus Torn in his office each day to discuss the past day's events and what was on the schedule for the day, as well as discussing concerns on the horizon, and brainstorming on matters that needed to be reviewed. All seemed pleased with the selection of the canine handlers, and it had been decided to let them work with the Virginia canine handlers for a few days before the visiting team had to depart, which worked out well for all. On several occasions, Ms. Vanis Goodson was invited to sit in, and discuss matters that were being handled in the personnel arena. Superintendent Colden studied his team, and was quite pleased; in fact, more pleased than he had been since his transfer to Glen Cove several years past. But the past year had been full of challenges, but he and his staff had come through with amazing success.

Over the new two weeks, he had begun to delegate more and more projects to Buddy McLeod, who was doing well, and was seemingly handling the associated stress at a satisfactory level.

As he drove into work one morning, six months later, he slowed down once he turned onto the asphalt entrance into the prison parking lot, glancing over to his right. He stopped, looking at the facility sign sitting in the corner, which read GLEN COVE CORRECTIONAL

INSTITUTION, with his name on the silver colored metal-plate under that. Breathing in a deep breath, he smiled; he proceeded on to park in his designated parking space. He proceeded through the gatehouse for the routine checks, and walked on to the main building, greeting his staff as he met them on the way in. Entering his office, he poured himself a fresh cup of coffee, and walked down the hall to the food services area, and walked into the kitchen, where he spoke with inmates who were preparing foods, cleaning tables, and working in the dishwashing area. He then spoke with the kitchen staff, who all seemed in good spirits and expressed pleasantries to him for his visit to the food services area and for talking with them. Realizing that he'd spend quite a bit of time in the area, he headed back toward his office, as he knew he had staff arriving in a few minutes for their meeting. Once he got back into his office, he picked up the phone and dialed home to speak with his wife. Darby Jane Colden answered her phone, "This is the Colden residence; may I help you?"

"Yes, ma'am, you can help me. What are your thoughts on my retiring, my dear lady? We can fix those rose gardens, take our fishing trips when we want, visit the boys, or whatever! Let's say I, no, no, not I, but we plan on my retiring the first of next month?" He seemed so excited that he didn't give her much time to speak, but he could hear her faint response when she became a bit emotional, and uttered "Oh, my, yes!" And then she followed that with, "Come home, J.T."

Slowly he hung up the phone, smiling. Moments later, his management team began to walk in, finding him with a fresh pot of coffee and a stack of Styrofoam cups on the corner table, which he offered to them. Mitch Steele, Buddy McLeod, Marcus Torn, and Vanis Goodson were busily greeting each other, while he summoned Ms. Brooks to join them. Sitting around the semi-round conference table in the front of his desk, he began to speak. "I want to say something to all of you this morning. Sometimes we can get so entrenched in our work, that we forget some of those persons who are so important in our lives. And sometimes our work can seemingly siphon the spirit right out of us and erode our love for the job. But we need to stay ever mindful of what is important in our lives, for life is short. With that said, I wanted you to know that I have decided to retire, effective next month. A rather difficult decision, for I love Glen Cove and I will miss all of you. It's difficult to let go of something you enjoy doing. I'll be calling my supervisor at the agency headquarters this morning to give him notice. You are a good management team; you work well together, and we have come through some tough times. And I do appreciate each and every one of you. If you don't mind, we will not have our morning meeting so I can attend to some things with Mr. Polk, but we can come back together around one o'clock this afternoon. We won't be long, for I plan to leave early and take Ms. Darby Jane out for dinner." He dismissed each of them and spent a few moments alone, before calling his supervisor to apprise him of the good news; good news for J.T. Colden.

———